A GUN IN EACH HAND

"If you locked the sheriff up," Sim Matson said harshly, "you're goin' back an' let him out. An' take your medicine. We're for law an' order around here. Tyner hit me when I wasn't lookin' yesterday. He ain't walkin' out like this, laughin' at me."

"I don't reckon Milt's laughin'," Shack said. "But I am. Who's gonna take me over tuh the jail?"

"I am!" Sim Matson stormed. He grabbed for his gun.

Both Shack's hands moved this time. One gun roared from his waist. The other fanned the men who scattered out from the bar. Sim Matson staggered back along the bar, holding his left arm from which blood was welling. His gun slipped from nerveless fingers and thudded on the floor.

"Who's next?" Shack snapped, crouching and weaving his guns. . . .

T. T. FLYNN

THE DEVIL'S LODE

LEISURE BOOKS NEW YORK CITY

A LEISURE BOOK®

November 2002

Published by special arrangement with Golden West Literary Agency.

Dorchester Publishing Co., Inc.
276 Fifth Avenue
New York, NY 10001

ISBN: 0-8439-5121-4

The name "Leisure Books" and the stylized "L" with design are trademarks of Dorchester Publishing Co., Inc.

Printed in the United States of America.

TABLE OF CONTENTS

Gallows Breed 7

Old Hellcat 77

The Devil's Lode 157

Gallows Breed

By 1934, Popular Publications' *Dime Western* (which went biweekly in October of that year) was a major market for T. T. Flynn's Western stories. Rogers Terrill, who edited *Dime Western*, kept urging Flynn to write short novels, so popular were his stories with readers. Of the five T. T. Flynn stories to appear in *Dime Western* in 1934, four were short novels. "Glory Blast" in *Dime Western* (3/34)—the one short story—and "Border Blood" in *Dime Western* (9/15/34)—the first of the short novels—have already been collected in DEATH MARKS TIME IN TRAMPAS (Five Star Westerns, 1998). The short novel that follows was originally titled "Gallows Breed" and was completed by the author on August 30, 1934. It was sent at once by Flynn's agent, Marguerite E. Harper, to Rogers Terrill who bought it for $500.00. It appeared in the issue of *Dime Western* dated December 1, 1934 under the title "Son of the Gallows Breed" and was showcased on the cover.

On November 17, 1920, having listed his residence as Washington, D.C., Ted Flynn had married Gertrude Allen in Landover, Maryland. He was, and would always remain, ruthlessly secretive about his life and his past, and little is known about this marriage except that it was apparently annulled because he was underage. However, his father was a witness on the application for the license when Ted married Mary C. DeRene at St. Francis de Sales Church in the District of Columbia on May 10, 1923. Mary, whom Ted always called Molly, had been born in Baltimore, Maryland on February 12, 1897. Ted may have seen Molly for the first time in lamplight or best remembered her that way, for that is how he first shows readers his literary recreations of her—Sally Jones in "Conquistador's Gold" collected in RAWHIDE (Five Star Westerns, 1996) and Gayle Barnes in this story. Molly suffered from tuberculosis, and Ted moved to New Mexico originally for reasons of her health. She would expire in his arms on August 11, 1929. T. T. Flynn would never forget her, nor could he ever entirely overcome his sorrow over her loss. When he was near death himself, he produced the photograph of Molly that he kept in a leather-covered frame and showed it to his daughter from a later marriage, saying that very soon now he felt he would be with Molly again.

I

"EL LOBITO"

When Jerry Carson ran past the dead body of his father toward
the smoking gun of Don José de Gama y Lopez and struck and
kicked the famous bandit until Don José's big, roweled spurs of
hand-hammered silver jangled under the onslaught, the thread
of Jerry Carson's life came very close to breaking. Don José's
nearest man swore in Spanish and whipped out a gun to stretch
the troublesome brat beside his father. But Don José stayed the
shot with a raised hand, and, holding off the miniature fury with
an arm, the great bandit laughed loudly.

"*¡Dios!*" he cried in Spanish. "*El Lobito* . . . the little wolf!
See . . . he is not afraid. He will grow into a man. Bring him
away from this coyote's den."

So the whim of the man who had killed his father snatched
Jerry Carson from that leprous little cluster of buildings.
Jerry's father had owned the whiskey station where passing
men had bought supplies and drank and gambled before they
went their way into the long, dry distances in every direction—and where some of them had stayed, vanished, forgotten, cheated, robbed, and killed by the man whose grave
was the looted, burning buildings where his sins had found
him out. His great mistake had been the robbing of a man
whom Don José called friend.

The elder Carson had been no better a father to his boy
than he had been friend to those he betrayed. But a boy, who

9

had known nothing else, knew no better. The worst sins of Carson's Crossing had been spared his early misunderstanding. And with no beauty to recall, no kindness to remember, the fast, wild life of the outlaw trail soon blotted out the past.

In those days Don José de Gama y Lopez was a rustler, a bandit, a killer, and a thief. Above all else he was a gambler—but not a liar. From the sandy shoals of the Colorado below Yuma to the brush thickets along the Nueces, Don José left his mark. Cattle were rustled, men were robbed and killed, posses were baffled or scattered with renegade lead. There were long, hard rides when men's throats parched and their bodies grew gaunt and starved—and nights under the bright, blazing stars with the high, shrill clamor of coyotes across the campfire telling of peace in the trail far from the haunts of man.

Don José had been a gentleman and a scholar, somewhere, sometime. It pleased his fancy—he never would admit to any deeper motive—to teach the stripling who grew up in the saddle with his men. But there was a greater teacher than even Don José. The outlaw trail had its lessons by day and night, and Don José de Gama y Lopez interpreted them. Shoot *first*. Shoot *straight*. Fight the flash of weakness that betrays. If you lose—lose quickly, cleanly, without feeling, for only a coward makes excuses. And above else—the truth always. For the weakling lies, the *man* keeps faith. That and much more did Don José instill into the boy through the years on the long outlaw trail; and the trail itself did its part. At nineteen, when Don José went the way of his calling with an old Sharps buffalo slug through his heart, Jerry Carson was a tall, broad-shouldered, young man of steel and leather, tireless, quiet, open-eyed, certain that his way was right.

Jerry Carson had killed men with his guns and with his

bare hands, and was resigned to killing more. In the outside world he took little part. Those who peopled it were a menace. He was a hunted man. But memory held little else, and the hunting did not trouble him.

After the passing of Don José, Jerry Carson was restless. Something had gone out of life. A bond of affection and companionship had vanished. He rode alone for two years, joining occasionally with others, but mostly keeping to himself. Always he sought something and never found it.

Where his money came from, he alone knew. Many men could account for parts of it. Wherever he went, Jerry Carson gambled—and won—as Don José had taught him. If there were gun fights and incidents better forgotten, those, too, were the way of the only life he knew. Even the stern chase of four days and five nights which followed the taking of the Mirage Mine gold shipment was only a passing incident. That his cloth mask had slipped from his face, as he shot the gun out of the hand of a guard who was throwing down on him, was a quirk of fate. The posse which quickly took to his trail and followed it stubbornly was only one more chance that he had to play out.

The Mirage Mine was up in central Colorado. Jerry led the posse day and night through the mountains, west, southwest, over the New Mexican border, across the great dry mesas where the streams gave place to sandy-bottomed arroyos, and water holes came farther and farther apart, then on through Navajo country into Arizona. Horses gave out under him, and he cinched his saddle on other horses, roped on the open range. There was little time to rustle food, cook, eat, or sleep. Men in that posse behind could ride and starve and struggle forward with as much fortitude as Jerry himself could show—and they were doing so.

Twice they almost caught Jerry, as he snatched brief bits

of sleep. Once he got away with bullets singing close, and only drew ahead because his horse, whose reins had been in the crook of his arm while he slept, was fresher than those which followed. In those flying days and nights Jerry Carson tried every trick he had ever learned to shake off the pursuit. None worked. Somewhere behind was a master tracker who unraveled every snarl in the trail.

First, Jerry abandoned the gold, tossing the small but heavy pack philosophically on the trail where it would be discovered. If that would stop pursuit, it was a cheap price—for he was one, and those behind were many. The ruse failed, and so he rode grimly, knowing that if horseflesh held out, few men in the West could keep up with him. His body parched by day and cried for moisture at night. There was never enough water or food along that far, straight trail he followed toward the border.

Hour by hour Jerry grew gaunter. Hollows deepened under dust-rimmed eyes that glowed brighter as his belt tightened and weariness fastened its increasing grip on him. Jerry laughed at times as he rode—and sang. This was life, the outlaw trail, the only thing he knew. Ahead, over the horizon, was the border—the border and safety.

His horse broke a leg in a badger hole and put him afoot miles from cover. Jerry had not passed a horse in half a day. He left his saddle there, took his rifle, belt gun, and all the cartridges he was carrying and went on afoot toward the high, rocky slopes of the nearest hills a good fifteen miles away. They overtook him in a rocky cañon near sundown, that posse which had started fifteen strong and by now had dwindled to four. Jerry shot two of the men, killed three horses, drove the two able survivors back in hasty flight, and trudged on into the hills with a bullet through his shoulder and a deep crease across his ribs where death had missed him by inches.

That was the end of the pursuit. Afoot, Jerry lost himself in the mountains—and a month later, still gaunt, but strong and easy once more, he rode a good horse across the New Mexico line toward the little cowtown of Quivado.

At the edge of town he reined up beside a pole on which a fresh, white notice had been tacked. It read:

THREE THOUSAND DOLLARS
REWARD
DEAD OR ALIVE
JERRY CARSON

II

"MIDNIGHT POKER"

Jerry whistled softly. In smaller print beneath was his description—a very good description, Jerry admitted ruefully. Colorado was offering the reward on behalf of the Mirage Mine.

Dusk was drawing a soft, dark mantle over the sprawl of adobe houses on the outskirts of the little town. The pungent smell of wood smoke was in the air. A dark-faced Mexican, leisurely driving half a dozen goats toward some nearby corral, loitered to stare and pass the time of day with a stranger.

"Buenas tardes," he greeted politely.

Jerry answered in the language with equal politeness. "Tell me," he questioned, jerking his thumb at the notice, "have they found this man yet, *amigo?*"

"No, *señor.* I have not heard, but the sheriff is looking for Jerree Carson. All men are looking for him. Three thousand *pesos* is a fortune. Me? . . . I am looking . . . for it is said perhaps this *hombre* will ride through these parts one day soon. These papers for him are everywhere."

Jerry shook his head in the deepening twilight. "This man," he said, "this Jerry Carson must be one bad *hombre,* eh?"

"Sí, muy malo," agreed the Mexican fervently. "I have heard it said that he has killed a hundred men. From his guns there is only death. There is much talk about him . . . much talk."

14

Jerry chuckled softly. "What would you do, *amigo,* if you came upon him?"

The man crossed himself hastily. "*¡Dios!* I would run like the devil was at my heels, *señor,*" he confessed. "And then I would run to the deputy of the sheriff in Quivado here and with him go to earn that three thousand *pesos.* It is much money. A man could almost die for that."

"*Sí,*" Jerry agreed gravely. "Much money. But watch out. This *hombre* is bad. I have heard of him. He will shoot you through the liver and leave you for the coyotes. *Adiós.*"

Jerry lifted his hand and rode slowly into Quivado—and on through. If a Mexican goat herder was looking for him, and reward notices were plastered around town, some sharp eye would recognize him—and there would be gun play and flight all over again.

Jerry swore under his breath as he rode on into the night with an empty stomach and a dry water bottle. The Mirage Mine was taking the business a little too seriously, considering that their gold had been recovered and that the posse men would not have been shot, if they had turned back then. The matter should have been forgotten by now—but, instead, notices had been scattered over several states offering a reward large enough to make every man watchful and alert.

An empty stomach might have had something to do with the sudden sense of dissatisfaction that gripped Jerry Carson as he rode on into the night. He had intended to eat and rest in Quivado. Now he had to move on—he must always move on. He wondered how men felt who did not have a price on their heads, men who did not have to run from posses, looking for them with guns ready to mow them down.

The next afternoon, fifty miles farther on, riding through the gloomy pine forests on a tortuous short cut through the Mogollon Mountains, Jerry was still wondering about the answer to that question. He had made a dry, hungry camp the night before, eaten at midday with a silent Mexican sheepherder who had not seen a man for weeks, and the coming night looked like another dry camp before the country pitched down toward the settlements in the Río Grande valley.

The sun dropped early behind the peaks to the west. Darkness was coming fast, when Jerry noted the flicker of a fire up a small, sheltered draw. He rode toward it. A fire meant food—probably another sheepherder—and back in here no reward notices would call for watchfulness.

He rounded a jutting outcrop of rock and came suddenly on the campfire. Three men were already on their feet, guns in their hands. But they were not Mexican sheepherders, these. Their hobbled horses staked out nearby, their watchful leanness told that they were hard riders who might have come from anywhere, who might even follow the twisted trails that Jerry knew so well.

With a grin Jerry saluted them. He was on familiar ground now. Men did not quit the food they had been eating and come to their feet, guns ready, at the approach of one lone stranger unless they were expecting someone.

"Hi-yah," Jerry greeted casually. "Got a bean to spare here? I was fixin' to sleep empty when I seen your fire and rode over."

Eyeing him closely, they waited until he rode up to the fire. The nearest man, short and stocky with visibly bowed legs cased in a pair of old batwing chaps, asked suspiciously: "Who's ridin' with you?"

"Nobody," Jerry admitted amiably. "A Mex sheepherder is all I've seen for two days."

The next man was tall, slender, wiry, about Jerry's size and age, and his black hair fell in a natural tangle over his forehead, as Jerry's did when his sombrero was off. He said curtly: "You been ridin' two days out this way with no grub?"

"Uhn-huh," Jerry assented, and waited in the saddle with his hands out in plain view. Not one of the three had yet holstered his gun.

The third man, who had not spoken, was the first to slip his gun in a low-slung holster. "Light," he said briefly. "Beans an' venison an' coffee is all we got, but it'll smooth yore belly and make you sleep easy. My name is Black . . . an' these fellers are Jack White an' . . . uh . . . Shorty Brown."

Jerry swung out of the saddle, stretched himself stiffly, and grinned slowly. "I'm Green," he said. "Tom Green . . . an' that makes the rainbow complete. I'll appreciate your beans an' meat, gentlemen, an' ride on tonight, if you figure the country around here is gettin' too crowded."

They exchanged glances. Some of the reserve vanished. The stocky man who had spoken first said colorlessly: "Stay right here tonight, stranger. There's beans an' meat in them two pans by the fire. You'll have to clean 'em out with your fingers or wait."

"I'll manage," Jerry said. "Is there water here for my horse?"

A seepage pool in a sheet of rock some fifty yards away was pointed out to him. Jerry watered his horse there, brought him back, unsaddled, and staked him out before he squatted by the fire and ate with the aid of his hunting knife.

Afterward, the four of them smoked in silence. No questions were asked. Presently the short, stocky man took a pack of dirty cards from a pair of leather saddlebags on the ground. "Care to play?" he asked Jerry. "And have yuh got anything to play with to make it interesting?"

"A little money," Jerry nodded. "Deal 'em and I'll try to hang on."

It started as a casual game, became earnest, with rising stakes. Jerry lost for a time. He noticed quick glances as he dug into the money belt under his shirt and brought out gold. But Don José de Gama y Lopez had been a mighty gambler, straight or crooked, as the need might be. Jerry noted a crooked deal. His face remained passive, but he played his cards closer, more carefully, and presently began to win.

Three pairs of eyes watched his every move—and caught nothing about which to protest as the gold he had lost came back, with more gold and silver and bills. The more they lost, the higher they raised the stakes. Sometime around midnight Jerry had over two thousand dollars of their money, and they began to stake their riding gear, saddles first.

"It's a long ride out of here bareback," Jerry reminded. "I didn't aim to get into a serious game like this. Anybody ready to call it a night?"

He was voted down—and in the next hour owned their saddles, spurs, blankets, and rifles. The slim, wiry one with the curly, black hair like Jerry's hurled his cards on the blanket in disgust after he lost his rifle. "I'm cleaned!" he announced wrathfully. "Stranger . . . Green or whatever your name is . . . you're too damned lucky at cards to sit right. I've got me a legal deed to a sweet little ranch down toward the border. She's got a few cows, a couple of sections of so-so land at the water holes, an' an adobe house. I'll put it up against your winnin's tonight. Cut the cards, an' high man takes all."

Jerry riffled the cards together. "I'm headin' for Texas, an' I'm a trail man . . . always movin' on. I can't use a ranch."

"You can use this one . . . if you win. Gimme them cards. We're cuttin'."

All three of them were glowering, surly, tense, now that

18

they were stripped of their possessions and faced with going on without them.

Jerry regarded them without expression—and tossed the cards over to the speaker. "Lemme see your deed."

The crumpled, travel-worn paper he held up to the dying fire seemed right and legal enough. It was signed, sealed, and witnessed, conveying the described property to Richard Galloway.

"Hmm," said Jerry, "you're . . . Galloway?"

"Yep . . . that's me," the slim young man admitted. His face was hard, challenging. "Mean anything to you . . . Green?"

All three were watching as Jerry tossed the deed on the folded blanket on which they had been playing. "I don't give two hoots what your name is or who you are," Jerry said calmly. "Let's go . . . my winnings against the deed . . . high card."

Galloway snapped the shuffled deck on the blanket. Jerry cut it with a deft movement of his hand. Galloway lifted part of the cards, looked at the bottom one, and turned it up. "Jack of clubs. Top that, stranger."

Jerry reached for the deck without looking, slipped off a thin cut, and tossed it face up on the blanket. "My lucky night," he said dryly. "Queen of hearts takes your jack, Galloway . . . and I'll take the deed as soon as you give me a bill of sale. Write it on the back. Here's a piece of lead pencil."

Galloway wrote mechanically on the back, scowling, muttering under his breath, and threw the deed violently on the blanket.

"Anyone at the ranch?" Jerry queried as he inspected the bill of sale, folded the paper carefully, and slipped it in his breast pocket.

"Only a Mexican family," Galloway growled. "You goin' there?"

"I'll probably sell it," Jerry said, getting to his feet. "I'll loan you back your gear and guns, men. Can't use 'em or take them with me now. Make it right, if we ever meet again. Thanks for the beans an' the card game. I'll be sashayin' along now."

"No, you won't! You're turnin' in here!" said the stocky, bowlegged one in the batwing chaps. It was an order, not a request.

Jerry, already on his feet, moved back, smiling thinly. "I'm traveling," he said. *"Adiós."*

From the corner of his eye Jerry saw them get to their feet as he unhobbled the horse. They were silent—ominously silent.

He caught the reins, turned the horse so he could watch them. Galloway was scowling. Jerry sensed tension growing to the breaking point. It erupted in a wrathful outburst from Galloway. "You fellows gonna let this skunk clean us an' ride off?"

Jerry ducked under the horse's head, drawing his gun. As he went, a hasty, crashing shot from Galloway's gun followed him.

III

"LONGRIDER LUCK"

The horse reared, lunged toward the fire, went down heavily, wounded in the head by the wild shot. Jerry whirled, crouching without cover as the three men at the fire exploded into action. The shot from behind the dying horse brought the muscles in Jerry's jaw ridging angrily. Otherwise, he was cool as he shot from the hip, carefully, with no wasted motion.

Galloway's second shot went wild. The curly-haired young man took one stumbling step—and pitched to his face beyond the kicking horse. The falling horse startled the other two. Jerry's menacing crouch when he should have been a dead man added uncertainty. Both their shots went wild—and Jerry's second .45 bullet found its mark an instant later. The stocky man yelled as it struck him. He lurched back, his gun falling from nerveless fingers. The third man whirled and ran for the safety of the black shadows beyond the fire. Two shots over his head made him run faster. A third one drove the stocky man with the wounded arm to awkward flight.

Galloway lay where he had fallen. He would stay there. The little dark hole of death had been visible in his forehead as he went down. The wounded horse kicked aimlessly. A bullet finished him. In the ringing silence which followed, the fire crackled softly. The crashing retreat of the two men through the underbrush snapped in the night.

Reloading quickly, Jerry jerked his rifle from the saddle

21

scabbard and stepped to the three horses, moving uneasily at the picket ropes. He chose a long-legged bay, clearly the best of the three, was in the saddle a moment later, and riding away from the spot.

No sense of victory went with Jerry. Another man killed, another wounded—no end to it. "Damn!" said Jerry aloud to the cool night breeze in his face. "They run a crooked game on me . . . an' then welshed. Nothing I could do about it." He spoke argumentatively, and cocked his head, as if waiting for an answer on the wind—an answer such as Don José might have made from his fund of wisdom. But there was no answer, and Jerry Carson headed into the night with a frown on his face. All the teachings of Don José, all the lessons of the outlaw trail gave no answer to the problems that became increasingly acute as he rode on through the darkness.

For the first time Jerry was tired of riding on, always on, through violent gun play, hair-trigger tension. His money belt was packed with bills, gold, silver. Behind him a dead man, a wounded man, and a badly frightened man offered nothing to worry about. Obviously on the run, they could add no further threat to that stirred up by the reward offered by the Mirage Mine. And yet Jerry was not at peace as he met the dawn and found water and shelter up a little side cañon. He unsaddled the horse, hobbled it, lost himself in the piñons on a nearby slope, and dropped off to sleep on a carpet of dry pine needles.

He reached El Paso a week later, riding in on a different horse and saddle than the ones which had carried him down toward the Río Grande settlements. He had left the saddle on an empty mesa, turned the horse loose, walked miles to the nearest town, and purchased what he needed out of the contents of the fat money belt.

El Paso held none of the Mirage Mine reward posters. Jerry hadn't seen one in the last two hundred miles down the valley. In the El Paso plaza the sun was warm. The bars were wide open. Gambling was in full blast, night and day. Honest gambling—crooked gambling. Jerry knew both kinds—so his money belt grew fatter. He drank, gambled, played—met now and then an old friend of the outlaw trail—met finally Segundo Smith, who had ridden three years with Don José. No man other than Jerry himself had ever been closer in the confidence of Don José.

Segundo Smith fell on Jerry's neck with a whoop, bought drinks, and over them lowered his voice. "I been lookin' for you, Jerry. Been sendin' out word for you. Half a dozen of us are ridin' down into the Big Bend next week. We need you. Throw in with us an' you'll have all the *dinero* you can use."

Segundo Smith was a big man, brawny, tireless, good-natured, until an enemy looked into his cold, black eyes. Segundo was grinning now—anything but an enemy—and his welcome was the old call of the outlaw trail.

Jerry smiled faintly. "You're wasting breath, Segundo," he said. "I've got other things to do."

"Let 'em go," Segundo urged.

"Nope. Got my mind made up."

Segundo cocked his head, knit his brow. "You look different, kid," he confessed. "Never seen you quite like this before. Something happened?"

"I've settled down, Segundo."

"I heard about that this morning," Segundo jeered. "You've busted half the faro banks in town."

Jerry grinned sheepishly. "I needed a little more money. Been gambling to win since I've been here. I've got a ranch, Segundo, and I aim to stock it with cattle an' settle down."

"You're lyin'," said Segundo with the flat assurance of an old friend who knew what he was talking about. "You ain't got a ranch, an', if you had, you wouldn't settle down. Our kind don't settle down, Jerry."

"Here's the deed."

Segundo Smith looked at the paper, whistled softly, and handed it back. "You can't do it, Jerry," he stated slowly. "You ain't the breed. It's too tame. An' if you could, they wouldn't let you. You're an outlaw. You ain't never been anything else. First sign of trouble you'll fight your way through it . . . an' then you'll have to hit the trail again."

"I'm through with gun fighting an' trouble, Segundo."

"Maybe," said Segundo. "Maybe not. It's bred in you, Jerry. You'll go out in a wave of gunsmoke or with a rope around your neck. Look at Don José. He couldn't get away from it. We're all in the same boat, an' we might as well take it high, wide, an' handsome while we can deal . . . 'cause there'll be a day when we won't have the deal, an' we'll have to take the cards as they fall."

Segundo Smith had never looked so serious, but Jerry smiled faintly again. "Maybe," he assented. "Maybe not, too. I'll have a whirl at it, anyway. Wish me luck, Segundo. An' forget it. Jerry Carson is leaving El Paso in the morning . . . an' that's the last of Jerry Carson."

Segundo Smith looked straight and hard into the faint smile—and suddenly thrust out a hand and gripped Jerry's hand. "Good luck, kid," he said gruffly. "You're young. Maybe you'll make it. I reckon Don José would say the same thing. Me . . . I've got fifteen years of sin on you, an' I don't hanker to own a ranch. So long."

Segundo Smith walked out without looking back, and Jerry bought another drink and went to his hotel.

The red ball of the evening sun was setting beyond the

slack, muddy current of the Río Grande when he rode east out of El Paso that night—and four days later a man named Green walked into the county clerk's office of San Saba and said: "I want to record this deed and bill of sale to the Galloway ranch."

The clerk cast a startled glance across the counter. Several men seated in chairs to right and left of the door stared at the stranger's back with quick interest. One of them, a tall, leathery man past forty, spat through a drooping, black mustache, got up quickly, and departed.

The clerk looked past Jerry at the departing man. A glint appeared in his eyes before he could look down and hide it. Jerry looked quickly over his shoulder and saw surprised interest among the seated men. He wondered, as he waited there by the counter, what that quick exit of one man had indicated—and was still wondering when he left the courthouse.

IV

"TROUBLE RANCH"

San Saba was crowded that day. Hitch racks were full. Wagons and buggies stood along the short main street which straggled up a foothill slope. Men and women—mostly men—crowded the walks, trooping in and out of the busy saloons and stores. A holiday spirit was in the air.

Outside the courthouse Jerry spoke to the first man he met, a bearded giant who looked like a miner from back in the mountains.

"Heap of folks in town today," Jerry said. "Election or something?"

The other shrugged, combed back his beard, spat in the dust. "Stranger, ain't you?" he asked.

"Sorta."

"Thought so. There's a double hangin' back of the jail this afternoon. Couple fellers held up the stage t'other day an' killed the guard. Posse got 'em an' Judge Simpson sentenced 'em to hang before they knowed what it was all about. Folks is sorta makin' a holiday outta the occasion. Ain't often you can see two jump off the same afternoon."

"I'll bet not," Jerry grinned. "This must be a peaceable range around here, if they hang men so quick."

"Well, sometimes . . . an' sometimes not. But Dick Creesy, the guard, was well liked. Folks got stirred up over his death. This'll be a popular hangin'. Better drop around an' see it."

Jerry smiled thinly. "Maybe I will," he agreed. "I've been interested in hangings for a long time."

The thin smile was still there as Jerry racked his horse in front of the nearest saloon and entered. The bar front was crowded. He stood at the end, ordered beer, drank slowly, watching the activity along the bar.

A mixed lot filled the place. Bronzed cowmen, swarthy Mexicans, brawny miners, bearded prospectors from back in the mountains, several soldiers on leave from the nearest post, and even a friendly Indian or so moving silently in the background. Back to the door, Jerry did not see the four men who entered, led by the tall man with the drooping, black mustache who had slipped out of the courthouse so hurriedly. Now he indicated Jerry and dropped back while the other three ranged themselves casually about the end of the bar. Jerry's first notice of them was when a voice spoke softly in his ear.

"There's talk that you've bought the Galloway Ranch, mister."

Jerry turned slowly and looked up. He had to look up to meet the eyes of the speaker. Cold eyes, they were, in a square face. The words had come from a thin-lipped mouth under a close-cropped, grizzled mustache. The man was at least fifty. He towered half a head over all others in the room, a huge, somber figure in black—black sombrero, black broadcloth coat and trousers, black, polished riding boots without fancy stitching. The square face was hard and forbidding, the voice curt and cold. The black coat was open in front, disclosing a pearl-handled six-shooter.

Jerry drank from his glass and put it down slowly before replying. He noted the slight frown of displeasure that brought. This somber-clothes giant had a temper. "I just came from the courthouse," Jerry admitted. "Talk travels fast in these parts."

His glance strayed to the black-mustached man who had abruptly left the courthouse after hearing the name of the Galloway Ranch—but Jerry's face was without expression as he idly turned the glass in his hand and waited.

The big man frowned at him. "Did you buy the ranch from Galloway?" he asked.

Jerry shrugged. "I filed a bill o' sale for it. That's enough."

Jerry turned his back to the bar as two men moved in beside him. A quick look found them smaller than the somber giant but, nevertheless, good-size men. Top hands by their looks, wearing belt guns and scarred leather chaps—and, although they scarcely glanced at him, it was plain that their attention was on every move he made.

The youngest, at Jerry's left, was no older than Jerry himself. His sombrero was canted at a jaunty angle, and the gay handkerchief around his neck was almost startling in contrast to the black garb of the big man. He was not smiling, but he looked as if he might at any moment, no matter what the moment brought.

It brought another frown, slow, heavy, and a cold-eyed stare from the big man. "Where did you see Galloway?"

"Last time I saw him," Jerry recalled, "he was startin' on a long trip. I guess he's still traveling. Friend of yours?"

"Friend!"

It was a harsh exclamation of contempt, not a question. "What are you doing with Galloway's land?" the big man asked.

"Settling down on it."

"What's your name?"

Jerry yawned slightly. "Look on the courthouse records an' you'll see it's Tom Green. What's yours?"

"I," said the somber giant, "am Amit Bristol." He said it colorlessly, flatly, as if the name was enough to place him.

"What's on your mind, Bristol?" Jerry asked. "And, if you're givin' orders to these two gun-toters who are crowdin' me, tell them to keep their distance. I'm touchy."

Amit Bristol stared hard at him. "I don't know you, Green," he said. "But if you had anything to do with Galloway, I know what cloth you're cut out of. I don't know what idea you have in settling down on that land, but I can guess. It's some more of Charley Starr's dirty work. He figures a new man can squat there and brazen it out fer a time. I'm warning you now . . . don't settle there."

Jerry's face grew bleak, cold, as he digested the warning. "I don't know what you're talking about, Bristol," he said. "I never heard of Charley Starr. If you've got a quarrel with him, that's your business. I'm not interested. If that land is mine . . . an' it looks like it is . . . I'm settlin' down on it. Savvy?"

Amit Bristol studied him for a moment. "I see you're a stubborn, young fool," he said harshly. "You tried to be clever, and now you're trying to brazen it out. But I've got you marked. Any man who takes Galloway's place is sure to be a killer, a rustler, a liar, an' a thief. You'll hear from me, if you squat on that land."

Amit Bristol turned and walked out, huge, formidable, and after him drifted his three men.

More than one eye had been turned to the end of the bar, while they talked. More than one glance followed Amit Bristol out—and then came back curiously to Jerry.

Jerry finished his drink and left the saloon thoughtfully. Amit Bristol had not been bluffing. Thought of the reward posters made Jerry grin. He had left them behind—and ridden straight into trouble that threatened to be as serious. Bristol's words had been those of a man who would kill if his hand were forced.

The old wariness returned. Jerry found himself scanning

passing faces. Casually he talked with various strangers. Amit Bristol, he found, owned the TVT outfit some miles to the north. Charley Starr's name brought evasion. Men seemed unwilling to talk much about Charley Starr.

The Lazy Teacup brand, northeast of the TVT, belonged to Starr. More than that men would not say, although their quick silence was proof that more could be said if they cared to—or dared to. Fear seemed to stalk with the name of Charley Starr.

Jerry let it go at that, as hanging time drew near. A big crowd began to mass behind the jail. Leaving the grim festival, Jerry rode north out of town, following directions he had gotten at the courthouse.

The distance was twenty-odd miles along the first slopes that piled up into the steep ridges of the mountains beyond. The sparse bunch grass, cactus, and Spanish bayonet of the south gave way through here to sparsely wooded hills that grew more verdant as the altitude increased.

The Galloway Ranch was back in the mountains a few miles, in the mouth of Ghost Cañon. Its few sections of land could not be worth much. But with the land as a nucleus, cattle stocked right, free mountain ranges at the back door, a man should be able to build up a nice little outfit. The law would not bother him; outlaw friends would not find him; there would be no temptation to take to the outlaw trail once more.

The afternoon was waning as Jerry rode down through scrub pine into a grassy little valley bisected by a willow-fringed thread of water that glinted now and then through the trees as the descending sun struck it. This, according to the directions he had been following, was the mouth of Ghost Cañon. TVT land lay to the east in a flatter country. This peaceful valley was Galloway land—his land—the first land

Jerry Carson had ever owned. It moved him more than he was willing to admit.

He was pondering this new feeling of possession when the sharp bark of gunfire broke out back up the slope to the left. Between the shots he heard the drum of fast-running horses, the crackle and crash of their reckless charge through the growth. They were not stopping to pick an open way. Trouble was sweeping down the slope grimly, furiously.

The riders were heading down into the valley, unaware that Jerry was near. He spurred to the edge of the trees, dismounted, ran the last few steps to a sheltering clump of scrub piñon, and looked out across the little valley. Half a mile wide, its floor was green and rich with grass. Near the center under spreading cottonwoods stood a small, low, adobe house, a pole corral, and an open-front shed. A curl of blue smoke hovered above the house. A peaceful scene—and yet giving it the lie was the crashing pursuit through the trees and the hammer of gunshots.

Waiting, Jerry saw a lone rider gallop out of the trees and head for the adobe house. Riding bareback, lying low along the horse's neck, guiding with a hackamore, the man was riding furiously. He looked over his shoulder, waited a moment, thrust back an arm, and emptied a hand gun, aiming carefully to make each shot count. The pursuit raced into view before the last shot was fired—two—three—four riders, spurring hard, shooting as they came. But they were using six-guns, too, and the shots were going wild. Jerry stepped forward suddenly, staring. A fifth rider had reined up sharply, lifted a rifle, aimed carefully. The shot cracked thinly. The fugitive flinched, lurched to one side. He was going down—falling—no—he regained his seat, holding on with both hands.

The next moment Jerry swore aloud. Out of the cabin a slender figure in a skirt and blouse came running. She carried a rifle. By the practiced lift to her shoulders Jerry saw that she knew how to use it, and she did not hesitate. Standing there in the open, oblivious to danger, she lifted the rifle to her shoulder and fired.

The first of the pursuers reined sharply around, galloped back toward the trees, weaving in the saddle. The others pulled up, uncertain what to do. She pumped in another shell and watched them. Jerry noted that wait. She probably could have shot another man at that distance, but she gave them a chance.

"Don't do it, damn you!" Jerry burst out harshly.

The man near him had lifted the rifle uncertainly. But shooting a woman was too much even for him. He lowered the gun, waited while the others cantered back toward him.

The woman sent a bullet over their heads by way of warning, and they withdrew slowly into the trees as their intended victim rode hard to the adobe house and brought up sharply around the corner. From his position Jerry saw what the others could not see. The lone rider slipped from the bare back of the horse and collapsed on the ground.

The woman did not see it, either. Slowly, watchfully, she backed to the side of the house. Only then did she look around and find the motionless figure on the ground. With no more thought of the riders she ran to the wounded man.

Jerry caught a glimpse of her dragging the man inside the house—too heavy for her to carry. Then the little valley was peaceful once more.

It was hard to believe that the sharp, furious tide of a gun fight had ebbed and flowed in the space of a few minutes. But it had—and the men who had been driven back did not stay to press the matter. As Jerry swung into the saddle once more, he heard them riding back up the slope, angling over toward him as they went. He listened. Voices carried far in this still, dry air, and they were coming nearer every moment.

The first thing he heard was savage, furious cursing. Another voice broke in on it. "Hell . . . Frank, she only plugged you through the leg. A clean hole like that ain't worth botherin' about. You're lucky. Now you got a chance to lay around an' take it easy."

" 'Sides," said another voice, still clearer as they cut along the slope, "Jack got in one good lick with his rifle. Barnes almost fell off his hoss."

The wounded man cursed again viciously. "Next time I aim to see he does. Jack oughta shot that gun-totin' female! Gawd, she like to busted my laig! I'll even up with 'em both!"

"You're a blood-thirsty cuss, Slim. I bet you'd shoot a woman."

"Why not? If she gets out an' shoots like a man, she oughta get man's treatment."

"Uhn-huh. Maybe. But not from you, Slim. This'll be all settled before you're ridin' again. Likely we'll be back in a day or so an' run 'em out with a whoop."

They drew away, voices fading. Jerry sat there on the horse for long minutes after the last sound. Who were those two in the adobe house? This was Galloway land, according to the directions. The valley, the trickle of water, the adobe house were right. But Galloway had said a Mexican and his wife were living on the land. Even across the distance it was plain that those two were not Mexicans.

Jerry rode slowly out across the open space toward the house, holding the reins breast high to show that he was coming peacefully. He was halfway across when a slight movement was visible at one of the windows. A moment later a rifle barked. A shot whined over his head. Jerry lifted his hands higher and rode on. A second shot warned him again—and he ignored it, also.

V

"NEIGHBOR'S WARNING"

The house was silent as he came up to it. It was a watchful silence, and the rifle muzzle still covered him from the window.

A clear, angry voice called: "Get back, Galloway, before I put a bullet through you!"

"I'm not Galloway, ma'am."

Silence for a moment—and then the woman said reluctantly: "I see you're not. You look something like him. But that goes for you, too, whoever you are."

"It's all right," Jerry assured her. "I'm not one of them." He walked the horse on toward the house as he spoke.

She cried: "Get back! I don't care who you are! You're not wanted here!"

"You've got a wounded man in there," Jerry said. "Hit pretty bad, too, I'm thinking. I reckon you need some help. You're alone, aren't you?"

He stopped a bare twenty yards away, keeping his hands in the air, and her voice addressed him angrily, with an undertone of tearful fury. "No . . . I'm not alone here! I have three men . . . and we're all holding guns on you! No one is wounded. No help is needed. You're not wanted, and you'll be hurt if you don't get away."

She was hidden behind a flowered curtain which wavered slightly in the breeze. Jerry smiled slowly. "I don't know who you think I am, ma'am. But if you think I had anything to do with that little fracas, you're wrong."

She said bitterly: "You seem to know enough about it."

"Yep," said Jerry. "I saw it an' waited until they rode away."

Her voice came more bitterly than ever. "You were there watching . . . and you didn't help when you saw four men riding down one man? And yet you come here offering help now?"

"I don't know what it's all about, ma'am. Fact is, I can't figger what you're doing here on my land."

"Your land?"

"Uhn-huh. I own Galloway's land now."

"This isn't Galloway's land! That starts two miles up the valley. Go there and stay there, if you own it, for I'll shoot anyone who is connected with Galloway as quickly as I will those who ride for Charley Starr. I'll give you ten seconds to be on your way . . . and I'll shoot then, if you aren't started!"

She meant it. Her voice was unsteady. Jerry doffed his sombrero to the curtained window. "Ten seconds it is," he assented. "And I'm on my way. But as long as we're neighbors, ma'am, call on me for anything you need. I've got a hunch you'll need help."

The low adobe house was quiet as he rode off. Jerry did not look back, but he felt that she was watching him until he was out of sight. He smiled thinly, wondered how the owner of that clear voice looked. She was slim, he knew, young she must be, and her husband, also.

The valley swung to the right, narrowing as it drove back into the mountains. The sides grew steeper as he advanced. But the forces which had scoured it out long ago had left the bottom flat, so that Ghost Cañon was almost like a wide trail carved back into the high hills. And it was traveled like such a trail. Over most of the valley floor the hoofs of passing cattle had left their mark.

One peculiar fact caught Jerry's eye in the fading light. Most of the tracks led the way he was going, back into the mountains. Many cattle went in . . . and few came out. He was pondering that when the narrowing valley made another swing, and he came in sight of the place which was to have been his home. It had, perhaps, been a home, when Galloway last saw it. The cottonwoods were there, under which the house had stood beside the trickle of water, and the remains of the house were there—but they would never shelter another man.

The adobe dwelling had been gutted by fire and razed to the ground. A few charred remnants of tree-trunk roof beams and heaps of crumbling adobe bricks were all that was left. At first sight, it might have been an accident, but a small pole corral had been thrown to the ground and burned, also. Men had done this deliberately.

Frowning, Jerry looked about. Through the purple dusk filling the cañon he saw another small house on the opposite slope. A man was standing before it with a rifle in his hands, peering from under the wide brim of a straw sombrero. Jerry rode across the trickle of water in the sandy streambed toward the house and man. He found a Mexican—Galloway's Mexican undoubtedly—wearing old, dirty overalls, a ragged shirt, and a low-brimmed, straw sombrero, weather-beaten and stained the color of old coffee grounds.

"Hello," Jerry said, stopping, looking down.

"No savvy."

The voice was soft, polite, as was the way with these people, and yet it did not match the face and manner. Short, thick-shouldered, powerful, the man had one of the ugliest faces Jerry had ever seen. The brown skin was heavily pockmarked. One cheek carried a livid weal of an old scar from cheekbone to jaw. The lips were thick, the nose broad and flat, suggesting more than a trace of Indian blood.

Jerry spoke in Spanish, turning in his saddle, indicating the house. "What happened there?" he asked.

The expressionless, Indian-like stare shifted past him to the house. The man shrugged. *"¿Quién sabe?"* he said.

A slatternly woman peered fleetingly from the doorway of the adobe shack and drew back quickly. In his hands the Mexican carried a new modern carbine. Unusual, too, for such a man was the gun belt and the gun he wore.

"This is Galloway's land?" Jerry asked.

"Sí."

"Galloway's gone . . . won't be back. I'm the new owner. What's your name, *hombre?*"

Puzzled, uncertain, the other stared. "Pablo Baca," he said after a moment.

"You work for Galloway?"

"Sí."

"You wish to work for me?"

"Sí."

"Tell your woman to fix me food and a place to sleep tonight," Jerry ordered, dismounting.

That was a queer meal in the squalid little house—flat tortillas, beans, leathery, jerked meat, and blazing red chile sauce to put over everything. The light came from a single, dim oil lamp. Baca's woman, a fat slattern with stringy hair, padded softly in bare feet from sheet-iron stove to table. Pablo Baca stood silently in the doorway, watching with a puzzled, undecided look. He had leaned the rifle against the wall—within easy reach, Jerry noticed.

Baca's answers to questions were vague. He knew nothing about Galloway. There were no cattle on the ranch. He did not know who had burned the house and corral.

"Bristol's men?" Jerry guessed.

A flash of intelligence illuminated the ugly face for an instant, then Baca shrugged. *"¿Quién sabe?"* he said vaguely.

Clearly the man would not talk. The squalid interior settled the matter of sleeping. An open-front shed a short distance from the house had a miniature loft stuffed with dried hay. Jerry chose that, turning in above his own horse and Baca's fine riding animal, kept here close to the house where it could be reached quickly. That was queer, too. A pole corral or a hobbled horse would have been more natural.

The night passed quickly. Jerry washed in a bucket of water which Pablo Baca brought him. The ugly fellow listened impassively as Jerry said: "I want a new house over there. Can you get men to build it?"

"Sí. When, *señor?"*

"Today."

"I go," Baca said.

The man seemed relieved for some reason or other, and, after a breakfast no better than the meal of the evening before, Baca rode up the valley on his fine horse. Shortly after noon he was back, followed by a small, creaking wagon drawn by two trotting burros. Four Mexicans with tools rode in the wagon.

They went to work at once, making mud bricks under the cottonwoods, laying them on the ground to dry in the sun. Jerry was watching them, when half a dozen horsemen swept down the valley.

Mounting, Jerry drew his rifle from the saddle scabbard and waited. His face was blank and watchful as the riders came up. These were no honest cowpunchers. The stamp of lawlessness was on them, unmistakable. The squint-eyed little man who rode at their head was no better, although his manner had a brisk air of authority. He reined in before Jerry and came to the point at once.

"I hear you've bought this place from Galloway."

"I got the deed."

"It wasn't Galloway's to sell!" the squint-eyed little man snapped.

"Whose was it?"

"Mine!"

"An' who might you be?"

"Starr is the name."

"Too bad," Jerry drawled. "Galloway was the name on the deed . . . an' it's Green now. I aim to squat right here."

Jerry noticed a lanky fellow on the right of the group, eyeing him closely. There was something familiar about the man, but he couldn't place it, not even when the other said: "What'd you say your name was?"

"Green."

A chortle greeted that. "Last time I saw you, it was Carson." The lanky one turned to Charley Starr. "Hell, this fellow used to ride with Don José. I watched 'em play faro in Yuma one night about four years ago. Don José busted the bank twice that night. An' I'm a muley cow if there ain't a reward out for Carson here. Most of Don José's men was wanted."

Jerry saw the men behind Charley Starr staring with more respect. The name of Don José was still potent. Charley Starr squinted harder. A sly grin came over his face. "I get it," he said. "Galloway is still smart. Why didn't you come to me, first off, Carson? I like to know where I stand."

"The name," said Jerry, "is Green. Tom Green."

Starr shrugged. "Sure . . . I can use you under any name, only I can't figure a man like you, settling down here."

Jerry swung his rifle slightly so that the muzzle covered

Starr. "The name," he said again gently, "is Tom Green. And you can't use me for anything, Starr, because I aim to squat here alone and raise cows. This is my land, deeded an' recorded . . . an' my advice is to get the hell off an' stay off."

Starr's good nature turned to quick, blazing anger. "You trying to threaten me?" he cried furiously.

"Nope . . . I'm tellin' you, Starr," Jerry snapped. "I don't know you, but I don't like your looks. I'm here to raise cows, not skunks. An' any man that'd send four gunmen after one man, like you did yesterday, is a first-class skunk to me."

Starr reddened, spoke calmly with an effort. "What do you know about yesterday?"

"Enough to know you oughta stink downwind, Starr," Jerry said. "See how fast you can ride back up the cañon."

Starr's look became venomous. He whirled his horse, spurred off, almost riding down one of the Mexicans. His men followed across the freshly molded mud bricks, ruining many of them.

Jerry half raised his rifle, then lowered it again sheepishly. Jerry Carson could have stopped them with a bullet . . . but Tom Green was here in Ghost Cañon to raise cows. Pablo Baca stood with a sagging jaw as Starr and his men rode off. Jerry looked toward him.

"Next time you report to Starr," he said in Spanish, "I'll skin you alive, *hombre*."

For the first time Baca ducked his head with a mark of respect. *"Sí, señor,"* he assented meekly. During the rest of the day Jerry noticed Baca, shooting furtive, uneasy glances at him.

Late in the afternoon Jerry rode to his neighbors'. He saw a slender figure step in the house as he came in sight, and once more, as he neared the house, a rifle barrel poked threateningly through the window.

Her clear voice warned: "I told you to stay away from here!"

Jerry doffed his sombrero, grinned at the window. "I got lonesome, ma'am. And I was wondering how your husband is?"

"Well enough," she answered. "And you'll find no company around here."

"I had a visit from Charley Starr today."

She replied scornfully. "That was to be expected. Birds of a feather."

"I don't take that kindly, ma'am."

"Maybe you'll take this kinder!" she called angrily—and Jerry ducked involuntarily as the rifle spat and the bullet just missed him. "I've warned you!" she called. "Do I have to drop you off that horse to make you understand?"

"It's plain enough in any language, ma'am." Jerry rode back up the valley, chuckling to himself.

Pablo Baca was gone, when he got back. The slatternly woman professed ignorance of his whereabouts, and Baca did not return for supper. After eating, Jerry said to the woman: "I'll ride up the cañon. When your man comes home, tell him to wait here for me."

She nodded dumbly.

Jerry rode up the valley, out of sight, and then back through the trees on the north slope, until he was above Baca's shack. He left the horse up there on the hillside, slipped down to the rear of the horse shed, and made himself comfortable. It was dark by then, although the moon was not yet up. The first silver glow was just appearing, when Baca galloped up, left his horse at the door, and went inside.

He came out again in a few minutes, walked to the horse shed, took up a position inside, and waited. There was a small, open window in the back. As the moon grew brighter,

Jerry looked through and saw Baca, standing with his rifle ready, watching the front of the house. The vigil was ominous, marked by deadly patience. It was plain enough that Baca was lurking there to do murder.

Jerry drew his belt gun, leveled it through the window. "You are waiting for someone, *hombre?*" he asked softly in Spanish.

Baca leaped like a cat and ran, dodging, ducking through the brightening moonlight. He leaped onto his horse like a squat shadow and galloped off up the valley without glancing back. The woman looked out and slammed the door.

Jerry stretched, grinning, walked up to his horse, and led it down to the shed. Starr had already shown his hand. Galloway's ranch was getting more unsafe by the hour. Two powerful men, Bristol and Starr, had declared their enmity. Jerry had been recognized by one of Starr's men. The sheriff might ride up at any time. A wise man would leave and keep going—but Jerry climbed up into the little loft with his rifle.

It was early. He lay on the pungent hay, smoking a brown-paper cigarette and pondering the puzzle into which he had stumbled, and listened to a galloping horse, approaching from down the valley. He was standing in the moonlight before the shed when she rode up—the woman whose gun had driven him off twice, whose clear voice had warned him angrily. In the moonlight she sat slim and easy in the saddle, reins in one hand, rifle in the other. A small Stetson shadowed her face, but her voice was clear as ever, and a little embarrassed now.

"I wondered if I would find you here," she said.

"Where else?" Jerry countered.

"I don't know . . . I thought . . . never mind." She hesitated. "My brother is worse," she said. "He asked me to get you. I'm afraid to leave him alone . . . and he insists that . . .

that I get you. Will you come down and stay with him?"

"Brother?"

"Yes."

"I'll follow you back," Jerry said.

VI

"RUSTLERS' MEDICINE"

The windows at the little ranch were glowing with light. The girl's saddled horse was standing by the house. She opened the door as Jerry rode up—and stood there in the lamplight with a .45 in her hand.

"My brother insisted that I ask you to come here," she said coldly. "You didn't bring that cut-throat Mexican, did you?"

"No," said Jerry.

He spoke briefly, because she filled his mind at the moment. Framed in the light, she was younger than he had thought, and prettier, far prettier than he would have believed possible. Her hair was dark, her face slightly oval, and she held her shoulders back, and her head high with a direct, fascinating honesty.

She made no secret of the fact that she distrusted him, disliked him as she stepped back for him to enter—and she made no move to put up the gun. The room, lighted with two lamps, was bright, clean, cheerful. A score of little touches in addition to the gay curtains at the windows reflected her efforts to make a home.

On a bed in the corner lay the wounded man, weak, motionless. He was a few years older than either she or Jerry. Pallor and weakness could not hide the hard, lank line of his jaw, the steady, estimating look in his eyes as his head turned slightly on the pillow and followed Jerry into the room.

44

He spoke with an effort, weakly: "Howdy. Hate to bother you. Got to have someone here. I'm Ed Barnes. This's my sister, Gayle."

"I'm Tom Green," Jerry told him. "What can I do?"

She came to the bed beside Jerry with an easy, graceful step, and again made no secret of the fact that she was hostile. "I'm going to ride off for . . . for some medicine," she said. "It may take me most of the night. Ed must be watched. He was shot through the side. It is a clean wound, but he has lost a lot of blood. I have done the best I can for him. I think he is going to be all right . . . but he must have someone here with him."

"I'll ride for the medicine," Jerry offered.

She gave him a hard, suspicious look. "I'll go," she refused shortly. "Ed . . . do you feel all right?" Her voice changed and her manner was tender as she leaned over the bed.

The wounded man nodded weakly, and she was gone a moment later, galloping down the valley through the moonlight.

Jerry closed the door slowly, turned to the bed. "She didn't go for medicine," he said.

Barnes made no denial. His feverish look was watchful. "Sit down," he invited.

Jerry nodded, remaining on his feet, moving restlessly about. "What do you know about Charley Starr?" he asked abruptly.

Barnes scowled weakly. "Plenty."

"What?"

Anger gave Barnes strength: "I know what a lot of men suspect. He's a snake . . . a killer, an' a thief. An' no one who draws his money is any better. Galloway was worse. I don't know about you. I heard you talkin' outside the window this afternoon, an' you sounded halfway decent."

"Thanks," said Jerry dryly. He added after a moment: "I

45

don't know Charley Starr. Haven't anything to do with him. Never saw Galloway before I got that piece of land from him."

Barnes did not believe him. He closed his eyes, appeared to doze. An hour, two hours passed. Barnes muttered for water several times. Greater weakness had replaced his burst of strength. But he struggled upright in bed as a pane of window glass shattered and a revolver barrel swept a curtain aside. A voice yelled into the room: "Hold still in there!"

Jerry was standing in the middle of the floor, his back to the windows. Only one lamp was burning by this time, and it was turned low. He lunged to it, knocked the chimney off, smothered the wick with his hand, and dropped to the floor as the man outside the window fired. The report was ear-splitting—but the bullet missed. Jerry rolled across the floor, clawing for his gun.

The bed creaked as Barnes fell to the floor, also, dragging blankets with him. It was well he had done so, for two livid flashes laced to the bed. Barnes would have been a dead man, if he had stayed there.

Jerry shot at the flashes. Barnes fired a gun at the same time. The window became silent. In ringing ears Jerry heard groans outside.

"You're handy with a gun," Barnes said.

"Not so slow yourself. Where'd you have that gun?"

"Under the blankets," Barnes confessed. "Just in case. . . ."

"In case the good Samaritan got nasty," Jerry chuckled.

He stepped softly to the window, looked out. The groans still came from the ground below. Silvery moonlight drenched the valley floor. Nothing moved between the house and the tree-studded slope beyond.

Jerry spoke under this breath. "That feller didn't come

here alone to shove a gun through the window."

"I'll bet not." Barnes spoke from the floor, then added bitterly: "Some of Charley Starr's doings."

"What's Starr got against you . . . or me?"

"I can't figure you," Barnes admitted. "But there's going to be trouble tonight, an' I'm wondering why you aren't in on it."

"Gimme a blanket," said Jerry.

He crossed to the door, jerked it open, dangled the blanket in the opening. Two blasting shots perforated it instantly. Jerry slammed the door, tossed the blanket on the floor.

"Couple of them outside. We're bottled in here. What's all the fuss?" he asked.

Barnes was silent for a moment, then muttered: "Looks like there's going to be trouble tonight." He was worried and did not try to hide it. "Hell, Starr's men are ridin'. I'll bet you knew this." Suspicion sharpened his voice.

"I don't know anything," Jerry said gruffly.

He was at the window again, watching close to the house as well as he could. A shadow moved to the right of the window. Someone was there, trying to reach the wounded man. Jerry flicked a gun muzzle out the open window and fired at the spot. A yell, feet stumbling back, announced that he had hit something.

"They're leading your horse away," Barnes said from the floor.

"I've rustled better horses than that. What are these jaspers up to?" Jerry asked again.

Barnes ignored the question, spoke his thoughts aloud. "I wonder if Gayle got through all right?"

"For medicine?"

"To Amit Bristol. If she did, there'll be help. If she didn't, no one rides back this way in a month of Sundays. I'm supposed to be watching things," Barnes whispered.

"Watching what?"

Barnes did not answer. The excitement had been too much for his strength. He had lapsed into unconsciousness. Jerry put a pillow under his head, left him there on the floor by the bed, and took up his post again by the window.

The wounded man outside was not groaning now. Perhaps he had crawled away. The minutes dragged—nothing happened. Jerry opened the door, flaunted the blanket—and two rifle bullets smashed through the door planking, barely missing him. The house was being watched, yet no attempt was being made to get in at them, no unnecessary shots were being fired. The first effort to get at them having failed, the men outside seemed content to bottle up the house and let no one out.

A half hour passed before Jerry heard a wave of sound coming up the valley. It grew louder, became the hurrying movement of cattle, urged on by men. Waiting by the door, Jerry heard the cattle come abreast of the cabin and pass. They were on the other side of the little creekbed, many of them—several hundred, at least—and men were driving them on at a swift pace.

Their coming, their passing toward the Galloway land and the frowning defile of Ghost Cañon fitted bits of the puzzle together. Jerry grinned thinly in the darkness. Many times in the past he had helped drive cattle through the night. They had not belonged to him at sundown—and it had not seemed so bad then, a game of wits, boldness, courage. At the time he had had no conscious feeling that he was doing wrong in rustling cattle. But now? The drive passed out of hearing. Jerry tried the door again. A bullet smashed through the wood once more and drove him back. He swore aloud—and on the floor Barnes groaned, stirred.

Kneeling beside him, Jerry asked: "How do you feel, old-timer?"

"Guess I've been asleep," Barnes muttered.

"Reckon so. You hear the drive pass?"

"What?"

"Cattle. A big bunch went up the valley a little while ago, traveling fast."

Barnes groaned. Jerry lifted him to the bed, made him comfortable, gave him water in the dark.

"I'll bet it's Bristol's cattle again," Barnes groaned. "I had a hunch today it was going to happen soon. They were too anxious to finish me off this time. That's why I sent Gayle to warn Bristol. But she didn't start soon enough. They'll be through the Roost an' gone before Bristol can get men after them."

"The Roost? Is that back in here?"

"You ought to know. Galloway worked with 'em until he got cornered, killed a member of the sheriff's posse, an' had to drift out until it blew over."

Jerry recalled tales he had heard about the Roost, that isolated little settlement back in the Guadalupes, almost impossible to get at, easy to defend, where there was no law, and the law did not intrude. Frowning cliffs, deep-slashed cañons, isolation so great that white men had never trod some parts of it lay beyond the Roost. Honest men did not venture back in there; too many had entered and never come out. The men in the Roost ruled that wild section of the mountains, and there were stories of little-known trails leading south to the border, west to the valley settlements, north through the mountains to the shipping towns. So savage were the men of the Roost that Don José had never gone there, no matter how badly pressed.

"So you figured I was tied in with the Roost?" Jerry said.

"Wasn't taking any chances."

"Charley Starr claimed this afternoon that my land really belonged to him. He's a rancher. Where does he tie in with the Roost?"

Weak as he was, Barnes grunted. "Rancher, hell!" he said with a flash of strength. "That's his screen. He's the outside man for the Roost, although nobody can prove it. He raises more gunmen than calves. He's kingpin at the Roost . . . an' nobody can prove it or do anything about it. Bristol's tried . . . but Starr can muster as many guns as anyone else. He's always ready to fight it out. An' he hates Bristol more than any man alive . . . he's afraid of him, too. Bristol horsewhipped him once when they were both young an' new in these parts. At least, that's the story. Anyhow, Charley Starr'd give his right arm any day to do Bristol a dirty trick."

Jerry asked bluntly: "Are you working for Bristol?"

"Yes . . . an' no," Barnes said. "This is my land. But the valley here is the best way back to the Roost. About the only way they can get cattle in from these parts quick. With a ten-mile start they're back out of reach before anyone can catch up with 'em. Gayle an' I try to keep hands off . . . but if there's anything Bristol ought to know, I take word to him. He's helped me. Yesterday I caught one of the Roost men running off a horse. When I jumped him, the others showed up an' lit into me. Wasn't till this evening that I figured there might be something to it besides the little fracas. Then I sent Gayle to warn Bristol. It's a fifteen-mile ride. Ought to be somebody back here by now," Barnes fretted. "Look out an' see if you hear anything."

"Couple of men, at least, out there, waiting to pot anyone who leaves."

"Damn them! If I was myself, I'd get out after her. You won't try, will you?"

"They wouldn't hurt her. Bristol's cows aren't yours or mine. They're only keeping us in here so we can't go for help. They'll ride off after a while."

Barnes moved uneasily on the bed. "You're taking it cool for a man who also claims he ain't tied in with the Roost."

"Might as well," said Jerry cheerfully. "If Bristol can't hold his cows, it's his hard luck."

There was silence on the bed, then Barnes spoke harshly. "You talk like a rustler yourself."

Jerry said nothing for a moment. Then: "I'm not wading out into a gun fight to prove different," he slowly told the sick man.

VII

"INTO THE ROOST"

Barnes fell into angry silence, and into that quiet a few minutes later beat the approach of hard-ridden horses. Listening, Jerry said: "They're coming up the valley. Your sister got to Bristol. Our watchdogs will hunt cover now."

Jerry lit a lamp and opened the door. No shots greeted him. His horse was gone, as he had expected. So he stood there in the doorway while five riders galloped up. In the moonlight the towering Amit Bristol swung down from the big black he had ridden to a lather.

"That you, Barnes?"—he called, and then looking closer —"Hell . . . you! Where's Barnes?"

"Inside."

Bristol crowded through the doorway, ducking his head. He saw Barnes on the bed, went to him. "What's wrong here?" he asked harshly.

Behind him, Jerry asked: "Didn't Miss Barnes tell you?"

Bristol looked around. "How could she tell me? I haven't seen her."

The other men came in. One was the young fellow with the jaunty sombrero and gay, silk handkerchief who had crowded close against Jerry's side in the San Saba bar. He was serious now.

Barnes tried to sit up, couldn't make it for weakness. His voice shook. "Didn't Gayle get to you?"

"No," Bristol repeated. "Haven't seen her for a month. What happened?"

"I sent her to warn you. Some of the Roost men potted me yesterday. Got to thinking today that they meant trouble. Tonight, after Gayle left, they bottled us up in here an' ran a big bunch of cows toward the Roost."

"We've been tracking them," Bristol said. "Circle D man cutting through the west pasture tonight saw some cows being driven and came over to ask if we had any men out. I started this way with what men I had handy. There's more coming. We found fresh sign leading this way. But . . . I haven't seen anything of your sister."

Jerry said softly: "She should have been there before you left. She had time enough."

Barnes was sitting upright in bed now. On his pallid face the cold sweat of weakness and effort glinted in the lamplight. But his eyes were feverish, his voice harsh with feeling. "Bristol, they've got her! They . . . they've done something with her! If she couldn't get through to you, she'd have started back here. An' if she was anywhere in the valley, you'd have met her on your way here. They've got her!"

Bristol's men moved uneasily. The younger one exclaimed: "They wouldn't dare! What good would she do them?"

"Maybe they didn't want her to carry out an alarm. Maybe they've taken her back to make sure they're not bothered," Jerry suggested. "They seem to want this cañon mouth cleared out an' private."

Amit Bristol wheeled on him, towering, grim. "How do you know so much about this? What are you doing here, anyway?"

Barnes spoke harshly: "God help me . . . I sent for him to stay with me while Gayle went for you. I heard him talking outside this afternoon, and he sounded like half a man . . . looked like he'd be all right to stay with me. But Gayle rode back here ahead of him. He knew she was going. He sent that gun-toting Mexican at his place to carry word. An' since he's been here, he's talked like one of the Roost men an' acted like one. He . . . knows what happened to Gayle. Damn him . . . he knows! Gimme my gun off the floor there! I'll make him talk!"

Barnes tried to reach over the edge of the bed—and collapsed, gasping with the effort he had put forth—and the five men who'd ridden up all believed Barnes.

Jerry looked into their faces and saw swift, rising hostility. Amit Bristol's mouth was a hard line beneath his grizzled mustache. His face was forbidding.

Jerry spoke quickly. "He's wrong. I tried to be a good neighbor this evening. Hell . . . I even shot one of the Roost men. He's outside that window."

Amit Bristol went to the window himself, opened it, looked out. His face was more forbidding as he turned back. "No one out there! Green . . . or whatever your name is . . . I warned you in San Saba yesterday. I know your breed. I knew there'd be trouble as soon as you took Galloway's place. A noose is the only cure for men like you. And, by God, if you've brought any harm to Miss Barnes, I'll put the rope around your neck myself!"

Jerry's own face was bleak, cold as he faced them. "I wouldn't blame you much, Bristol, if it was true," he said. "Only . . . I don't know any more about Miss Barnes than the rest of you. I told you in San Saba that I was settling on my land to raise cows. You branded me a rustler, a liar, an' a thief then before I had any chance to show what I was. I didn't call you on it because I wanted peace. I'm calling you now, Bristol. You lied in San Saba. You lie now, if you put this at my door."

Bristol was still somber in black—and his quick, blazing anger would have cowed most men, but most men had not ridden with Don José de Gama y Lopez. It was Jerry Carson, outlaw pupil of Don José de Gama y Lopez, who faced them in the lamplit room.

Bristol could not know that. It probably would not have mattered if he had. His rasping order filled the room. "Bring him outside, boys! We'll see how he talks with a rope around his neck! I've had enough of Charley Starr and those varmints at the Roost! If this one won't talk, we'll hang him up for the buzzards!"

They were five to one, armed—but Jerry Carson was quicker. It was not the first time a flashing draw had been needed. Amit Bristol, almost as fast, did not hesitate as did the others when Jerry's gun came up.

"Drill him!" Bristol bawled. His own intent was plain.

Jerry shot first—and was already dodging back as the shattered lamp plunged the room into blackness.

Bristol's roaring shot was a wink behind, flashing lividly in the darkness. Jerry's back leap saved him. He felt the bullet graze his coat front, just missing the flesh beneath. He fired no more as the others shifted in confusion to escape random shots. A flying leap took Jerry through the window Bristol had opened. He sprawled heavily on the ground, rolled, stumbled to his feet, lunged for the corner of the house.

Bristol's yell followed him: "Outside, after him, boys!" And Bristol, leaning out the window, fired quickly, accurately. Once more Jerry felt the numbing shock of a bullet, ripping into the hip flesh, high up where it would bleed and throb with pain but would not be serious. He missed his stride for an instant, only that, and then he was around the end of the house to the horses.

Bristol's four men came tumbling out in confusion as

Jerry's flying leap carried him to the nearest saddle. The horse bolted before Jerry got the reins. It ran under the cottonwoods, across the sandy streambed, while Jerry stretched low over the horse's neck, the bullets whining close with the buzz of angry hornets. None found the mark. With his feet in the stirrups, reins in his hands, he swung up the valley.

Seldom had Jerry ridden as he did now. Bristol's men were after him in a few moments, firing as they came. Had it been daylight, they might have dropped him. They were trying to. Their hatred of the men at the Roost, of rustlers, outlaws, and those responsible for Gayle Barnes's disappearance concentrated on him.

Jerry grew bitter as he rode. The warning of Segundo Smith came back: *You can't do it, Jerry. You ain't the breed. It's too tame. An' if you could, they wouldn't let you. You're an outlaw. You ain't never been anything else. First sign of trouble you'll fight your way through it . . . an' then you'll have to hit the trail again.* The day Segundo Smith had forecast had come quickly, and now Jerry rode the horse at a killing pace up the valley toward the outlaw haven. They knew him there—Jerry Carson, who had ridden with Don José.

The horse was still strong. It drew ahead slowly while the pursuit swept across the Galloway land, past the ruins of Galloway's house, past Pablo Baca's hovel. The valley narrowed, and the sides grew steeper. The way led him into the frowning Ghost Cañon. The pursuit dropped back out of sight. Jerry never did know when the men turned back, but, as he reined in presently, he heard nothing behind.

He padded his wound the best he could with a handkerchief and galloped on up the cañon. The sides grew precipitous, barren of trees and bushes. The craggy walls were bare, forbidding. It was obvious now why it was called Ghost Cañon.

Narrower, deeper, the cañon wound back into the mountains. The thread of water trickled over a stony bed. The broad, grassy trail gave way to a rocky path, winding, too, at times rising high above the water. Abruptly the cañon turned, apparently ending in a barrier of rock. Jerry, examining the walls carefully, found high overhead a moment later a spot where the moon-drenched sky entered a narrow cleft that extended down into the blackness of the cañon bottom. Jerry's horse splashed into the water, kept on.

Ahead a harsh voice called: "Who's that?"

The speaker was invisible against the black, rock wall.

"I'm Carson, who took over Galloway's land! Is Charley Starr at the Roost?"

"What makes yuh figure Charley Starr'd be at the Roost?"

"He dropped by to see me this afternoon."

"Stop that horse, damn you, or I'll put a bullet through yuh! What you want with Charley Starr?"

Jerry was abreast of the other horse by then, gun in hand. He stopped there. "What I want with Charley Starr is my business, an' his," he said. "If you want to argue it out with a gun, cut loose. But get me the first shot, *hombre,* or I'll bring you down off that rock like a buzzard off a dead limb."

"Nobody gets by here without orders."

"I'm passing," Jerry said. "You'll get orders from Starr later. Didn't the last two men through here tell you Bristol was bringin' men up?"

"Bristol ain't bringin' anyone past here. He knows it ain't no use. I heard about yuh this afternoon, Carson. Yuh rifled Starr aplenty."

"Damn Charley Starr," Jerry said calmly. "I don't like him . . . but I've got business with him now. Hell is ridin' this way. Bristol's collecting men to raid the Roost. He started on me . . . ran me up through the cañon and put a bullet in my hip."

"Yuh don't say! Maybe it oughta been through yore head."

"Look," said Jerry. He flicked a match, held it over the bloodstained area of the wound.

The guard climbed down, confessing: "I figured it was hot air. So they plugged yuh? Don't blame yuh for wantin' to see Starr. He's up at the Roost tonight . . . an' he'll know how to handle Bristol an' his men, if they try to get in. I'll ride in with yuh."

The man spurred into the narrow cleft. Jerry kept close behind, ignoring the growing pain of the wound. The horseshoes struck hard against smooth rock underfoot, echoing and reëchoing in the narrow defile. He found it hard to believe that a herd of cattle could be driven through here—and yet it had, for once in Ghost Cañon there was no other way out.

At the other end a gruff voice challenged them. Jerry's companion called: "It's all right, Jake. I'm takin' a man up tuh the Roost."

"Who now? The last two through was the only ones out."

"This is Carson, who settled on Galloway's land. Bristol put a bullet in him. You better ride down tuh my post. The boys were right. Bristol's bringin' some men up."

"They won't come this far."

"Carson says they will. Bristol's on the warpath."

"The boys better git up an' stretch, then. They oughta left some men here, anyway. They're gettin' too damn' careless around here."

The speaker fired three shots in the air, spat audibly as the echoes died away, and grunted: "That'll shake 'em up."

"We'll meet 'em," Jerry's guide said.

He rode on into moonlight. Trees cast shadows ahead. The horses walked out on grass. Jerry looked down the mile-long length of a little mountain valley. It sloped sharply up toward cliffs at the other end but was not more than half a mile wide.

Bristol's cattle were not in sight, which was puzzling. They had come this way—and there seemed no other way out as the guide rode toward the black shadows at the base of the left wall of the valley. Before they reached the steep rock the clatter of hoofs drifted out to meet them—and the rock itself seemed to vomit horsemen.

The lead man yelled: "Who fired them shots?"

"Bristol's bringin' men this way. You rannies better get down there an' meet 'em. Where's Starr?"

"Talkin' to Red Mike in the back of the store. Did you bring us down here to hear about Bristol? We just heard he got as far as the Barnes place. He ain't comin' on."

"Looks like he is this time. Better get down there. This man just brought word."

Once again Jerry had to be identified. His presence convinced them. The bunch rode hard toward the narrow entrance to the valley. Jerry's guide headed for the rocky wall and rode into it—for once more a fissure opened before them, this time more of an open chute that led steeply up. It was a hard climb. The horses were panting, when they reached the top, coming out onto a huge natural shelf on the side of the mountain. Jerry stared in amazement.

From the valley floor this looked like the top, but it was not. The shelf was some hundreds of yards wide. At the back, another rocky wall rose so steeply that a man on foot could hardly have climbed it. Scattered haphazardly before them in the moonlight were a score or more of low buildings, mostly built of logs, with one larger structure dominating the rest. Here and there small corrals held horses. Windows were lighted. Dogs barked at their approach. It was a small com-

munity, clinging here on the side of the mountain like an ea-
gles' aerie, perfect in its isolation, its means of defense.

"I'll be damned," Jerry said frankly. "I wasn't lookin' for
anything like this."

"Snug up here, ain't it?" His guide chuckled. "Two ways
in an' out . . . the one yuh come through an' the back way. It's
a seventy-mile ride around tuh San Saba the back way, an' a
man can't hardly get through, at that. The old Teacup mine
usta be up here. The rock was so rich they could afford tuh
freight it out through Ghost Cañon. Vein ran straight in from
the heading beyond the store there. Big one, too . . . about
eight feet high. But when they cut through the hill tuh the
other slope, that's all there was tuh the vein. So they left the
outfit tuh rot until the boys found this was a good place tuh
lay. Lead a horse through the mine tunnel an' yuh can get
'most anywheres you want without being bothered."

"Cattle, too?"

"Yep. Tricky business gettin' 'em through, but the boys
are pretty good at it now. Most of them make their *dinero*
other places an' come here tuh rest up. Red Mike sorta runs
things and keeps the store stocked. If a man's got a woman,
he can usually find a empty cabin. San Saba ain't no better
place tuh live in . . . an' they don't ask questions here. Starr
oughta be in Red Mike's store."

VIII

"GUNS IN THE MOONLIGHT"

It was getting late, but the Roost was wide awake. In several of the cabins women stood in the doorways and watched the two men ride past. Horses were racked before the log-built store. Several armed men, standing in front, eyed them sharply as they went in, and inside other men, armed also, turned to stare as Jerry limped through the door.

The Mexican, Pablo Baca, was standing at the bar, nursing a drink. Baca's jaw dropped, his hand made an involuntary movement toward his gun, then relaxed as Jerry grinned at him.

"Yep, you look all right," Jerry said to him in English. "I thought you had a fit, when you lit out. Feeling better now?"

Baca looked puzzled, humorless. "I don't feel bad," he denied.

"You will one of these days," Jerry comforted. "Glad to know you speak English anyway. I figured this no-savvy stuff was dumb."

The other men were sweepings of the *malpais*, rough-looking, crafty. Don José would not have ridden with one of them. The store itself was old, dirty, and disorderly. Scantily stocked shelves and a counter ran down one side. A stained, unpainted bar stood against the opposite wall, and the wide floor in between was unswept and dirty in the light of the two brass lamps hanging from the ceiling.

Jerry saw now that his guide was lanky, square-faced, slouching as he walked with his rifle in the crook of an arm. He grinned as a bearded man sitting on the counter mocked: "Where'd you git young handsome, Pete? You make him limp thataway?"

"He rode in. Bristol shot him up."

"Ain't that too bad. We'll make a man of him around here."

Jerry smiled thinly, said nothing as he followed through a door at the back into a smoke-filled rear room. The place might have been called an office. It held a battered old desk— evidently left from the mining days—a cot against the wall, and a round table with chairs. A bottle and glasses stood on the table. Two men were sitting opposite each other, smoking and talking. One was Charley Starr. He looked up and, seeing Jerry, came to his feet with an oath, reaching for his gun.

Jerry grinned. "I rode in to see you, Starr."

The other man would have made two of Starr. Not as tall as Amit Bristol, he looked broader, fully as powerful. Long, red hair came down around his ears, and a great ragged, red beard swept his chest. His hands, thick and powerful, were matted on the back with coarse, red hair, and his voice to Starr was a heavy rumble. "Who's this?"

Starr's mean, squint-eyed face twisted in a grin of malicious satisfaction. "This is the young squirt who claims the Galloway place. By God, I'm glad to see him here. I've been wanting him ever since this afternoon."

"I'll bet," said Jerry. "Still a skunk, aren't you, Starr? And you still stink to me. But I came here to tell you Bristol is going to clean out the Roost tonight."

Starr snapped his fingers. "Bristol? Damn Bristol!" He grew suspicious. "You came here to tell me that? After this afternoon?"

"Bristol's men figured I was in with you. They shot me up, ran me off. So I came here to you, Starr."

The blood was there to see. Starr squinted at it, grinned. "If they hadn't shot you . . . I would have," he said.

"I thought so." Jerry grinned back.

Starr rubbed his hands. "And so Bristol's really coming to fight for his cows?"

Jerry shook his head. "Not his cows, Starr. It's Barnes's sister."

Red Mike swore a mighty oath through his beard. "I told you, Charley, it was a damn' fool stunt to bring her here!" he bellowed. "Cows is one thing . . . a woman's another!"

Charley Starr's squint-eyed face grew vicious. "I've had enough of those two squatting there in the cañon, carrying tales to Bristol. I've tried to run 'em out, and they won't run. She was on her way to Bristol tonight, when the boys got her. She's worth more to us now than a dozen men. They won't break in here as long as we hold her."

"But," said Jerry gently, "when you have to let her go and she's back safe, what then?"

"Who asked you, Carson? She's Bristol's niece, his sister's child. He hasn't any children, and he'd give his right eye for her. I've got him where I want him now. I'll make him sweat."

Jerry thought of anger he had seen on men's faces, anger of all kinds, but never had he looked on such malignant viciousness as he did now. Only hate, old and deep, could make a man look like that. "And what," said Jerry, "will happen, when Bristol has her back?"

"Happen?" Starr shouted in sudden fury. "Maybe he won't get her back! What they can't find, they can't prove! I know the law."

Jerry grinned. "You seem to. But Bristol's coming. Try to

stop him by spouting the law."

"I don't like it," Red Mike said heavily. "You've gone too far, Charley."

Starr's rage grew greater. "I haven't started yet! Mike, I'll kill you, if you turn yellow on me." Starr drew his gun—and he handled it like an expert.

A killer, Jerry thought. *He'd shoot from behind as quick as in front.*

Red Mike could have smashed the smaller man with his bare hands, but he became placating before Starr's rage. He spoke hastily. "I'm with you, Charley. What do you reckon we'd better do?"

"Leave two or three men in the tunnel. We'll meet Bristol with the rest. Too bad we haven't got the ones who're hazing his cows." Starr turned to Jerry. "You, too, Carson. You'll earn your way, and, if you stop another bullet, it won't be too quick for me. Got a rifle?"

"No."

Starr looked at the guns racked on the wall, changed his mind. "You won't need one. Skaggs, you go along with him. If he won't fight, shoot him. I don't trust him."

Jerry's guide nodded, patted his rifle, and Charley Starr stormed out to the bar, calling to the men there. Red Mike caught a rifle and two belts of shells off the wall and followed stolidly. Jerry limped after, his guard a step behind.

"We'll let them come through to the valley," Starr was saying loudly. "In the moonlight we can pick them off. Damn them. We'll teach Bristol a lesson he won't forget."

Men were mounting at the hitch rack. Starr hurried out and shot into the air.

Jerry mounted his horse. Red Mike, on a big bay beside him, loaded a rifle silently. Several more men galloped up while Starr waited, swearing under his breath.

"Let's go!" Starr burst out finally. "Carson, lead off! I'll see you don't hang back!"

Jerry laughed at him. "You're going to get a big surprise tonight, Starr. Keep your eyes on me."

The guard barely kept up, as Jerry rode hard for the rocky chute. Abreast, they began the steep descent. Behind them came the others, invisible in the black shadows, but the clash of hoofs on rock, the creak of saddle-leather were loud in the chute.

Jerry laughed aloud as he leaned back in the saddle and gave his horse its head. The old exaltation was sweeping him. Danger! Action! And yet it was different this time—far different.

"Going to be dust raised tonight," Jerry called to his guard.

"And you're going tuh be in it!" Some of Starr's animosity had gotten into this man.

"Watch me," Jerry promised.

They burst out of the chute, riding side by side through the black shadows at the base of the cliff. Jerry reined over sharply into the horse and rider beside him.

"Hey . . . what'n hell you tryin' to do? Get over there!"

Jerry's hand found the shoulder it reached for. He yanked, leaning far over and chopping to the head with his gun. No more was needed. The man came out of the saddle limply, dropped. His horse swerved off.

Starr rode up, yelling: "What's the matter with you two?"

Starr slackened as Jerry pulled up. The others went past with a rush toward the moonlight just beyond, and Starr, a vague blur in the shadows, edging close, demanded angrily: "What are you two holding back for?"

"For you!" Jerry called—and he crowded against Starr, hooked an arm around Starr's neck, and dragged him from the saddle, jamming a gun against Starr's body as it came over. "Keep quiet, you squint-eyed snake," Jerry warned as Starr came out of the saddle.

It was over in a moment.

The other riders were out in the moonlight, riding hard toward the valley entrance. Jerry dragged Starr across his own saddle horn. Starr's arm moved convulsively toward his gun. Jerry hit him on the back of the neck with a clenched fist. Starr quieted—and Jerry got the gun and threw it away. Catching the reins, he turned back toward the rocky chute.

Face down, Starr choked with rage. "I'll kill you for this, Carson."

"I know," said Jerry. "You're a mean *hombre*."

Starr cursed. "You won't get out of here alive," he gasped.

Jerry hit him on the back of the neck again. "You talk too much," he suggested cheerfully. "Don José used to say that a man who used his mouth too much might be hell at grub time . . . but he was usually short rations in trouble. Keep quiet or I'll take out that rotten little heart of yours an' fit it in a peanut."

Charley Starr was fairly sobbing with rage. "If I had a gun an' half a chance, I'd put daylight through you in a dozen places."

"Moonlight," Jerry corrected. "I'll bet you're just a rootin'-tootin' he-badman." Jerry hit him on the back of the neck again. "I've killed worse than you'd ever want to be, just because they talked like that, Starr. An' I'm itchin' to kill you. Go on an' egg me on to it."

The request was so cold, so calm, that Starr's frantic anger vanished abruptly. He lay quietly, limply, as the horse bunched its muscles and started back up the chute with its double load.

Halfway up, Starr asked uneasily: "What are you going to do?"

"I thought you guessed it, *hombre*. Miss Barnes."

"You're a young fool. You'll never get out of here with her."

Jerry chuckled. "You'd be surprised the places I've gotten out of. They'd make this two-bit outfit of yours look like a joke."

Starr's manner changed. "I thought Bristol's men put a bullet in you."

"They did."

"Then what are you makin' a play like this for? They'll give you another bullet for your trouble."

"Maybe," Jerry agreed. "But I'm not doing it for Bristol."

They topped the chute, met another rider starting down. Frantically Starr yelled: "Kill this man! I'm Starr. I . . . !"

Jerry brought his gun down. Starr collapsed limply, and in the white moonlight the other rider's gun glinted as he drew it.

"Drop it!" Jerry shouted.

But as he spoke, he saw that the man was going to shoot. Jerry's gun blasted first. There was nothing else to do. He thought fleetingly, as the man fell, that this was one killing the law would not protest.

Starr was a dead, limp weight. "Damn!" Jerry swore with sudden chagrin. "I've gone and done it now. Ought to have my ears pinned back."

Starr would not talk for some time. Meanwhile, there was no one to say where Gayle Barnes was.

IX

"BACK ROAD TO HELL"

The thin crackle of gunfire came drifting up out of the valley. Bristol and his men had arrived. But Jerry, who had been through that dark, rocky fissure, had little thought that they would break in and clean out the Roost. It couldn't be done that way. Willingness to fight would count little against those high barriers of rock.

Four other riders galloped toward the head of the chute. As they came up, Jerry yelled: "Bristol's men are breakin' in! Get down there quick! Charley Starr had an accident! I'm takin' him to the store!"

The distant gunfire convinced them. They went on with a rush. Jerry rode through the cluster of cabins, ignoring the women and children who had been drawn out into the night.

One woman called shrilly to him. "Are they gettin' in?"

"Not yet. Can't tell what'll happen."

The store was lighted, deserted. Jerry tied his horse, limped inside with Starr, laid him on the bar. There might be a chance Starr would come out of it.

The squint eyes were closed, breathing hardly noticeable. Breaking the neck of a whiskey bottle against the bar edge, Jerry slopped whiskey on Starr's face, pried open his mouth, and put a little inside. It had no immediate effect. Starr evidently would be unconscious for quite a while.

A foot scraped softly in the doorway. Turning, Jerry saw

Pablo Baca, standing there covering him with a rifle. The brown, ugly face was set hard with suspicion.

"W'at you do weeth him?" Baca demanded.

Jerry's smile had no mirth. "He had an accident, Baca."

"Funny. I see you hit him on your horse."

"Hmm, I wonder," Jerry said. "Hanging back up here, were you? . . . watch your finger on that trigger."

Baca's brown hands gripped the rifle tensely. His trigger finger was crooked, ready. On his broad, pockmarked face was a curious mixture of hate and fear. It was hard to tell whether he would shoot or talk.

"Help me with him," Jerry ordered.

Baca shook his head. "I watch you," he said. "I watch you until all come back. You fool these men . . . but not me, Pablo Baca."

"You working for me, Baca?"

"No," said Baca. "I work for *Señor* Starr. Eight years I work for heem. An' now I watch heem . . . and you."

Jerry was standing on the inside of the bar, looking at the rifle muzzle. He set the whiskey bottle on the bar edge. "Baca, where is Miss Barnes?"

Smoldering satisfaction came over the pocked face. "How I know?" Baca said. "I don' know w'ere she is."

But he did. He could not hide it, and Jerry grinned at him. "You're a smart Mex," he said. "But . . . not smart enough."

Baca was puzzling that, when Jerry dropped behind the bar. Baca shot—an instant too late. The whiskey bottle shattered, scattering whiskey—and Jerry came up through the shower with his gun in his hand, smiling.

Baca was pumping in another shell. Fear and horror ran across his face as he looked at the big .45 and the mirthless smile behind it.

"A smart Mex," Jerry said, resting his gun on his raised left arm almost leisurely.

Baca squealed with sudden fright, turned to run toward the door. The gun blasted across Jerry's arm, and Baca sprawled on the floor with a shattered ankle.

Vaulting the bar, Jerry caught up the rifle and looked down with an expressionless face. "Not so smart, Baca," he said. "Where's Miss Barnes?"

"I don' know!" Baca gasped.

"Too bad," Jerry stated regretfully. "I didn't want to kill you. But . . . here goes."

"¡No! ¡Ah, Dios, no!" Baca screamed, cowering from the gun and lapsing into his native Spanish. "She is above." Baca's shaking hand pointed up to the second floor.

An open door at the front end of the bar gave into a narrow, little hall from which the stairs went up. Jerry took them two at a time, into the dark hall at the top.

"Miss Barnes?" he called.

Her answer came muffled from the back of the hall. Running there, Jerry found the door locked. He burst the door open with his shoulder, staggered into the room. By the light of a small lamp on the table, Gayle Barnes stared at him.

"So it's you." She grinned coldly.

Jerry motioned with his gun. "Come along, ma'am. We've got to hurry."

She said: "I heard you talking to them in the room below. I knew you were no good, when you settled on the Galloway land. But I didn't think you were as bad as you turned out to be. You sent men to head me off, didn't you?"

Jerry thought that in this blaze of anger she was prettier than ever. He shook his head. "I didn't know anything about it," he said. "I came here to get you."

She cried: "Don't lie any more to me! I heard you warn

them! You're a thief and an outlaw, too! You didn't even use your right name. You pulled a sneaking trick on me . . . a woman . . . and stayed behind to handle a sick man. And when my uncle came along, you ran here to warn them. If . . . if I had a gun. . . ."

"Your uncle an' all the men he could collect couldn't fight their way in here to the Roost," Jerry said. "Charley Starr's a crazy man . . . crazy from hating Bristol. You aren't safe here."

"I'd rather take my chances with Starr and his men than with you. Don't . . . don't touch me!"

She backed to the wall, as Jerry advanced. She tried to fight him off, but Jerry caught a wrist and dragged her to the door.

"Even a mule wouldn't balk at a time like this," he said. "If you were a man, I'd club some sense into you. Keep quiet and come along."

She fought all the way along the hall and down the stairs. Jerry was disheveled and panting, when he dragged her out into the big room below. Several women had slipped to the door and were looking in fearfully at the moaning Baca, who had left a bloody path as he dragged himself to the door.

Gayle Barnes ceased struggling and looked sick. "He's dying," she gulped. "Who . . . who did it?"

"I did," said Jerry. "Those women will take care of him soon as we get out of here."

Charley Starr was stirring on the bar top. His eyes opened. He rolled his head to look at them. Jerry left Gayle Barnes, went to him, and jerked him upright. Starr shrank away. Jerry jerked him off to the floor, held him upright as he staggered.

"Savvy now?" he snapped.

Starr gulped, nodded.

"Then pay attention," Jerry said in a brittle, cold voice.

"I'm going to kill you, if you look cross-eyed, make one move, or open your mouth unless I tell you to. Kill you, Starr, before you can explain. Get me?"

Starr rolled his eyes at Gayle Barnes, nodded. His face was pale, drawn. His hands kept going to the back of his head.

"Stand there," Jerry ordered.

He went behind the bar, caught bottles, and smashed them on the floor and back bar until there were no more bottles. Stepping back, he struck a match and tossed it. The explosion drove a scorching blast into his face. A sheet of blue flame leaped toward the ceiling.

"Outside!" Jerry snapped to Starr—and he followed the man past Baca who was crawling to safety.

Behind them a lurid fountain of fire was attacking the bar and the wooden wall behind it. Jerry cast an estimating glance back through the door. "Nothing'll stop it now," he said.

His horse was at the hitch rack. A second horse, saddled, stood in the moonlight some twenty yards away. Jerry herded Starr and the girl toward it, leading his own. He recognized Baca's fine animal.

"Ride this one, ma'am," he said to Gayle Barnes. "Starr, get up behind her. I think I know where there's a horse for you. If we meet anyone, I'll do the talkin' an' you back me up. An' don't forget, I'll kill you the first time you speak out of turn."

In the moonlight Starr nodded. Weakly he managed to mount behind Gayle Barnes. She was passive, obedient now. Her glances were wondering.

Jerry rode beside them, back between the cabins toward the head of the rocky chute leading down into the valley. There he found the horse whose rider had been dropped with a bullet.

Catching the horse, Jerry ordered Starr on it. When that

was done, he took the reins and said curtly: "We're going down to the fight. But you won't be any safer among your men than you are here. Get it?"

"Yes," said Starr with an effort.

They went down the chute, Jerry holding Starr's reins. Not until they were out in the moonlight on the gentle valley slope did he surrender them.

"Keep close," he ordered. "Miss Barnes, you stay behind."

Down at the end of the valley, sounding as if it came from the black cañon beyond the fissure, gunfire was still blasting the peace of the night. As they rode fast that way, straight to the men of the Roost and their guns, a crimson glow broke out on the great, high shelf behind them, rising, spreading until the flames could be seen leaping up.

Jerry rode with his leg almost touching Starr's, belt gun ready in his hand and Baca's rifle in the saddle boot. Behind them sparks began to spew toward the sky, and a dull, red glimmer reached out over the valley after them. The big log structure, dry and impregnated with pitch, was burning like tinder, and the fire seemed to be spreading to adjoining cabins.

Men rode out to meet them, the leader shouting: "What happened up there?"

"Men from San Saba got in through the tunnel," Jerry yelled. "They're burning out the place! Where's Red Mike?"

"At the cañon head with most of the boys! We drove 'em back down the cañon through the tunnel!"

"Take a look at what they're doing!" Jerry answered without stopping. "We're turning the girl loose. She's made all this trouble. Get up to the Roost and do what you can!"

Starr said nothing, as they went on. Riding close to him, Jerry cast a look over his shoulder and saw Gayle Barnes behind. She was riding into danger, death perhaps, without a word of objection. With bullets flying in the darkness ahead, there was every chance she might stop one. Jerry knew it, shrank from it for her sake, but saw nothing else to do. Bristol's men had failed. If she didn't get out now, she might never leave the Roost, for as soon as the men reached the burning buildings and found out the truth, they would return, ready to kill.

More men appeared as they neared the mouth of the fissure, men who shouted for information—and got it from Jerry as he herded Charley Starr past.

The narrow fissure yawned before them. Riderless horses were being held there by two men. Their own animals splashed down into the water. Jerry caught Starr's reins once more and rode leg to leg, his gun over Starr's body.

Twice they passed riders in that narrow way, men who went by in the blackness without questions. The firing continued in front, echoing and reëchoing along the rocks. More horses were being held near the other end, where a slight curve shielded them from stray bullets. Jerry crowded past with difficulty, and the man, watching the horses, told him that Red Mike and the others were just ahead.

Moonlight marked the end of the fissure. The firing was very close. A ricocheting bullet knocked down chips of rock from overhead. Jerry stopped, spoke over his shoulder: "Afraid, ma'am?"

"No," she said clearly. "Are you?"

He chuckled. "You bet I am. I'd sooner pet a rattlesnake, but it's got to be done. Maybe we'll be lucky. Get down flat on your horse's neck an' follow us."

"I'll try," she said steadily.

Wrapping Starr's reins around his left hand, Jerry sent both horses trotting out into open space.

"Red Mike! Red Mike!"

The men of the Roost were scattered out among the rocks to right and left, firing at gun flashes several hundred yards away where the cañon made its first bend. Bristol's men had retired to there. From the right, Red Mike answered.

"Hold everything! They're burning the Roost out! Charley Starr's going out to talk to Bristol!"

Red Mike bellowed: "What's that? You there, Charley?"

"Tell him," Jerry rasped.

Charley Starr choked: "That's right, Mike."

"Hey . . . wait! You're crazy!"

But they were already on their way—and the surprise, the uncertainty of what was happening, held the outlaw guns silent as they went.

Jerry had counted on that. With the guns silent behind them, Starr and himself were shielding Gayle Barnes. The clatter of their advance over the rocky trail was loud in the sudden silence at this end of the cañon. Bullets whined about them, then slackened, stopped as Bristol's men waited.

"Call your uncle, Miss Barnes! Keep calling him until we get there! They don't know but what the whole gang is coming down on them!"

Her clear voice rang out, echoing down the cañon. "Uncle Amit! Uncle Amit!"

Amit Bristol's mighty shout answered: "Gayle!"

There was moonlight around the bend of the cañon. Amit Bristol himself swung his niece to the ground.

"Thank God!" he said prayerfully. "Who brought you?" And then Bristol's voice hardened, grew ugly. "By the living dead . . . Charley Starr and that young renegade he put on the Galloway land. Drag them down, boys!"

"I'll drop the first man who touches me!" Jerry warned.

But Gayle Barnes said: "Not him, Uncle Amit! You're

wrong. Brought me out himself . . . and dragged Charley Starr here to you! He fought them, shot them! I . . . I don't believe any other man could have done what he did!"

"God bless me!" Amit Bristol rumbled. "He went in and got you?"

"Yes."

"I can't figure why."

Charley Starr found his voice then, harsh, sneering. "He did it to curry favor with you, Bristol. He used to be an outlaw. They never change. His name's Carson. Probably got a price tag on his head."

Jerry swung stiffly to the ground.

"You're all wrong," he said shortly. "I rode into the Roost after Charley Starr an' Miss Barnes because a low-down cow-thief an' woman-snatcher made trouble on my land. I aim to raise cows in peace, if I have to clean out every skunk in a day's ride. I set the Roost on fire. It's burning up now. Bottle 'em in there, starve 'em out, an' you'll have a clean range around here before you know it."

Amit Bristol answered unashamedly before his niece: "By God, I can believe talk like that. Raise your cows, Green, and you'll find us all good neighbors."

"All of us," Gayle Barnes said calmly.

Jerry grinned then, grinned at her through the moonlight. "I never had neighbors before . . . but I can understand talk like yours. I'm liable to be riding over 'most any time to hear more of it."

"Why not?" Gayle Barnes asked.

She was smiling, and in that moment Jerry knew finally that Segundo Smith had been wrong.

Old Hellcat

About once a year in the 1930s Marguerite E. Harper, T. T. Flynn's agent, would sell one of his short novels to *Argosy*, then published weekly on Saturdays. It was one of the most prestigious of the so-called rough-paper magazines, although in the next decade, after its purchase by Popular Publications, it would join the ranks of the smooth-paper, or slick, magazines. After the transition Flynn would continue as a contributor. Perhaps because Flynn already knew where this short novel was going when he wrote it, he did not give it a title but, instead, entered it in his author's journal as "Shack Anderson Western." It was bought for $495.00 and appeared under the title "Old Hellcat" in the *Argosy* issue dated March 7, 1936.

I

"THE WAR-HORSE"

Shack Anderson pulled off his white cotton nightgown and looked out the hotel window at the warm morning sunshine over Stinking Springs. An explosive oath burst from him.

"Seven o'clock," Shack said angrily, stamping over to the chair which held his clothes. "Dang my worthless old hide! Gettin' up at seven o'clock. I oughta be ashamed o' myself . . . an' I damn' well am. I ain't a man no more, layin' in bed tuh this hour o' the mornin'."

Shack hauled clothes on his gaunt, big-boned frame, growling to himself. When he turned to the mirror, he saw white hair, a lean, weathered face, and a wide mouth under a close-clipped mustache. There was no doubt he was old this morning, and it made him angry. He tucked his trousers into polished riding boots and snorted disapproval.

"All duded up like a Saint Louis gambler. By golly, I never thought I'd get so low."

Standing before the mirror, Shack made heavy work of the black, string tie with his gnarled fingers. He had messed it up twice, when someone knocked at the door. "Come in!" Shack yelled without looking around.

In the mirror he saw who entered and swung around, forgetting his tie.

"Great snakes, I never thought I'd live to see Soogan Kate up so early in the morning!" Shack exclaimed. "Yo're a sight for sore eyes, Kate. Set down. What's the matter? Yuh in trouble?"

Soogan Kate Conners closed the door and looked at Shack. Kate's hair was white, also. Why, it seemed only yesterday that Soogan Kate had been the prettiest dance-hall girl in two states. The good wives had lifted their noses and looked the other way, when Soogan Kate had swung by in her elegant finery. But Kate, queen of her own world, had only laughed at them. In those days Kate could drink the ordinary cow waddie under any table and dance all night, every night. A square shooter, too, Kate had staked many a man when his luck ran out. A great girl, Kate had been.

"Yo're a sight for sore eyes, Kate," Shack said heartily. "Want I should pour yuh a drink?"

"I stopped drinkin' twenty years ago, Shack," Soogan Kate said, taking a chair. "I never did put away half as much as the boys thought, anyway."

"I'll have one fer both of us," Shack said sociably. He took a half-full quart from his suitcase, pulled the cork, held the bottle up. "Mud in yore eye, old-timer. Here's to us an' all the hell we raised together."

Kate watched him, smiling faintly as he put the bottle back. "Those were wild days, Shack," she said.

"I reckon so," Shack agreed. "Things have changed a heap, Kate. Look at me . . . all duded up an' rollin' outta bed at seven o'clock, gruntin' with my rheumatiz. Yep, things has changed."

Kate nodded, and mused: "First time I knowed you, Shack, you had patches on your britches. Now you're a retired cattleman with plenty of money, taking life free, wide, an' easy."

"I'm retired, anyway," Shack said sorrowfully. "Turned out tuh pasture." He looked at Kate closely. Her clothes were good. She did not look particularly worried. "What can I do,

Kate?" Shack asked. "If it's money, speak out. I c'n let you have all you need."

"The same old Shack," Kate smiled. "Pockets wide open to your friends. It ain't money, Shack. I've got enough of that, thank God. I saved an' hung onto it. I own my own saloon, an' it's makin' me money. It's you, Shack. Right after I got up this morning I heard you was in town, so I came over to see if you had the news."

Shack grinned at her. "Sounds serious."

"Maybe it is," said Soogan Kate, with a worried frown. "How are you and Hondo Matson gettin' along?"

Shack stiffened at the name—then remembered and sat down. "I reckon me 'n' Hondo are gettin' along," he said. "Two old men who've hung up our chaps, banked our money, an' left our ranches. Hondo give his Hangin' Noose tuh his boy, Sim . . . an', when my Flo got married, I turned over the Bar A spread tuh her 'n' her husband. Times has changed. Things ain't the same no more. I was forkin' a dead bronc', Kate. It was time I got outta the cow game. They've made it a dern banker's business these days. Hell! Wire strung all over the range like a schoolmarm's chicken yard, an' cowhands orderin' fancy neckties an' forgettin' there ever was such a thing as guns. Shucks! Us old-timers don't fit in no more. Even the cows are all duded up. It's been years since I've seen a honest tuh God ory-eyed longhorn. An' a railroad sidin' stuck right up tuh yore back door tuh take the beef. I never figgered I'd live tuh see it."

Shack put down another drink to oil his injured feelings.

Soogan Kate had listened with a faint smile. "That's a long speech, Shack. You must feel pretty strongly about it."

"Why shouldn't I?" Shack replied indignantly, tossing the bottle back in the suitcase. "Three weeks ago I passed that fox-faced, mealy-mouthed Hondo Matson, an' he had the nerve tuh stick out his paw and allow we'd let bygones be bygones. I come tuh myself, walking on t'other side of the street and thankin' the Lord I didn't have my gun on. Offered tuh shake hands with me, he did."

Soogan Kate chuckled.

"It spoiled my victuals fer a week!" Shack snorted. "That low-down cow thief should've been hung forty years ago. It's always been a wonder tuh me his gizzard wasn't shot out the first year he come on this range."

"You've throwed enough lead at him to do your share," Kate said. "Hondo's still carryin' some of it, ain't he?"

"Not enough," Shack said regretfully. "I got two bullets in me that come from that son's gun. If my gun hadn't busted that night, it would've been all over with Hondo. I'm still ashamed of the way I high-tailed it."

"Well, it ain't all over with Hondo."

"Just as good as," Shack snorted. "Like me, Hondo's wore out, played out, an' got out. That rawboned, buck-toothed colt o' hisn's runnin' the Hangin' Noose, an' Hondo's sportin' dude clothes, too, takin' it easy an' tryin' tuh pretend he's respectable."

Kate sniffed. "Your eyes ain't what they used to be, Shack, or else you been snoozin' a lot lately. Didn't you know young Sim Matson has took in two partners, an' the Hangin' Noose is spreadin' out and lookin' for trouble? They've hired a lot of cold-eyed brush-wallopers that are wearin' their guns low an' pinin' for trouble. Sim Matson has let on the Hangin' Noose is takin' no backtalk from nobody."

"I have heered some such damn' fool talk," Shack admitted. "Likely Sim was drunk an' shootin' off his mouth like Hondo used to."

"Hondo Matson has bought up control of the Lone Pine Bank," Kate said.

"The dickens, Kate! I never heered that."

"I pick up things," said Kate. "Jack Lawson, the sheriff at Lone Pine, is powerful friendly with Sim Matson."

"Lawson's taste for company never was worth a damn."

"Shack," said Kate, "it looks like I got to be the one to bring you the news. Your son-in-law, Milt Tyner, had words with Sim Matson yesterday afternoon at Lone Pine. Milt knocked Sim down . . . an' one of Sim's cowhands shot Milt through the right arm. And then Jack Lawson throwed Milt in jail for disturbin' the peace. If you want my opinion on it, Shack, your Bar A is gonna make about two juicy bites for the Hangin' Noose crowd with you outta the way."

Shack stood for a moment, blinking. His hands began to stiffen. His mouth opened soundlessly—and then a blast of indignation erupted. "Milt throwed in jail for punchin' Sim Matson in the jaw? An' he let hisself get put there?"

Soogan Kate said nothing.

Shack groaned. "That's just like Milt! He was raised on peace and pap . . . an' Flo's egged him on in it. Trouble gives 'em both goose pimples. Peace an' plenty is their motto. I might've knowed Hondo Matson's mouth'd water at a set-up like that."

Soogan Kate's look was queer. "You better be glad you're out of it, Shack," she sympathized. "You ain't got nothin' to lose."

"Who ain't got nothin' to lose?" Shack yelled, glaring at her. "I got my pride, ain't I? I got the Bar A, ain't I?"

"Your kids own the Bar, don't they, Shack?"

"Hell, no!" Shack snorted. "I ain't a fool. I kept title to the Bar A. Flo, my oldest girl, an' her husband is only runnin' it on shares until I die. I must've had a hunch somethin' like this'd come up."

Shack ripped off his black string tie and hurled it to the

floor. Diving into his suitcase, he hauled up two worn, old gun belts and two cloth-wrapped packages. Tossing the belts on the bed, he tenderly unwrapped the packages. They held two single-action .45s, oiled against moisture.

"I've been a damn' fool," Shack said darkly, "but I still had sense enough tuh keep my hawg-laigs close."

"Shack," said Kate, "what are you aimin' to do?"

"Do?" Shack snorted. "I'm goin' back to ranchin', Kate. Somebody kidded me outta my senses. I ain't old. I'm never gonna grow old. A heap o' folks are gonna be surprised, when I hit the Lone Pine range."

Soogan Kate's eyes were shining as she stood up. "Shack, I knowed they couldn't bluff you. Only don't get reckless. There's only one o' you, an' there's a heap o' them."

"I c'n put my hand on a dozen good men I usta ride with!" Shack snapped. "I'm good fer another dozen myself. If the range around Lone Pine needs a touch of old times, it's gonna get it. Thank you kindly fer bringin' the news, Kate."

Soogan Kate's smile was good to see. "I thought you'd be wantin' to know, Shack. Good luck." Kate held out her hand.

Shack took it, saw her out the door, and then finished his preparations feverishly. They consisted of kicking the string tie under the bed, strapping the gun belts around his waist, testing the guns, and filling the cylinders with cartridges. But other things had happened of which Shack was only dimly aware. A stoop in his shoulders had vanished. When he cocked the sombrero on his head, he was a tall, gaunt, weather-beaten man with a hard, purposeful mouth under the white mustache. Shack had come into the hotel room the night before old. Leaving the suitcase at the foot of the bed, he strode out of the room with a young man's spring in his feet.

Downstairs at the desk he paid the bill and gave the clerk a curt direction. "There's a suitcase full o' dude clothes up in my room. Give 'em away to any old fool who's willing tuh wear 'em."

"I beg your pardon?" said the clerk. His face was soft, smooth, his black mustache was carefully trimmed, and the look he cast at the two guns showing under Shack's open coat was somewhat uneasy.

"What're yuh beggin' my pardon for?" Shack snapped. "You got ears, ain't you?" He stamped out of the lobby and made for the livery stable.

Harmony Higgins, the old-timer who ran the livery stable, greeted Shack jovially. "Want the team harnessed to your buggy, Anderson?"

"I'm leavin' that baby cart here, Harmony. Where's that big bay saddle horse yuh was showin' me?"

"Back in the same stall," Harmony Higgins said, blinking.

"I reckon he's for sale, huh?"

"Uh . . . mebbe," said Harmony cautiously. "If I can get my price."

"Yo're gettin' it," Shack said. "I'll spoil yore day by not hagglin' over it. You got a second-hand saddle there in the office, too. I'm buyin' it. That Texican saddle."

"That's my old saddle," Harmony protested. " 'Tain't for sale."

"I'll borrow it, then. Texican way is the only way I'll ride."

"Seein' it's you," Harmony yielded. "But if you're goin' home, what's the matter with your buggy?"

"No use tryin' to explain tuh an old idjit like you, Harmony. I ain't half a man, when I get tucked in a buggy. Anyway, I'm cuttin' across country tuh Lone Pine."

"Don't make sense," Harmony Higgins said frankly. "But you've bought a bay an' borrowed a saddle. I'll get 'em *pronto*."

While that was being done, Shack walked to the nearest store and bought a pair of spurs. A few minutes later in the livery stable he shoved a bill of sale in his pocket, swung into the saddle, and sent the big bay galloping down the street.

II

" 'YUH AIN'T A SHERIFF.' "

The sun was a blinding ball in the cloudless blue sky. Shack Anderson's corded body soaked up the heat gratefully. For forty years he had been used to it. Shack's eyes roved across the brown, rolling sweep of the range. Mountains made massive dikes against the horizon. Flat-topped mesas stood up here and there in the distance. Off to the right, tall cottonwoods and willows along Jacksnipe Creek snaked a band of green across the dun-colored grassland.

A great country, even if the old days were gone. Ghosts of the past stole in as the bay's driving legs put the miles behind. Memories of a time when white men were few on this Southwestern range, and the Apaches ran riot with death, torture, destruction. In those days men worked, laughed, and loved with guns ready and death close.

Shack snorted as he dismounted to open a Texas gate set in wire, stretching out of sight in either direction. He had passed this way when a man could ride from Paso del Norte to the headwaters of the Arkansas without striking a line fence. Now Milt Tyner, the son his daughter had brought him, the boy bred of wire fences, towns, and fat, white-faced cattle, had let a weak-chinned sheriff lock him up on a trumped-up charge.

Shack spoke aloud bitterly. "I ain't gonna think about it. I'll ride myself useless, if I keep on."

Noon was past, and Shack's belt was tight about his lean middle, when he rode the sweat-streaked bay into Lone Pine. Man-planted cottonwoods grew in Lone Pine now, and there was one block of brick sidewalk. Shack knew every brick, every building. He'd watched them come year by year.

Men lifted hands, called greetings, as Shack rode along the main street. Others stopped and watched him silently. Like a lean, wise, old hound, sampling the wind, Shack sensed an undercurrent of expectancy. He read it right and smiled mirthlessly under his close-cropped, white mustache. They knew about Milt Tyner. They were waiting, wondering what old Shack Anderson would have to say. Old Shack—busted-down cowman, retired, softening and useless on the fat of the land he had won by sweat, work, and daring. A familiar buggy and sorrel team stood before the brick jail. Shack tied his horse and walked into the sheriff's office. He was prepared for what he found there. Flo started up from her chair in surprise.

"Father! What are you doing here? I wasn't expecting you back for a week." Flo looked anxious. "I hope there's nothing wrong, Father?"

Shack masked his feelings by coughing. "Wrong? Ain't Milt in jail here?"

Flo at twenty-four was a little heavier than she had been when she had married Milt Tyner, a little more complacent and satisfied with life. But she was good-looking, well-dressed, a woman any man would be proud to have for a wife or daughter. Shack eyed her closely as he waited for her answer. Flo's eyes were red. She had been crying and looked worried—but not angry, not determined. Her answer was uncertain, almost ashamed.

"Yes, Milt's here, Father. He . . . he got in a fight and was wounded in the arm. It isn't bad. He'll be all right with some rest. I'm waiting now to see if some arrangements can't be made."

Shack opened his mouth soundlessly. His face reddened. When he spoke, the words came with difficulty. "Yo're waitin' tuh see if it can't be arranged? An' Milt'll be all right if he can get some rest after he gets out?"

Flo nodded. "We'll take care of everything, Father. Drive on out to the ranch and don't worry about it."

Shack gagged—and unleashed his feelings with a roar of wrath. "Rest myself an' don't worry! Dang my dirty, old, cowhide britches! It's a good thing I come back! The two of yuh ain't got any more spunk than a pair of chipmunks. Where's the sheriff? Where's Milt?"

"Please, Father," Flo begged. "You'll only make it worse. We . . . we don't want any more trouble over this. It's disgraceful enough as it is. I've money for Milt's bail as soon as the sheriff can find Judge Cornwell."

Shack fanned the air and glared at his daughter. "Sit down!" he yelled.

Flo subsided on her chair abruptly, mouth open in astonishment. "W-why, F-father," she stammered.

"Don't 'why, Father' me!" Shack stormed, stamping about the room. "I'm plumb ashamed I ever raised a gal like yuh. I should've licked yuh more when yuh was a young 'un. I've seed yore mother let fly with a Sharps rifle at a snoopin' Apache an' never bat a eye. And here yo're beggin' me tuh keep quiet so's not tuh make any trouble."

Flo pressed her lips tightly together. Shack knew the signs. Flo was getting ready to put her foot down. She had been doing it increasingly the last year or so. "I feel sure Mother never approved of the life she was forced to lead," Flo said primly. "And times have changed, Father. We have law and order now, and everyone is proud of it. I have no doubt Milt will bring charges of assault against the ruffian who shot him. But I insist that you calm down and let us handle it."

"Yuh insist?" Shack barked, advancing on his daughter. "Yuh insist, huh?" His gnarled finger wagged under Flo's shrinking nose. "Yore days of insistin' are gone, Daughter. Yore preachin' and orderin' an' mollycoddlin' me has ended. I'm takin' charge of the Bar A from now on. If there's any backtalk from you or Milt, yuh both can pack yore things an' hit the road. I was a man till I give in tuh yore damn' fool milksop ways. It stopped this mornin' sudden, over at Stinkin' Springs. From now on I'm ridin' yuh an' Milt with a curb bit."

Flo began to dab her eyes with a handkerchief. "I th-think you've gone crazy," she wailed.

"I've just gone sensible," Shack snapped. "Yuh say the sheriff has gone lookin' for the judge an' left yuh sittin' here?"

"I didn't have to wait," Flo wept. "I wanted to be near Milt."

"Jack Lawson wouldn't let Milt in here tuh talk tuh you while he was out?"

"He said he couldn't take chances with a prisoner that way, and, of course, he couldn't leave me back in the cell with Milt. It's against the law."

"God Almighty!" Shack snarled. "If yuh talk law to me ag'in, I'll dust yore bottom like I used to when yuh was a freckle-faced little chit. Sit there an' drip in yore handkerchief, if it makes yuh feel any better."

Shack turned to the back of the room, jerked open the heavy door giving admittance to the cell block, stalked in, and confronted his son-in-law who was sitting morosely on a cot along the side of his cell.

Milt Tyner was a tall, broad-shouldered, young man with a square, good-natured face and mild, blue eyes. He looked pale and worried now, but he stood up and smiled as Shack stopped outside the bars. "I thought I recognized your voice in the office, Shack. Sounded like you was angry about something," Milt said.

Shack glared through the bars. "I'm plumb ashamed tuh own yuh for a son-in-law, Milt," he said witheringly. "First time yuh needed tuh be a man, yuh fell down flat. Didn't yuh have guts enough tuh keep from lettin' yourself be locked up thisaway?"

Milt looked unhappy. "It's a disgrace, isn't it?" he said. "But it'll come out all right in court. Sim Matson said things I couldn't take from any man. I knocked him down, even if I had to pay a fine for it."

"Yo're killin' me," Shack choked. "I'm hearin' what yuh say . . . but I ain't believin' it. What sort o' man are yuh, anyway?"

Milt Tyner frowned in puzzlement. "I don't understand you."

"No, you wouldn't," Shack snarled at him. "I'll give it tuh you so yuh *can* understand. I just told Flo the same, an' she's leakin' in a handkerchief. If yuh want mine tuh cry into, yuh can have it. I'm takin' over the Bar A! I'm handlin' everything connected with it, includin' you an' Flo. If yuh can't be a man, I'll do it for yuh."

"Now, Shack," Milt protested with a pained look, "aren't you getting excited?"

"Don't 'Shack' me, darn you . . . !" Shack broke off as the door opened, and the sheriff walked in.

Jack Lawson was tall, thin, with a long neck and a long head that was flattish in the back. His chin was a little too rounded off, his smile a little too ready as he spoke heartily. "Howdy, Anderson. Your daughter told me you were in here. I suppose you know it's against the rules. But we'll forget that."

"Will we now?" Shack said ominously.

Lawson failed to notice anything out of the ordinary. He spoke to Milt Tyner blandly. "I haven't been able to find the judge yet. I expect he'll show up along towards suppertime."

Milt frowned. "Does that mean I'll have to stay in here until then?"

"I reckon it does," Lawson said, grinning.

Shack growled in his throat. "Why did yuh lock him up, Lawson?"

"He knocked Sim Matson down. We can't have anything like that."

"One o' the Matson men shot him, didn't he?"

"He was trying to protect Sim Matson."

"Did yuh lock *him* up?"

Lawson frowned. "Tyner here started the whole thing," he said shortly. "I handled it the way I saw fit."

"Now, did yuh?" said Shack. "Well, well, well." He spat on the floor and took a step forward. The sheriff moved back uncertainly, frowning, and then jumped as Shack yelled: "Unlock door an' let him out, yuh rabbit-faced skunk! Yuh hear me!"

"You're talking like a crazy old fool," Lawson snapped angrily. "I've given you too much rope now. Get out of here and stay out. I'll let Tyner out, when the judge comes back and takes some bail for him."

Shack dropped his voice to an ominous calm. "Want me tuh take them keys away from yuh, Lawson?"

The sheriff made the mistake of starting to reach for his gun. Shack's gnarled right hand moved amazingly fast. Lawson jumped back and held his hands away from his body as the big, single-action six-gun covered him.

"I've seed the day when yuh'd been a dead man, messin' like that," Shack said sourly. "Yore breed can't handle a gun,

Lawson. Yo're a joke as a sheriff. Let Milt out."

The sheriff was pale and angry. "You've gone too far, Anderson," he choked. "A trouble-making, old fool like you can't do this sort of thing any more."

"I'm doin' it," Shack said. "An' damned ef it don't feel good. Watch yore tongue with me after this, Lawson. Jump with them keys, damn yuh."

The sheriff hesitated, then stepped to the cell door, and unlocked it. "I'll have something to say about this later on," he warned angrily.

Milt Tyner gulped. "I think I'd better stay in here," he said uncertainly.

"Don't argue with me," Shack ordered. "Go out there tuh Flo an' drive her home tuh the ranch. Talk over what yo're gonna do on the way out. If yo're stayin', wait till I get home tuh give yuh orders."

Milt started to say something, then after a look at Shack's face, remained mute. He walked out into the jail office.

"Get in his cell," Shack said to the sheriff.

"Listen, Anderson, I'll. . . ."

"Yuh'll talk yoreself into somethin' yuh can't finish," Shack said. "Get in there."

Lawson looked into Shack's leathery face—and, as Milt Tyner had done, he obeyed silently. Shack slammed the door, turned the key, tossed it on the floor.

"That'll keep yuh out of mischief for a while," he said, holstering the gun. He shook a warning finger. "Maybe yo're thinkin' what yuh'll do when yuh get outta there. Lemme set yuh straight, Lawson. Yuh ain't a sheriff. Yo're a rabbit-chinned fake what's been gettin' by on talk. Yuh handed Milt a dirty deal, an' yo're gettin' it back. If yuh come after me over this, I'll meet you with guns smokin' instead o' talk. Think it over. I've took all the foolishness I aim to. I'm a rattler, rattlin' loud. If yuh want to get bit, yuh know what to do."

Shack left the cell block, slamming the door behind him. Milt and his wife were outside, getting into the buggy. Shack stalked out to his horse and eyed them coldly as Milt gathered up the reins.

"Don't yuh two get any foolish ideas on the way home," Shack warned.

"I think he's out of his mind," Flo whimpered.

"I'm just gittin' my mind back," Shack replied darkly. "An' it's a good thing fer both of you. Yuh need a guardeen."

III

"ONE-SHOT BATTLE"

Shack swung into the saddle and loped down the street, as they drove off the other way toward the ranch. The Lone Pine Bank occupied a one-story building at the next corner. Shack's new spurs jingled as he walked inside. No customers were there at the moment. Eben Briggs, the vice president and cashier, spoke cordially through the grilled window. "Good afternoon, Mister Anderson. What can I do for you today?"

"How much cash have I got in here, Briggs?"

"Just a minute." Briggs stepped back to a ledger, searched a moment, and turned back. "Forty-four thousand, three hundred, and eighty dollars, Mister Anderson."

"Get it," Shack ordered.

Briggs stared. "I didn't understand," he said uncertainly.

Curtly Shack said: "I'm drawin' it out, Briggs. Takin' it away with me. That plain enough?"

"But . . . but this is unusual," Briggs protested. "We'll honor your check, of course."

"I'll bet you will," said Shack. "You're honorin' it now. I'm closin' my account. I ain't leavin' my money in a bank that Hondo Matson controls."

Briggs was florid, full-faced, with a large, carefully tended mustache. His florid face reddened now. "Mister Matson's connection with the bank hardly calls for closing out your account," he said stiffly. "Mister Matson is a well-known

95

rancher with ample means and well thought of by everyone."

"Don't tell me what tuh do with my own money," Shack said disgustedly. "You only been around here three or four years, Briggs. Maybe yuh mean well. I dunno. But I've knowed Hondo Matson over forty year . . . an' I'm takin' my money away. Trot it out."

Briggs shrugged. "If you wish," he replied curtly. "I'll have to give you a sack of gold. I'm afraid we haven't enough bills in the safe to make up the full amount."

Ten minutes later Shack emerged from the bank with a newspaper-wrapped bundle of currency under one arm and a heavy sack of gold pieces under the other. The gold was heavy, but Shack carried it easily as he walked down the block. At Tom Craig's Seven-Up Bar a line of horses was hitched. The flank brand of the first one caught Shack's eye. He looked at the others. All but one were Hanging Noose horses. Loud voices and laughter came from inside. Shack turned stiffly and entered.

A sudden hush fell as he appeared. Then a young man in old leather chaps and a battered Stetson lifted his voice carelessly. "Ain't that old man Anderson?"

Shack marched stiffly to the end of the bar, dropped the bag of gold heavily on it, and slapped the package beside it. "Tom, put these on the back bar an' gimme a shot o' yore best whiskey," he said. "I got a bad taste in my mouth I want tuh wash out."

"Sure thing, Shack," Tom Craig said readily. He was a grizzled old-timer, too. It was hard to remember when Tom hadn't been selling whiskey here in Lone Pine. Not as tall as Shack, Tom Craig was broader, heavier. Easy living had fleshed him comfortably around the middle. His face was expressionless now, but his glance was keen as it shifted from Shack to the other men along the bar. Shack turned on his heel and surveyed them.

Sim Matson was the tallest. A powerful young fellow with a tanned, bold face, handsome in a sullen, savage sort of way, Sim Matson always seemed to swagger a bit as he moved, to eye the world with a faint challenge. A man about Shack's size and age stepped out from the others with a cordial: "Howdy, Shack, old-timer. How's the world treatin' yuh these days? Nothin' tuh complain of, I hope."

Shack edged away from the bar, so both his elbows had plenty of room. His lazy response remained the same, but his eyes narrowed. Under the speaker's fine black hat, white hair showed. Little wrinkles of humor radiated from sharp, peering eyes. The close-trimmed white beard and mustache gave the smiling face a fox-like look. And for all the cordial greeting, no hand was extended. The situation seemed to amuse the others. They were grinning.

A bottle and a glass slapped on the bar top. Tom Craig said: "Here's yore whiskey, Shack."

Shack kept his eyes on the man before him. "Hondo," he said, "are you lookin' for trouble?"

Hondo Matson continued to smile behind his beard. His voice was surprised. "What'd I want trouble for, Shack? I'm just an old coot, tryin' tuh get along peaceable . . . like you. We buried the hatchet long ago, didn't we, Shack?"

Hondo Matson's sly smile vanished as Shack's reply slapped on the silence. "We ain't friends, Hondo. We never was. We never will be. Yo're a skunk, a cow thief, an' a liar. Yore kind never changes. For forty years I've despised yuh. You've pulled on a sheep's coat the last few years, but yuh never fooled me, Hondo. I dropped in tuh tell yuh I'm runnin' the Bar A again. I've drawed my money outta yore bank an' got my son-in-law outta jail. Keep away from me an' mine from now on, an' you'll keep outta trouble."

Sim Matson shouldered forward. His right cheek was bruised, and a blue-black swelling puffed the corner of his right eye. His challenge grated. "What's that you said about Tyner being outta jail?"

"He's out an' gone, mister."

"Damn Lawson!" Sim Matson said furiously. "What'd he mean by doing that?"

"He didn't mean," Shack said. "I threw a gun on him an' left him locked up."

Sim Matson's sullen face darkened. "So you've started wavin' your guns like an old fool," he rasped. "Listen, you old moss-back, I'll. . . ."

Hondo Matson broke in hastily. "Son, maybe yuh better calm down. We'll talk this over later."

Sim Matson gestured his father away impatiently. "Now's as good a time as any!" he said angrily.

Shack smiled grimly. "Yo're talkin' sense," he approved. "Don't look so nervous, Hondo. Yuh raised the whelp. Yuh oughta taught him better."

"If you locked the sheriff up," Sim Matson said harshly, "you're goin' back an' let him out. An' take your medicine. We're for law an' order around here. Tyner hit me, when I wasn't lookin' yesterday. He ain't walkin' out like this, laughin' at me."

"I don't reckon Milt's laughin'," Shack said. "But I am. Who's gonna take me over tuh the jail?"

"I am!" Sim Matson stormed. He grabbed for his gun.

Both Shack's hands moved this time. One gun roared from his waist. The other fanned the men who scattered out from the bar. Sim Matson staggered back along the bar, holding his left arm from which blood was welling. His gun slipped from nerveless fingers and thudded on the floor.

"Who's next?" Shack snapped, crouching and weaving his guns.

Men stood there with guns in their hands which they had drawn as they dodged, but no man lifted a muzzle toward the gaunt, crouching figure that faced them.

In the uneasy silence Sim Matson backed against the bar and looked at his men. "Are you yellow, lettin' him get by with this?" he raved.

A short, bowlegged man whose pinched face and flaming red hair made him stand out from the others answered bluntly. "It was yore play, Sim. Yuh asked fer it. The barkeep an' this damned grub-line rider has took sides. I ain't gunshot hungry over such a damn' fool argument."

Shack had noted the young stranger who had backed against the bar with his gun covering the Hanging Noose men. Tense, silent, watchful, with a youthful face, the man was strangely threatening.

Sim Matson's voice lashed at the stranger. "So you come beggin' for work, an' at the first trouble you pull a gun on us? Who cut you into this play anyhow, damn you?"

The young stranger replied without taking his eyes off the Hanging Noose men. "You turned me down on the job, Matson. No loud-mouthed trouble-hunter with a pack of gunmen at his back is goin' to rawhide an old man while I can throw lead."

"You better get scarce quick," Sim Matson snarled. "I don't forget easy."

Tom Craig spoke from behind the bar, where he had been covering the room with a sawed-off, double-barreled shotgun. His easy-going face had hardened, and his voice was cold. "Are you handin' me that same warnin', Matson?"

"I wasn't talkin' to you, Craig."

"That's sensible," Tom Craig said. "You started this,

Sim. There'll be no ganging on Shack Anderson, while I can sling buckshot."

Hondo Matson had leaped back without drawing his gun. Now he spoke reproachfully. "You oughtn't to have blowed up like that, Sim. I've told you Shack is one of the orneriest gun-slingers that ever hit this range. Yuh ain't handled a gun long enough tuh outdraw him. Go get yore arm fixed an' forget about it."

Sim eyed his father sullenly.

"Go on," Hondo ordered.

With a muttered oath Sim jerked a bandanna from his neck, wrapped it around his arm, and strode out of the saloon.

Hondo addressed Shack placatingly. "Put up yore gun, Shack. There's no hard feelin's. We'll forget about it."

"You're lyin', Hondo," Shack said coldly. "Yuh won't never forget it. Get outta here with yore men. I'm goin' tuh enjoy my drink. All of you toss yore guns on the bar as yuh go out."

"I'm backin' it up," Tom Craig said stolidly.

Hondo nodded to his men, spoke mildly. "Boys, if it'll make Shack feel any better, leave yore guns here till he gets outta town."

Hondo set the example by stepping over to the bar and putting his own gun down. The red-headed man followed suit. With muttered oaths and black faces the others did the same and followed him out. Shack holstered one gun and spoke gratefully to Tom Craig and the young stranger. "Drink up on me, boys, an' thank yuh both kindly. I reckon yuh saved my gizzard. If they'd all cut loose, I'd've dropped two, three . . . but the rest would have got me."

The young stranger reached for his drink with a grin. His overalls were bleached, worn, and patched, riding boots were old and dirty with dried mud, and shirt, leather vest, and sombrero had long ago seen their best days, but Shack noted approvingly that his eyes were clear, steady, and he was unworried now as he said: "My name's Kit Erwin. It did me good to put a burr under that big fellow's saddle blanket. I'd just asked him for a job, an' he wasn't any too polite about turnin' me down."

"He's tryin' to be a badman," Shack said, smacking his lips over the drink. "Maybe you'll do well tuh keep outta his way."

Erwin shrugged carelessly.

"So yo're ridin' the grub line, huh?" Shack asked.

Erwin chuckled. "I'm ridin'. There hasn't been too much grub lately."

"Want a job?"

"You don't have to dig up a job because I yanked out my gun, mister."

"I like yore style," Shack declared. "If yuh can pull that gun again, when it's needed, I can use yuh."

"Expectin' trouble?"

"You seen it."

"I'm your man," Erwin said promptly.

"You sure galloped in here with your ears pinned back for trouble, Shack," Tom Craig said, as he swamped off the top of the bar. "I thought you was takin' things easy."

"I got crowded outta it, Tom. Hondo stopped blowin' off his mouth the last few years, but he's still a fox. He's brewin' a mess of trouble, if yuh ask me."

"Seemed meek enough in here, Shack."

"Hell, that's Hondo. When he made noise, yuh always could turn yore back on him, but when he got quiet an' sly, he was fixin' tuh bite. Who's that red-headed little waddie? He didn't have much tuh say, but he looked like a bad actor tuh me."

"Calls himself Red Davis. He's one of Sim's new partners. The other partner's a chunky, black-haired fellow named Weis. Only seen him once. He's cold and watchful, an' looks like a bad actor, too. I guess he didn't make it to town today."

"How come the Hangin' Noose has took on partners?" Shack said. "Those buckaroos with Sim looked like they were a heap more familiar with trouble an' guns than cows."

Tom Craig shrugged. "By me, Shack. Maybe the Hangin' Noose needed money, an' the men come with the new partners."

"Hondo didn't need money bad, if all he could do with it was buy hisself control of the bank."

"Funny, ain't it?" Tom Craig agreed. "What you aimin' tuh do, Shack?"

"Keep my eye peeled," Shack snorted. "Pass the word tuh some of the old-timers tuh drift out to the Bar A an' draw gun wages from me, Tom."

Tom Craig cast a sharp look, nodded, asked no questions. "Anything I can do?" he asked casually, as he washed a glass.

"Guess not. Keep yore ears spread. I was gonna leave that money on the back bar in yore safe, but I reckon I'll save yuh the worry. Over forty thousand there."

"Yuh oughtn't tuh keep that much cash around the ranch," Tom Craig protested.

"It'll be safe," Shack said grimly. "Lemme have it now. I'll get outta town before the sheriff listens tuh Sim Matson an' starts somethin' he can't finish. Erwin, grab that bag of gold an' tote it for me."

Erwin lifted the heavy sack of gold and grinned. "First time I ever had my hands on so much," he remarked. "Ain't you afraid I might start ridin' with it?"

"I'll take a chance. Watch yoreself as yuh go out. No tellin' what dirt that bunch of skunks'll break out with."

IV

"A NEW FOREMAN"

The shot had been heard outside. Several men pushed into the saloon as young Erwin and Shack started out. The first man blurted: "What happened?"

"Nothin'," Shack said without stopping. "Pull in yore eyes, Ed King. You've heered a gun pop before."

The bundle of bills was under Shack's left arm and his right thumb was hooked in the cartridge belt just over the gun as he stepped outside. The Hanging Noose horses were still at the hitch rack, but the men had disappeared.

Erwin looked inquiringly at Shack. "My horse is here at the rack," he said.

"Ride to the bank."

As Shack started along the walk, ignoring the gathering crowd, a thin, wizened man with a seamed, leathery face fell into step beside him and spoke under his breath. "Trouble, Shack?"

"Nuthin' tuh speak of, Jeff."

"Somebody said yuh tangled with Hondo Matson. If yo're expectin' trouble, I'll get out my six-gun."

Shack chuckled. "Feel like yuh got one more good fight in yuh, Jeff?"

"Hell, I got a dozen!" Jeff Ryan snorted.

"Git a horse an' yore guns an' come out tuh the ranch. I c'n use yuh, Jeff."

"Mean that, Shack?"

"Come an' see."

"I'll call yuh," Jeff Ryan said, and turned off across the street.

Young Erwin, riding a long-legged red roan, caught up. Shack noted the young man's eyes were wary and watchful. He was ready for trouble.

As he unwrapped his mount's reins from the bank hitch rack, Shack saw two of the Hanging Noose men come out of the sheriff's office and look down the street toward him. They hurried back in as Shack climbed into his saddle. Shack spoke to his companion as he led the way leisurely down the street. "If anything starts, lemme call the plays, son."

"Sing out an' I'll be with you," Erwin said.

The crowd on the sidewalk before Tom Craig's saloon watched them ride by. Shack could see them talking to one another, could sense them speculating among themselves. He smiled faintly under his white mustache. It had been a long time since such an air of uncertain threat and expectation had been seen in Lone Pine.

They were only a mile or so out of town, when Jeff Ryan came up at a gallop. Jeff wore a cartridge belt and gun, and a rifle was thrust in a saddle scabbard. His seamed, weathered face was grinning as he pulled into an easy lope beside Shack.

"Who's the first one to get shot up?" Jeff called.

Shack chuckled. "Yuh bloodthirsty old coot! Maybe yuh'll get all the action yuh can handle before long."

Jeff spat in the white road dust. "I c'n handle a hell of a lot," he said.

Shack nodded. "That's why I wanted yuh, Jeff."

Presently Shack led them at an easy lope across country. They were evidently not being followed. Young Kit Erwin rode in silence. Jeff Ryan asked no questions. Shack said little. In the past he had often ridden like this with Jeff. It was characteristic of Jeff that he came blindly now without knowing what lay ahead.

In a week's ride no range was better than the Bar A land. Shack had searched long and carefully before he filed on his first modest holding. The long miles of thick bunch-grass pasture had never been overgrazed. Foothill ridges of juniper and piñon pushed up to the mountain pastures where grass could always be found in the dry seasons. Arroyos and dry, boulder-strewn washes were balanced by windmills and tanks which seldom went dry.

The setting sun was a blaze of golden glory, when they rode slowly down a gentle slope toward the windmills, the corrals, feed stacks, and adobe buildings which formed the Bar A headquarters. Jeff Ryan eyed the scene and said: "You shore done well, Shack. I never would've thought all this would be here when I first met you."

Shack rolled a brown paper cigarette, lighted it, and eyed the scene before him. "I was lucky, Jeff," he said soberly. "But today I've been wondering a heap what it's all got me."

Jeff snorted. "Yo're talkin' like an old fool now. It's got yuh somethin' tuh be proud of. Yuh started with nothin'. Yuh fought an' worked an' built an' saved. Yuh made somethin' outta nothin', Shack."

Shack smiled dreamily. "Yuh would say the right thing, Jeff. I *am* proud of it. Proud of every bunch of grass an' calf an' cow an' horse. My wife an' I put our hearts here an' give all we had. It was hard on us. I reckon you know how hard, Jeff. We was both proud, when we began to get somethin' . . . an' I aim tuh keep on bein' proud."

Jeff Ryan nodded silently.

But young Erwin looked at Shack queerly. "This ain't none of my business," he said. "But I want you to know, mister, I can tackle plenty for a man who feels like that."

"Thanks, son," Shack said. "I like yuh for sayin' that."

They rode up to the long, adobe house which had grown room by room through the long years. As they dismounted, Flo emerged from the front door with Dot, her younger sister.

Flo's eyes were still red, but she was calm now. "Are you all right, Father?" she asked.

"I reckon so."

"I was afraid you'd get into trouble," Flo said.

"I told yuh to forget about me."

Dot said: "I've got to hear all about it. Did you really pull a gun on the sheriff, Dad?"

Shack eyed his younger daughter indulgently. He could have been Dot's grandfather instead of her father. Dot was twenty. But for all the difference in their ages, they were close, seeing eye to eye on many things. Dot was like her mother, golden-haired, slim, alert with life. She could outride and outshoot most of the cowhands, and would rather ride circle any day than work in the house. In her tailored riding skirt, soft leather boots, silk blouse, and neckerchief, Dot looked, Shack thought, prettier than any girl had a right to be.

Flo nodded reluctantly and eyed Jeff Ryan coldly. She never had approved of Jeff because of his periodical hell-roaring drunks. She hesitated, and then spoke almost unwillingly. "Did you have any trouble in town, Father?"

"Not much," Shack said carelessly. "I put a bullet in Sim Matson's arm. Should've killed the young pup. Erwin here drawed his gun an' helped hold 'em off."

"You . . . you got into a shooting scrape?" Flo gulped.

Shack eyed her coldly. "Yuh heered me, Daughter. Never mind tellin' me what yuh think about it. I know already . . . an' I don't give two whoops."

Flo flounced into the house, dabbing at her eyes.

"You've disgraced her," Dot said solemnly. "Did you really shoot Sim Matson in the arm, Dad?"

"I did," Shack said severely. "An' I'm not tellin' yuh about it. Yuh got too much interest in such things. I'll be out in a minute."

Shack took the gold from young Erwin and carried it and the bills into the house. When he came back out, Dot was questioning Erwin.

"I thought so," Shack snorted. "Got tuh know all the gory details. Git in the house an' forget such things, Dot. Yo're too pretty tuh be thinkin' about shootin' scrapes. Boys, come on back tuh the bunkhouse."

Seven men occupied the bunkhouse. Milt had hired five of them and appointed his own foreman. Jaspar Bell, the foreman, was standing beside the bunkhouse door as Shack walked up. Milt Tyner's voice was audible inside.

"We don't want any trouble, if we can keep out of it, men. When you go to town. . . ."

Shack shouldered inside. "Shut up, Milt! I told yuh to keep yore hands offen the ranch!"

Some of the hands were standing, some sitting on their bunks. Shack eyed them critically. Good cowhands, most of them—but that was all. They looked uncertainly at him.

"I reckon Milt has been pumpin' yuh up with soft soap an' milk," Shack said. "Maybe he's been tellin' yuh tuh humor the old man an' not tuh pay much attention tuh him."

Several sheepish grins admitted the truth of that.

Reddening, Milt Tyner said: "I was tellin' the men you lost your temper today, and might not be cooled down when you got home. I suggested we have no trouble with the Hanging Noose men."

"Uhn-huh," Shack said. "An' now that you've had yore prayer meetin', I'll take charge. Men, all orders on the ranch are comin' from me after this. If I catch any of yuh listenin' tuh Milt, yo're fired *pronto*. Jeff, come in an' show yoreself. This," said Shack, "is yore new foreman, men. His orders is the same as mine."

Jaspar Bell's square, stolid face reddened. "You firing me?"

Shack regarded him without rancor. "Not unless you quit, Bell. Yo're a top hand . . . but yuh ain't the man I want right now. Yo're too much like Milt. Take Jeff Ryan's orders or pack yore war bag."

Burly, slow-moving, with heavy, blond eyebrows and a full red face, Jaspar Bell hesitated, frowning. "I'll stay," he decided gruffly.

"How many of yuh are willin' tuh buckle on yore guns an' fight, if I need yuh?" Shack asked.

Only one of the five men Milt Tyner had hired, Jack Barr, spoke up quickly. "You can count on me."

Barr was young, stocky, good-natured, but his eyes were cool and direct. Doughball Daley and Longo Ross, old-timers who had worked on the Bar A for years, answered in the affirmative without hesitation. The others, including Jaspar Bell, hesitated.

Shack smiled coldly at them. "I reckon we know where we stand," he said. "Erwin, get a bunk an' grub with the boys. Ryan'll give yuh orders in the mornin'."

V

"SHORT TALLY"

Life took a new turn on the Bar A. Shack and Jeff Ryan were out at daybreak, in the saddle until dark, driving at a rough tally of all the cattle.

"Milt figgered three strings of wire around the place made everything all right," Shack snorted to Jeff. "We'll see."

Jack Lawson, the sheriff, made no move.

Men began to drift in with blankets and guns—elderly men, lean, weathered, whose legs were bowed, who rode easily, talked softly, said little to the younger cowhands. They bunked in the house.

Flo wore a martyred and disapproving air. Milt Tyner disapproved, too, but did his share of the work and was civil enough. Milt had some good points, Shack had to admit, even if he wasn't much use in trouble.

Evenings Shack and his guests gathered on the long, front *portale* and yarned. Flo left them alone, but Dot hung on every word. Day times Dot helped with the beef tally. She was almost a top hand herself. Shack noticed her riding in, talking, laughing with young Erwin. The third time it happened, Shack had a word with her out by the corral.

"Yuh seem to like Erwin, Dot."

"To talk to," Dot said carelessly.

"I don't know nothin' about him."

"He's from San Antonio, Dad. His family has a ranch."

"Funny him ridin' the grub line with a home ranch."

"I wonder if he hasn't had some trouble," Dot speculated. "Sometimes he acts as if there's something on his mind. He asks a lot of questions about people in this part of the country."

"Yuh don't say?" said Shack. "See if yuh can find out what's on his mind."

The beef tally worked out short of what it should have been. "Hondo Matson," Shack said bitterly to Jeff Ryan. "I might've knowed that old cow thief couldn't reform long. Hold Barr, Doughball Daley, an' Longo Ross back in the morning. We'll sashay over tuh the Hangin' Noose an' talk turkey tuh Hondo."

They started after breakfast the next morning, eleven strong, including Shack, on the sixteen-mile ride across country to the Hanging Noose headquarters at Palo Verde Cañon. Before they were off Bar A land, young Erwin caught up with them.

Shack reined over to him. "Somethin' wrong?"

Erwin grinned. "I thought maybe you'd need another gun."

"Itchin' for trouble, huh?"

"Just ready for it."

"I won't deny you the pleasure."

In grassy Palo Verde Cañon were the adobe buildings, corrals, and haystacks of the Hanging Noose. Tin cans and cast-off litter lay about in the open. The adobe buildings were in disrepair. Shack looked about contemptuously as they rode up.

"Ain't it a hawg pen?" he said to Jeff Ryan. "For an outfit with so much money, they ain't showin' much interest in the ranch."

"A mud hole always looks good to a hawg," Jeff retorted.

"Wonder where everyone is."

The place wore a deserted air. In a corral two horses stood listlessly, a lean dog barked half-heartedly. But as they rode up to the front of the house, a window was suddenly thrown open. A rifle barrel poked out. Inside the window a man with a white bandage around his head yelled: "What do you want?"

"Where's Hondo Matson?" Shack asked curtly, riding nearer to the window.

"Gone to Lone Pine."

"Where's Sim?"

"What the hell do you care?"

"Stranger, yo're makin' big talk for one man an' a rifle," Shack said coldly. "I'm Shack Anderson of the Bar A. I've got business with the Matsons."

Tom Craig's description of the second new partner fit this man in the window. Chunky, black-haired, cold-eyed, his rasping reply bore it out. "I'm Weis, one of the owners. What's on your mind?"

"I'm talkin' to the Matsons," Shack said curtly. "Are they both in Lone Pine?"

"Take yore bunch of broken-down old coots home an' stay outta trouble!" Weis exploded. He slammed the window down and put an end to the conversation.

Shack reined his horse around and addressed his men calmly. "We'll keep on across the Hangin' Noose tuh Lone Pine, boys. Scatter out an' look for any beef that looks hungry for Bar A grass. If yuh run into any of Matson's men, let 'em start the trouble first."

As they rode off, Jeff Ryan said: "Funny, that fellow bein' bandaged up thataway."

Shack's look was shrewd. "Got somethin' on yore mind, Jeff?"

111

"I was just a-wonderin'," Jeff confessed. "Ben Tikeman was a-yarnin' to me yesterday. Two weeks ago Ben was runnin' some wolf traps out north of Little Bald Mountain. One day-break he heered some riders foggin' through Black Sheep Cañon. Ben's bedroll was up the slope by that little spring. Bein' a curious cuss, he edges over an' looks down at the trail. It was Sim Matson an' half a dozen men ridin' dead-beat horses. They looked like they'd come a long ways in a hurry, an' they was plastered with guns an' primed for trouble."

"Sounds interestin'," Shack said dryly.

"You ain't heered it all, Shack. Pinto Harris put the cracker on it. Four, five years ago Pinto was over in the Gila country. There was an outlaw bunch over there called the Black Jack Emery gang. Pinto seen a posse tangle with 'em in a little minin' town. Pinto never spoke out about it till he heered Ben Tikeman, an' then he told us one of the Emery gang that high-tailed past him that day, throwin' lead at the posse, was Sim Matson or Sim's twin brother."

"It couldn't have been Sim, of course," Shack said sarcastically. "Even if Sim *was* away from here five or six years ago. Hondo had a different story tuh tell about Sim every time he opened his mouth on it."

"I been studyin' it," Jeff declared calmly. "If Sim was ridin' the outlaw trail then, how come he bedded down so quick to cow raisin' on the Hangin' Noose . . . but still goes foggin' out over the country with them ornery gun-slingers he's put on the Hangin' Noose payroll?"

Shack canted his sombrero toward one eye, against the sun. "Cow raisin', new partners, buyin' the bank, grabbin' for more land, an' bustin' out on long rides at night makes a funny mess in the kettle. Go get me Pinto Harris an' Ben Tikeman, Jeff. I'll be over that rise there where Howdy Daniels rode."

★ ★ ★ ★ ★

Ten minutes later Shack faced three old-timers like himself. Ben Tikeman was stooped, gray-haired, with a scanty beard. Pinto Harris was clean-shaven, lean, wrinkled, and Howdy Daniels had a smooth, cheerful face despite his age and wore the brim of his flat-crowned hat pinned up in front.

"Boys, I got a job for you," Shack said. "Go back tuh the ranch, get yore blankets an' some grub, an' scatter out around the Hangin' Noose. Keep outta sight an' peel yore eyes for anyone ridin' off Hangin' Noose land. I want tuh know who goes an' comes."

As the three men galloped off, and he rode on with Jeff Ryan, Shack said: "A jack rabbit won't get past Hangin' Noose wire without them three old buzzards hangin' on its tail."

Beyond Hanging Noose land Shack's men came together. They had not found any suspicious beef and had not seen any Hanging Noose men.

"I reckon we'll find 'em in Lone Pine," Shack said.

Two hours of steady riding put them in Lone Pine. Erect and watchful, Shack led them down the main street; and, as before, people stopped, stared, passed remarks to one another. Shack pulled up and questioned a man on the sidewalk.

"Where's Hondo Matson and his men, Sam?"

"Hondo was in the bank a little while ago, Shack. He come tuh town alone."

"Ain't Sim or his men here?"

"Not as I know of."

Shack addressed his men. "I guess yuh can scatter out an' suit yoreselves for a little."

Doughball Daley uttered a yelp: "First drink's on me, boys! I been dryin' up fer six weeks!"

Shack rode on to the bank, dismounted, and entered. Half a dozen customers were inside today. He ignored them, men and women alike, and walked stiffly to the iron grillwork, beyond which Hondo Matson was standing. Dressed in a black suit today, Hondo's white hair was combed neatly, and his small, pointed beard was trimmed. He looked law-abiding and business-like as he scanned a sheaf of papers in his hand. As Shack approached, Hondo looked up. His cordial greeting was audible over the lobby.

"Howdy, Shack, old friend. I'm glad to see yuh. Anything we can do for yuh today?"

Shack's reply rasped just as loud. "I ain't doin' business with the bank while yuh got an interest in it, Hondo. Come outta that cage and listen tuh me."

Eben Briggs looked up from the passbook in which he was writing. All eyes went to them.

Hondo fingered his beard and spoke mildly. "I see yo're wearin' guns again today, Shack. An' yuh seem tuh be lookin' for trouble. I'm a man of peace. Are yuh figgerin' on throwin' down on me?"

"Nothin'd make me feel better, Hondo, but yuh can choke off that sanctimonious talk an' come out with an easy mind. If I was after yore hair, I'd come in and get it."

"Yo're makin' a heap of trouble these days, Shack," Hondo said sorrowfully. "But I still look on yuh as a friend."

Hondo unlatched the door and stepped out.

Shack regarded him coldly. "Where's Sim an' his men?"

"They've got a heap of work to do at the ranch," Hondo said mildly.

"When you get back, yuh'll find I've been there," Shack rasped. "They ain't around. I come here tuh give you warnin', Hondo. The Bar A's losin' beef. Yore mousy ways has fooled a heap of folks lately. But I can remember when yuh was a common cow thief, an' as far as I'm concerned yuh still are. The warnin' yo're gettin' now has gun talk behind it. Hangin' Noose men caught on Bar A land after this'll get shot first an' spoke to afterwards. An' if I can pin any cow stealin' on yuh . . . an' I'll try hard, Hondo . . . I'll rawhide yuh till yuh break out in a cold sweat when yuh think of a cow. I'm meetin' yuh in the only way yuh understand . . . gunsmoke an' plain talk."

A woman across the lobby gasped and spoke under her breath to a woman companion indignantly. Shack heard a little of it. ". . . disgraceful. . . . Something should be done. . . ."

Hondo Matson looked hurt. "Yo're doin' me a great wrong, Shack. Yuh know such talk is damagin' before folks who've got their money here in the bank. I reckon that is why yo're shootin' yore mouth off so loud. But if yo're tryin' tuh egg me into a fight, it ain't gonna work. I'm a cowman an' a banker, not a gunfighter."

"Yo're a skunk!" Shack said violently. "Watch yore step after this." He turned and strode out, spur chains jingling, and the last thing he heard was Hondo Matson's sorrowful voice saying: "Friends, I hope you'll overlook this. . . ."

Shack snorted and headed for Tom Craig's Seven-Up Bar.

VI

"TROUBLE"

Young Erwin was coming out of the post office, engrossed in a letter. Shack waited until the other crossed the street and joined him.

"Got yore mail, I see," Shack commented.

Erwin grinned. "Just one letter."

"Yore mail reaches yuh in a hurry, for a feller who was ridin' the grub line."

Erwin's reply was rather lame. "I aimed to be around Lone Pine here for some time and had it sent on."

Shack made no comment. "Need any money?"

"Five dollars be all right?"

Shack gave him the money and went on to Craig's bar alone. Longo Ross and Doughball Daley were there. A poker game was going at one of the back tables, and several men were at the bar.

"I was wonderin' if you'd drop in," Tom Craig said as he put a bottle and glass down.

They were alone at the end of the bar. Shack lowered his voice as he poured his drink. "Anything I oughta know, Tom?"

"Some of it'd make your ears burn, Shack. The sheriff and Hondo Matson have been working their tongues. You ain't so popular around Lone Pine right now. They're sayin' you've turned into a trouble-huntin', old fool, livin' in the past, an' something oughta be done about it."

Shack grinned coldly and put down his drink. "What do they aim tuh do?"

"Pass a law or make a rule or somethin'." Tom Craig chuckled. "It's this gun talk an' gun play they object to. It was all right before everybody got respectable, they say, but times has changed. They're in favor of hobblin' you some way, Shack. I understand the judge says he'll tame you if they get you in court."

Shack grinned again. "I tame hard, Tom."

"If you ask me," Tom Craig confided, "the sheriff ain't itchin' to tackle you alone. He's waitin' for you to make a move so he can crack down with a posse. He's still burnin' over being locked up. They've laughed him ragged."

"Ought to kick him outta office," Shack said disgustedly. "Which reminds me. I've got to look him up an' lodge a complaint about rustlers workin' on my beef. I'll ride along that far with him."

"He's out east with a posse, Shack. Last night a train was held up about eighty miles out. Blew up the express car, killed two men inside, an' got sixty-eight thousand in gold an' bills. Lawson got word some of the bandits might be headin' this way."

Shack grabbed the bottle and poured himself another drink. He tossed it off and looked at Tom Craig speculatively. "So there was a train robbery last night?"

"Third one in four months in this part of the country. An' every time the sons-of-bitches got away slick. Don't that beat all?"

"It starts me thinkin'," Shack said slowly.

Tom Craig looked at him queerly. "Here's something else to make you think. There was a fellow in here this mornin', askin' me if I had any new Eighteen Ninety-Two twenty-dollar gold pieces. He seemed powerful anxious to see one."

"Whyn't he try the bank?"

"I told him so . . . an' he said he'd done so, an' they didn't have any."

"They gave me a sackful t'other day, Tom."

"Now, did they?" Tom Craig mused under his breath. "I had this fellow pointed out to me once in El Paso. He's a Pinkerton man."

They looked at one another. Neither said anything. Shack turned, caught Doughball Daley's eye, and motioned him over. "We're startin' back tuh the ranch as soon as I eat at the hotel."

Doughball's face fell. "Yo're shore makin' quick moves today," he sighed.

"Switch yore mind from a whiskey bottle tuh business," Shack advised.

They started on time, and, as they rode away from the hotel, Longo Rosso chuckled. "Yuh must've built a fire under Hondo Matson, Shack. He started home quick after yuh talked to him. They're tellin' around as how yuh damned near throwed a gun on him in the bank."

"By the time Hondo gets through lying about it, he'll be shot in the back an' ready tuh bury," Shack snorted. He rode a short distance and spoke his thoughts aloud. "Funny, Hondo lit out so quick. He's crooked as a gopher's tunnel an' meek when it suits his play. But he ain't afraid of hell er high water. My talkin' never scared him outta town. I'd like tuh know what that foxy-lookin', old skunk is cookin' up."

They reached the ranch in time to hear Powder Ike, the cook, hammering out the supper signal on a dangling crowbar. There was a rush to get unsaddled and washed.

Dot met Shack as he walked to the house. She was smiling

ruefully. "You're in for it," she said. "Flo and Milt just got back from town. They're packing."

"I'll see 'em," Shack said. "Might as well get it over with. Yuh go on an' eat."

Flo and Milt Tyner were in their bedroom, packing. Flo's nose was red. Milt Tyner looked troubled, determined.

"Makin' a trip?" Shack asked, closing the door.

Flo faced him indignantly. "Milt and I were in town today, when you had that disgraceful scene with Hondo Matson. It was the final straw. You have made an armed camp out of the ranch. Heaven knows what will happen next. We'll all be outlawed. Milt and I are leaving until you come to your senses."

Shack smiled grimly. "That the way you feel, Milt?"

Milt Tyner nodded. "You and these old men you've gathered here will kill someone next. I don't want anything to do with it."

"Yuh know some of our cattle has been rustled, Milt?"

"The law can take care of that," Milt said doggedly.

"It ain't helped that bullet wound in yore arm."

Milt frowned. "I went around to the judge today, paid a ten-dollar fine, and filed charges against Sim Matson. We're not living on the frontier any more. Trouble with you, Shack, you haven't grown with the country. It don't take a gun to defend your rights any more."

Shack blew up again. "If I'd've been a man like yuh, Milt, there wouldn't't've been any Bar A here today! Yuh ain't got sense enough tuh see that country never grows up so there ain't somebody wantin' tuh gobble somebody else. Yo're like a maverick calf, bloated out with milk yuh didn't make, standin' with yore eyes closed, waitin' for someone like Hondo Matson tuh drag yuh down. If yo're bein' disgraced by men ready fer trouble, yuh better herd with yore kind. Yuh don't belong on the Bar A. Are you leavin' tonight?"

"Flo's tired. We'll leave in the morning, if it's all right with you."

"Suit yourselves," Shack snapped. He stamped out of the room and slammed the door. As he sat down at the table, he said: "Boys, are yuh ready tuh start ridin' again?"

Rick Jones, who had come in with the soldiers in the 'Fifties and stayed in the country after his discharge, swallowed a mouthful of food and brushed his long, gray mustache: "Any time, Shack. What yuh hatchin' up?"

"There's some things I want tuh find out in a hurry, Rick. It'll take ridin' tuh do it."

"Are you going to do any fighting, Dad?" Dot asked.

"Fightin'?" Shack said, lifting his eyebrows. "My stars! Ain't you heerd? There's a sheriff tuh do all that, Bright Eyes."

"I've heard there's a sheriff," Dot admitted. "But I'm not sure who he's working for . . . the taxpayers or Sim Matson."

Clem Mason, who had appeared three days before with a brace of six-guns and a rifle, chuckled through a grizzled beard. "She's learnin' fast, Shack. It beats me how an old sinner like yuh ever had such a sweet kid."

"She's the spittin' image of her mother an' a fire-eater, too," Shack said.

"I ain't never forgot when the Apaches chased yore buckboard," Clem said. "Yore wife laid leather on the hosses, an' yuh laid lead back on the Apaches, an', when we come along an' turned the devils back, yuh was cussin', an' yore oldest girl was cryin', an' the little one here was laughin'. Thought all that was fun, she did."

And they were off, yarning of the old days. Milt Tyner put an end to it by coming in and speaking accusingly. "All this running around with guns has stirred up some kind of trouble, Shack. Erwin says you'd better come out right away."

Young Erwin was waiting at the back door. "There's a black horse just come in with an empty saddle," he said. "It's wounded on the flank. Jaspar Bell says that Ben Tikeman changed to the black when he came back today."

"Finish eatin' an' saddle up," Shack snapped. "Ben's butted into trouble."

VII

"TWO DEAD MEN"

Milt Tyner came out while the horses were being roped and saddled. "If there's trouble, don't you think you'd better send for the sheriff, Shack?" he said dubiously.

"Yuh *would* think of the sheriff!" Shack exploded. "There ain't no time tuh fool with that. I'll leave yuh in charge while we're gone, for what yo're worth. Better get out yore guns."

"I guess I won't need anything like that," Milt said tolerantly.

"Yuh need a new backbone," Shack rasped.

The black horse stood tied to a corral bar, leg lifted off the ground. Sweat streaks and white flecks of foam showed on the black hair. A grazing bullet had left a raw, ugly furrow on the flank.

"If you mean to handle it your own way, there's nothing I can say," Milt responded stiffly.

"Yo're damned right," Shack bit out. "Keep back outta the way. Ben Tikeman never fired a shot until someone opened up on him. If gun play has started, we'll stop it the quickest way . . . with hellfire an' brimstone. That's talk gunslingin' skunks can always understand."

Young Erwin stepped over. "You are takin' me, too, aren't you, Anderson?"

"Yuh may get shot up, son."

"I hired out for that, if I was needed."

"Fork yore horse, then."

Shack noticed that Dot said good bye to Erwin before they left, and her face was troubled. But there was no time to think of that as they thundered away from the corrals. Only Erwin and Jack Barr were young men.

Twilight was deepening, when they reached the first gate in the Bar A wire. It was closed. Shack veered off to the left, following the wire. Darkness had come, when he reached the third gate. It was a Texas-style gate, formed of three strands of wire attached to poles at each end. The end bar was lying on the ground.

Leaning from the saddle, Shack examined the wire loop which had held the top of the end bar up to the post. Black hair and traces of blood were visible on the outside barbs of that loop, which had to be lifted to open the gate.

"I knowed that black horse had tuh get inside our wire some place," Shack said. "An' a woman taught him tricks before I bought him. He's a gate-opener. I've seen him nuzzle around an' open a Texas gate slick. He come in from the north an' worked this one. If I was tuh head tuh Black Sheep Cañon, I'd use this gate, an' Ben Tikeman had reasons for layin' up toward Black Sheep Cañon."

Jeff Ryan snapped: "Don't yuh think we know enough? I'm in favor of ridin' tuh Palo Verde Cañon and havin' it out quick."

"We'll try to find Ben first," Shack decided. "Maybe he ain't dead yet. Howdy Daniels an' Pinto Harris are over this way. Maybe they know something. An' because folks seem willin' to brand us outlaws, we'll make sure first."

Shack led them at a fast pace into the north. Night closed down. They were on Hanging Noose land, well west of Palo Verde Cañon. The country was rolling, open, gashed by arroyos, covered with hard-grazed grass. A full moon slipped up, revealing occasional bunches of cattle.

They reached the foothills, where junipers dotted the landscape like man-planted bushes. Presently taller piñon trees were about them and the mountains were ahead, and in the moonlight the dark gash of Black Sheep Cañon opened up. The dry, boulder-strewn bed of Black Sheep Creek glistened whitely in the moonlight as they rode down into it. They paused there a few minutes, while the horses drank sparingly in the narrow trickle of water, and then rode up to the trail which followed Black Sheep Creek back into the cañon.

"I was hopin' we'd see Pinto Harris or Howdy Daniels," Shack said. "We'll ride in a ways an' fire a couple of shots. Ben'll answer, if he's around."

Black Sheep Cañon widened to some extent as it cut back into the mountains. Softer rock and soil had washed faster back in here. The moonlight reached the cañon bottom. Looking back, Shack saw his men strung out behind. The creak of saddle leather, the thud of hoofs were the only sounds. Around their advance hovered something grim and purposeful. Shack knew what was in their minds for the most part. Not a one but wouldn't share his last bite with a hungry man as quickly as he'd draw his gun to kill if crowded.

A moment later Shack rode around a point of rocks beside the trail and saw the fitful red glow of a small campfire up the slope to the left. He lifted his hand, and the men pulled up—just as a rifle cracked sharply up the slope. The bullet whined close overhead. A warning hail followed it. "Stay on the trail, yuh sons, or I'll shoot tuh kill!"

"Hell, he's shore on the prod for trouble!" Shack exclaimed. He cupped his hands to his mouth and bawled: "Watch yore shots, Pinto! We're comin' up!"

Pinto Harris's reply held relief. "Why didn't yuh say who

yuh was? I wasn't lookin' for yuh so quick."

The slope was rough, rocky, but the horses made it. Shack swung out of the saddle near the small fire and met Pinto Harris.

"Yuh got here in a hurry," Pinto said. "Howdy must've run into yuh."

"Ain't seen Howdy, Pinto. Was he lookin' for us?"

"He started to the ranch less'n an hour ago."

"We missed him. We're lookin' for Ben Tikeman," Shack explained. "Ben's saddled horse came in with a bullet wound in the flank. We rode quick. I figgered Ben might have come toward the cañon here. Seen him?"

The red fire glow struck against Pinto's clean-shaven, lean face. It was gaunt, hard now. Pinto's answer had a raw edge. "Ben's here, Shack. Over beyond the fire there."

Shack stepped quickly to the spot, where lay a dark form he had not noticed. Ben Tikeman lay on his back, with Howdy's coat rolled up under his head. The bearded face was peaceful and calm. Ben Tikeman had ridden many trails, and the last one had ended here in Black Sheep Cañon.

"We found him at sunset, shot through the back," Pinto said, with that raw edge to his voice. "We'd agreed tuh watch for smoke signals from each other. Ben's smoke got high enough for me tuh see it. I made smoke for Howdy an' rode this way. Ben was lyin' there by the fire, unconscious. He was hit too bad tuh move. The blood trail was plain where he'd dragged hisself up here tuh the first green stuff that'd make smoke. He'd been shot in the back."

The men had gathered silently around them. They were silent as they looked down at Ben. War, death, violence were an old story to these old-timers. What they felt, they kept inside.

Shack's voice was wire-hard as he said: "Shot in the back,

huh? That'd be the only way most men could down Ben. Did he talk?"

"Never opened his eyes," Pinto replied heavily. "I stuck with him, hopin' he would. Howdy Daniels seen my smoke an' come. He stayed with Ben while I went down an' read sign. I found where Ben had been shot outta the saddle an' laid in the trail for a time. I reckon he was left there for dead. Tracks came down tuh that spot from some rocks up on the slope. Empty cartridges was up there, an' the tracks cut off along the slope tuh another dead man. Looked tuh me like he'd been killed about the time Ben was shot."

"Did Ben get the son that shot him?" Jeff Ryan asked quickly.

"Nope," said Pinto. "That other fellow had been carried up there outta the way. Looked tuh me at about the time Ben came ridin' along, and the fellow who did the killin' snuck along tuh the first handy rocks an' cracked Ben, too. Don't know why he didn't carry Ben outta the way, too."

"Maybe he took off after Ben's horse an' didn't catch it," Shack guessed. "Who's this other man?"

"Never seen him before, Shack. I'll show him to yuh."

They all went, scrambling over rocks and crashing through the growth on the slope. Ben stopped and struck a match, revealing a bold-nosed man with straight, coarse, black hair. Two empty holsters showed that he had been well-armed.

Young Erwin uttered a soft oath.

"Know him?" Shack asked quickly.

"Yes," Erwin said harshly. "We were friends."

"Who is he?"

Erwin hesitated an instant, and then said: "His name is Osage Jim Conners. He's a quarter-breed, and he was white clear through."

"Where's he from?"

"All over. We were together in Indian Territory once."

Shack struck a match and held it down to the empty holsters and belts. "All the loops are full. He wasn't doin' any fightin'. Did yuh look in his pockets, Pinto?"

"I didn't take time," Pinto declared. "As soon as I got back tuh the fire, Howdy started tuh the ranch, an' I stuck with Ben. He lasted till about twenty minutes before yuh come along. When I heard the lot of yuh stop down there on the trail, I was sure trouble was comin' . . . an' I didn't feel like dodgin' it."

Shack knelt and went through the dead man's pockets, piling his findings in the crown of his hat. Still kneeling, he lit a match and looked through them. One object held his attention for a moment, and then he put it in his pocket without comment.

"This is somethin' for the sheriff to handle," Shack decided. "We'll leave him here. But I want Ben to go home. Two of yuh take him, an' the rest ride with me. Pinto, you an' Jack Barr go back tuh the ranch with Ben."

"Not meanin' to run out on Ben," Pinto protested, "but I'd rather go along with yuh, Shack. Yuh see . . . I stood an' watched Ben die. I'm itchin' tuh do somethin' about it."

"I'd rather go with the rest of you," Jack Barr said. "But if somebody's got to do it, I'll handle the body myself."

"I won't forget it," Shack promised.

They put Ben Tikeman on Barr's horse, and then rode ahead of him out of Black Sheep Cañon to Hanging Noose land, and Palo Verde Cañon.

The Matson place was dark, silent, deserted, when they rode up. No windows or doors were open; no voices hailed them. Only the dog barked from the moonlight back of the empty corrals. Bunkhouse and house were locked. Hammering on the doors brought no response.

For the first time that evening Shack lost his temper and swore. "There's something wrong!" he declared harshly as he swung into the saddle. "The Matsons ain't hidin' out. But they didn't lock this place up an' take off tuh the last man for nothin'. They're up tuh somethin'."

Jeff Ryan said regretfully: "An' we won't have much luck trailin' 'em tonight, either."

Shack was silent for a moment, and then he spoke slowly: "I got an idea. An' if I'm right, I'll be cold and shaking with fear for the first time in my life. Erwin?"

"Here," young Erwin answered, riding forward.

In the moonlight Shack regarded the young man. "I reckon all cards had better be laid out open," Shack declared bluntly. "In the pocket of that Osage Jim yuh used tuh know, I found a badge. He was a Pinkerton man. What kind of work was yuh doin' with him in the Indian Territory, Erwin?"

Interest rippled through the listening men. They moved their horses closer. Young Erwin did not reply for a moment, and then his answer was reluctant. "We were selling whiskey, Anderson."

Shack's voice lashed at him. "I want the truth from yuh, Erwin. Yo're a Pinkerton man, ain't yuh?"

Erwin's sombrero moved in the moonlight as he nodded slowly. "I guess there's no reason why you men shouldn't know now," he said. "I'm a Pinkerton man, Anderson. I hated to take advantage of your kindness, but I needed a job around here."

"I knew there was somethin' funny about yuh," Shack grunted. "Yuh asked too many questions. An' yore mail came too quick for a grub-line drifter. Yuh knew that other Pinkerton man was around, didn't yuh?"

"I found out in the mail this morning," Erwin said.

"No need tuh ask you what he was after. I c'n tell yuh. He was in Lone Pine lookin' for new gold money."

"Yuh seem to know a lot," Erwin said calmly.

"Things are just fittin' in together. Why are the Pinkertons interested in new gold money around this range?"

"I'm not saying any more," Erwin refused.

Shack leaned toward him and snapped: "I've got tuh know. Are they lookin' for gold money that was stole out of express cars?"

"That's a good guess."

"It's all shapin' up," Shack groaned. "I've done the one thing tonight I shouldn't have. I've left the Bar A with no one lookin' after it. There's a sack of new Eighteen Ninety-Two gold pieces in the house an' a bundle of bills that'd choke a flock of goats. An' Hondo Matson knows the Pinkertons are lookin' for that gold, an' he knows I've got the sack of it. Eben Briggs must've handed 'em tuh me in the bank by mistake. I knew Hondo was up to somethin' when he rode outta Lone Pine so quick today. Longo, yuh stay here an' keep an eye on the place for two, three hours. The rest of yuh ride like hell with me tuh the Bar A. You've all had twice as much ridin' today as yuh should've . . . but I'm afraid, boys, I'm afraid."

VIII

"A NEW MAN"

Clem Mason's sharp eyes first saw the rising red glare against the sky ahead of them. "Fire at yore place, Shack!" he yelled.

Shack looked, and drove his horse into full gallop. The men needed no orders. They knew what fire at the Bar A meant tonight.

Shack knew fear as the pistoning legs of his horse drummed hard. It wasn't the fire. Houses could be rebuilt, haystacks renewed. They couldn't burn the rolling miles of land, couldn't take the cattle in an hour. But they could kill, callously, as the Pinkerton man had been killed, as Ben Tikeman had been wiped out. Only Milt Tyner and the few peace-loving hands he himself had hired were there at the ranch to hold them off. Milt who was worse than useless, with his blind faith in the law, his scorn of guns and violence. That sinister red light leaping to the sky ahead told its story. Milt hadn't been ready; Milt had been weak; Milt had failed.

The men had strung out behind Shack. The thunder of their passing shook the night. But one man drew abreast, forged ahead. In the moonlight Shack saw young Erwin, riding madly. Something in Shack warmed and went out to the fury of that other rider. Only a bitter vision could make a man ride that way. Only a vision as cruel as Shack himself faced with that red glare in his eyes.

Erwin got there first. It didn't matter. As Shack rode his

reeling, lathered horse down the long slope, he saw that they were too late. The buildings were glowing ruins now. The haystacks were burned down. The barn was gone. The bunkhouse was in ruins, and the big house was a gutted, glowing shell. Flames still licked up, smoke billowed, sparks whirled high, but the fury had struck and gone. The dying flames were macabre ghosts of the hell which had raged here.

No shots greeted their arrival. In the wavering red glow Shack saw, as he galloped up, two still forms between the house and the bunkhouse. Both men were dead. Erwin had leaped from the saddle and looked at the dead men. He was staring wildly about as Shack rode up. Suddenly he ran toward the corrals. Shack rode after him.

As he rounded the corral, he saw what had drawn Erwin. On the far side, a row of figures had been tied to the poles. Erwin was cutting at the rope which held Dot as Shack flung himself out of the saddle, barely noticing the three bound men beyond the women.

"Dot! Flo!" Shack gulped. "Are yuh all right?"

Dot staggered free. Erwin caught her, and they clung together.

"See to Milt. I think they killed him," Flo cried.

Jaspar Bell was the nearest. Milt was beyond, sagging limply against the ropes that held him. Arms spread-eagled, legs tied to the bars behind them, Milt stood with his head hanging forward to his chest. He looked inert, dead. Dark, wet bloodstains covered the front of his shirt. When Shack pushed up Milt's head, he swore with bitter rage. Milt Tyner's face was a bloody mess.

Jaspar Bell spoke thickly. "They beat him with their guns an' held matches tuh his hands, and swore they'd kill him if he didn't talk!"

Shack opened his knife and cut at the ropes that held Milt

up. The others had come up with a rush. They caught Milt's limp figure and laid it on the ground.

Jaspar Bell talked on thickly. "They wanted to know where yore money was, an' Milt wouldn't tell 'em."

Flo, freed by Erwin, staggered to the spot, crying—"Milt, darling!"—and went to her knees beside her husband.

Shack knelt by her. All differences were forgotten now. "Let me look at him, honey," Shack said to her. "He should've told where the money was. It's all gone now, anyway."

"I told them where it was!" Flo sobbed. "They got it before they started the fire. I would have told them where anything was to make them stop torturing Milt!"

"Yuh did right, baby," Shack said huskily. "I wouldn't've had yore man treated this way for all I own. I've misunderstood him, too. He's shore a man tuh stand out against 'em thataway."

Shack felt Milt's heart and pulse, and said: "He'll come outta this. His heart's steady. Somebody get some water from the pump."

Flo was in no condition to answer questions at the moment. Shack stood up and stepped to Dot, who was still with Erwin.

"They didn't hurt the women," Erwin said huskily. "Dot says they rode up and started shooting before anyone knew what was happening. Tyner ran out to see what was the matter and was roped and dragged on the ground."

Dot shivered. "Did the Matson men do this, Dad?" she asked.

"Didn't yuh see 'em, Dot?"

"They were all masked. I didn't see anyone who looked like Hondo or Sim. They hurried us back here to the corral at once. I wouldn't recognize any of them again." Dot hesitated.

"Except that one man's hat fell off while he was dragging Flo along, and I saw that he had a white bandage around his head."

Shack started a cigarette with gnarled hands that were unsteady. "I reckon that's enough," he said in a brittle voice. "It's all the proof I need. Hondo Matson an' his men have pulled their last dirty trick. If I never do anything more on earth, I'll smash 'em like I would a nest of rattlers. I knew Hondo'd never die peaceful till he worked off this grudge ag'in' me. He made one big mistake by not waitin' here tuh stop me tonight."

"Funny we didn't meet 'em," Erwin jerked out.

"They seemed to scatter out an' ride in all directions, when they left here," Dot said.

"They ain't far away," Shack snapped. "Hondo's too sly tuh do a trick that'd make him an outlaw, if there was any way outta it. Seein' as he an' Sim kept outta sight an' everybody wore masks, it ain't hard tuh figure he's aimin' tuh keep this off his doorstep."

Jeff Ryan had joined them. "Hondo must've needed money bad tuh get it this way," he said savagely.

Erwin met that thoughtfully. "I think Hondo only wanted that sack of gold pieces, but took everything while he was at it. The Pinkertons have been pretty sure that outlaws were laying up somewhere in these parts. They vanished after every hold-up. Pinkerton men have scattered out to watch for them. Those new Eighteen Ninety-Two gold pieces were the first sent out this way, and they were stolen from the express car. Matson must have heard at the bank that the Pinkertons were looking for them. A sack of them had been handed to Anderson. Matson had to get them back."

"That's about the how of it," Shack agreed. "It's plain enough now yore outlaws have been holed up at the Hangin'

Noose. It was outlaw money that was makin' the Hangin' Noose so prosperous. I reckon Hondo aimed to control all this part of the range before long." Shack's cigarette end glowed red as he inhaled deeply. "Hondo took one bite to-night that's gonna choke him for good. Let's see about Milt first."

Flo had been working over her husband. He stirred, opened his eyes. A few minutes later he was sitting up, groggy, weak, but trying to reassure his wife. Milt's head and face were cut, gashed, battered, but his skull was sound, and strength was returning rapidly. Powder Ike, the cook, and two of the hands were dead. As the fire burned down and the red glow faded, their bodies were placed side by side in one of the empty corrals.

That had hardly been done, when Jack Barr rode in with his sad burden. Ben Tikeman, too, was laid in the corral beside the others.

"Four of 'em," Shack said bitterly, looking down at the row of bodies while the other men gathered around. "God knows how many more there'll be, men, if yuh keep on with me."

Clem Mason spoke harshly through his beard. "It's got beyond *you* now, Shack. Ben Tikeman was enough for all of us. Ain't that right, boys?"

The replies left no doubt about the matter.

"We'll need more horses," Shack said. "Scatter out an' get 'em, men. The womenfolk'll have tuh go away from here to-night. There's no home here for a while."

Getting the horses took time, but finally a small covey was run into one of the corrals. Shack was tired, the men were all dead-beat, but there was no lack of energy in saddling fresh mounts. The saddle shed had been left untouched. Saddles were put on for the women.

"Milt, will you take the girls into Lone Pine?" Shack said. "They'll have tuh stay there for a while."

Milt had gotten most of his strength back, although his face looked bad, even in the moonlight. His reply was savage. "I'm going with you, Shack!"

"What did you say?"

"I'm cured!" Milt said in a tone new to him. "Tonight, when I saw Flo an' Dot grabbed by those masked sons and didn't know what was going to happen to them, I wanted to kill for the first time in my life. And when they gun-whipped me on the head until I passed out, they beat that lesson in to stay. All I want is to get at them with a gun."

"I don't know whether tuh shake yore hand or cuss yuh out," said Shack. "But I'm gettin' along, Milt. What happens tuh me don't matter much. Somebody's got to be left tuh look after the girls. Yuh got to do it, Milt."

"No," Milt refused. "I told Flo I was going. She said whatever I think best goes with her."

"I've seen a miracle come tuh pass," Shack admitted ruefully. "I still don't believe it. But who's gonna take the girls tuh town while we go the other way?"

No man spoke up for the job.

Shack laughed grimly. "All of yuh have lost yore manners, I see. Yuh'd rather kill a Matson than be polite tuh a lady."

"That goes for me," Rick Jones stated calmly.

Doughball Daley's voice rose loudly. "Great saints an' prairie dogs! Look what Longo Ross's bringin' in on his rope."

Around the glowing, crackling shell of the house two riders had come unnoticed. The lead man rode with a rope around his neck. Longo Ross rode close, holding the other end of the rope. The prisoner was a stranger, dark-faced, sullen, with one arm hanging limply at his side.

"What yuh got here, Longo?" Shack demanded.

"He rode up tuh the Matson place alone, an' I snuck up on him," Longo said. "When I found he was shot in the arm, we pow-wowed a bit. He wouldn't talk, except tuh say the Hangin' Noose men had gone tuh Lone Pine tonight. I seen fire in the sky, so I brought this jasper along."

"Get this fellow down an' we'll see what he knows about it," Shack said harshly.

The man was hustled off the horse, and his surly voice defied them all. "Yuh got me. I'm wounded. But I ain't talkin'. Suit yourselves what yuh aim to do."

"Anyone recognize this snake?" Shack asked.

"I wouldn't know him," Jaspar Bell said, stepping close and peering. "But Powder Ike fired a couple of shots before they riddled him. It's likely one hit this fellow's arm."

"More'n likely," Shack grated. He spoke to the prisoner. "So yore bunch is in Lone Pine?"

"That's where they started."

"An' that's where yo're goin'," Shack told him. "Boys, Hondo's hit for town, where he'll deny everything. If we come shootin', chances are he'll claim we forced the trouble. So be it. Heist this snake on his horse, boys. We'll start for Lone Pine now."

IX

"THE SHOWDOWN BEGINS"

Midnight was past when they got to Lone Pine, but the town was not asleep yet. Saloons were running full blast along the main street; hitch racks were filled. Shack led the Bar A men in by a side street and turned over beside the hotel. Flo and Dot got down and went inside.

A man was sitting on the side verandah of the hotel. Shack called to him: "What's everybody up for tonight?"

"Sheriff's posse got in late. They're makin' a night of it, seein' as how the Hangin' Noose men are celebratin', too."

"Yuh don't say?" said Shack. "Celebratin', are they? Did the posse get any of them bandits they were after?"

"Nary a one."

The man was leaning forward, staring curiously at the prisoner who drooped sullenly in the saddle with the rope still around his neck. As they rode on, Shack saw the man get up quickly and enter the hotel. He had to tell what he'd seen.

At the corner Shack turned right. "Sheriff's office, boys," he said, and rode ahead of them the half a block to the jail.

Horses were at the hitch rack. The sheriff's office was lighted, and men were inside. Shack climbed down stiffly. The day had held almost too much riding. Tying his horse, Shack called for the prisoner's rope, and ordered the man down.

"Wait out here for me," he told the men. Drawing a gun, Shack prodded the prisoner ahead of him.

The door of the sheriff's office had been open. A man had looked out, seen them, said something to others inside. Men crowded into the doorway as Shack drove his sullen prisoner at them.

None of the men in the doorway was a Hanging Noose man. They stepped back and let the newcomers in. Jack Lawson, the sheriff, was on his feet in the middle of the office floor, holding a cigarette in his fingers. Lawson's ready smile was absent. He was scowling as he demanded: "What the devil's this? You been up to more trouble, Anderson?"

Shack tossed the rope end to him. "Lock him up, Lawson. He's one of the bandit gang yo're lookin' for. That is, if you're really lookin' for 'em."

"What d'you think I've been doing all day?" Lawson snapped. Boots, black trousers, leather vest were dusty. Lawson was tired, unshaven, irritable.

Shack looked at him from eyes bloodshot with fatigue. "I don't know what yuh been doin'," he said with dangerous calm. "An' I don't rightly give a damn. Yuh didn't get anything, did you?"

Lawson passed a soiled hand to his chin, that chin which was a little too rounded. "We looked hard enough," he said ill-naturedly. "What have you done to this man? He's wounded. You been stirring up trouble again, Anderson?"

The prisoner spoke sullenly. "Get this old fool away from me. My gun went off accidental an' hit my arm, and they dragged me away from Matson's place on some fool idea."

Shack yanked the man's neck back with the rope. "That'll be enough outta you. I didn't shoot yuh, but I wish I had. Yore outlaws have been on the Hangin' Noose, Lawson.

Hondo Matson an' Sim Matson are thick in it. I'm callin' on yuh tuh lock this man up . . . an' keep yore hand away from yore gun."

The sheriff stood there with his face reddening. Four other men were in the office. Shack knew them. Carl Tate, attorney-at-law; Deacon Billings, skinny merchant who ran a store; Jed Keenan, who clerked in the store; Ropey Dale, Lawson's deputy. Good, solid, respectable citizens. Before them Lawson let his anger flare.

"I don't know what damn' foolishness you got on your mind now, Anderson. But this has gone far enough. You can't work out your grudge against the Matsons by any play like this!"

"Listen tuh me, Lawson," Shack said with that same dangerous calm. "The Hangin' Noose men burnt out my ranch this evening. They kilt three of my men, beat Milt Tyner up with their guns, an' stole mighty near forty-five thousand dollars outta the house before they fired it. And before that they kilt Ben Tikeman an' a stranger out at Black Sheep Cañon. I'm layin' the charges ag'in' the whole Hangin' Noose bunch. What are yuh sayin' about it?"

"I'm sayin' you're crazy!" Jack Lawson blared angrily. "Hondo Matson has been in town since before dark. Sim Matson almost as long. Their men have been here for some time."

"How long?"

"A couple of hours, anyway. Sim told me he was havin' them come in for another posse, if I needed 'em. If you've had trouble at your place, I'll take them out there and see about it. The bandits we're looking for must have ridden that way. But don't lay it on the Matsons."

Shack's face was wooden. "So you'll take the Matson men out tuh settle my trouble? Is that yore final word?"

"It is!" Lawson said angrily.

Carl Tate, the lawyer, said: "Anderson, you're making yourself ridiculous by this itch for trouble with Hondo Matson. Don't you think you'd better get some sense?"

Shack turned his head, and the lawyer fell silent before the look he received. "I've got all the sense I need," Shack said harshly. His big-boned frame moved like an uncoiling steel spring. His gun flashed up. The steel barrel crunched against Lawson's temple. As the sheriff dropped where he stood, Shack whirled. One gun covered the deputy, the other menaced the other men. "Turn around an' drop yore hardware on the floor! Hell has started in Lone Pine, an' yuh ain't wanted in it!"

Paling, Tate wrenched out: "You've lost your mind, Anderson."

"Don't argue with me, damn yuh. Jump! I'm in a hurry!"

Clem Mason's big beard loomed in the doorway. Clem's booming voice filled the room. "Shuck yore guns an' stay healthy, men. You're gonna see more hell in two shakes than yuh ever dreamed could happen in Lone Pine."

Guns thudded on the floor. Shack let them lay. "All of yuh get back in a cell. I'll save yuh from any foolish ideas about buttin' in on this little picnic."

"You're gonna get in trouble over this," Ropey Dale, the deputy, protested angrily.

"Get, before I put yuh on the floor beside Lawson," Shack barked at him.

A minute later Shack turned the deputy's key in the cell door and walked out. Clem Mason had already gathered up the guns and taken them outside. Shack strode after him. The men were waiting on the sidewalk.

"We're wastin' a lot of good time," Jeff Ryan remarked. "I thought yuh wasn't gonna fool with the sheriff, Shack."

"I give him his chance, Jeff. An' I wanted him outta the way. His posse is still underfoot. If he'd throwed 'em in with Hondo, we'd have too much to handle. Are yuh ready tuh start huntin' Hangin' Noose men?"

Yellow light from the office window washed against Howdy Daniels's smooth, cheerful face, showing it utterly guileless as Howdy asked: "I just got in from the Bar A, Shack. Shall we shoot 'em on sight?"

"Give 'em a chance tuh surrender an' be locked up. After that, let yore conscience be yore guide."

"I left my conscience back with Ben Tikeman," Howdy Daniels affirmed.

Within the memory of many living people, Lone Pine had never seen a march such as the Bar A men made from the jail. Shack Anderson led them, gaunt, big-boned, erect. His leathery face was hard, wooden. Gnarled hands slowly flexed and unflexed as the muscles limbered for the work ahead. Old men for the most part, they advanced stolidly, like ghosts out of a past that would not die. Gaunt, bearded, and mustached ghosts, carrying a code they had learned in years long past.

Men stood on the hotel porch as they came along—armed men, younger men who had been in the sheriff's posse. Scanning them as he came up, Shack saw no Hanging Noose men. Abreast of the hotel verandah, he stopped for one cold sentence.

"Hondo Matson or any of his men in the hotel there?"

A man replied uncertainly. "Haven't seen any of them in the last half hour. Any trouble, Anderson?"

"Keep outta this," Shack said curtly. "Any man who sides with the Matsons tonight gets the same medicine we're bringin' them."

Shack walked on, scanning the horses at the hitch rack. As

an afterthought he threw over his shoulder: "Don't kill Hondo Matson or Sim, if yuh can help it. Hondo especially. He belongs tuh me."

The Hassayampa Bar was first. Its hitch rack was full of horses. The windows were lighted. Bellowing laughter rolled out from within. A man stepped out of the front door, looked idly their way, suddenly stiffened, and retreated inside. Light from inside limned his chunky figure, showed a white strip of bandage under the edge of his hat.

"That's Weis, one of the new partners," Shack threw over his shoulder. "I'll take him. Don't crowd me, boys."

In the Hassayampa, bluish layers of tobacco smoke drifted about the hanging lanterns. Eight or nine men were inside. Six of them Shack knew as he stepped in, arms swinging loosely at his sides. They were not Hanging Noose men. The chunky figure of Weis was backing slowly toward the rear of the room. His gun was out. His cold-eyed face was drawn into a sneer. Two more men, wearing leather chaps, ranged out behind him, drawing their guns.

"Hey!" the bartender said loudly. "Don't start any trouble in here!"

Shack ignored him. "Kinda skeery, tuh duck in here an' yank out yore gun, ain'tcha, Weis?" he asked.

The sneering smile remained on Weis's face. "You looked like you're huntin' trouble with that busted-down pack of old fossils," he said. "Turn around an' keep walkin', Anderson. I ain't wantin' you in here tonight while I'm drinkin'. Your dried-up old face riles me."

"Does it now?" Shack said noncommittally. "I've come tuh lock yuh up in a jail for raidin' my place tonight, Weis. Are yuh comin' peaceable?"

Milt Tyner loomed up beside Shack. Milt's battered face was not pleasant to look at. His voice was shaking with anger.

"I'd know that voice anywhere! You laid your dirty hands on the wrong woman tonight, mister!" Milt jerked out his gun, reckless with fury.

Weis's gun crashed. Milt staggered over toward the bar. Shack's sudden shift to one side had the flowing speed of a young man. Two hands snapped to his guns in a blur. They fired hip-high, roaring with Weis's second shot and the guns of his two companions.

A bullet burnt the top of Shack's shoulder. Another went through his hat. But Weis collapsed where he stood. An ugly hole had appeared in his face. The man at his left reeled back, struck a chair, and went down to the floor on top of it. The third man whirled and dove for the door into the back room while Shack's guns were still roaring. A bullet caught him in the back. He pitched to the floor, sliding through the doorway on his face. He was still kicking as Shack whirled with smoking guns. Men had piled over the bar. Others were standing petrified. It had happened so quickly that the Bar A men crowding in from outside were too late.

"My Gawd!" the bartender swore loudly. "Yuh killed 'em all!"

"Any more Hangin' Noose men in here?" Shack rasped.

"That's all. Ain't it enough?" one of the men before the bar stammered.

Shack stepped to Milt, who was supporting himself against the bar, holding his side. Milt's face was white, drawn with pain. "Busted my rib and cut me up some inside," Milt gasped. "I guess I ain't so good, after all."

"Yuh took yore chance, an' I'm proud of yuh," said Shack. "But yuh ain't a gunman, Milt. It was a fool stunt tuh jump in against them gun artists. Can yuh get tuh the hotel?"

"I reckon so. Don't waste any time on me."

"I ain't," Shack said, turning to the door. "Hondo's hell has started, an' it's gonna be finished quick."

Outside Jeff Ryan yelled: "There's Hondo Matson comin' outta the Seven-Up!"

X

"THE GOLDEN CLUB"

The moon flooded the street with light. The Bar A men were scattering as Shack shouldered out and saw the crowd of men boiling out of the Seven-Up. Hondo Matson's tall, white-bearded figure stepped off the sidewalk over there.

Shack raised his voice. "Weis an' two of yore men are down, Hondo! Tell yore outfit tuh put down their guns, an' there'll be no more shootin'."

Hondo Matson's laugh rasped against the night. "So yuh finally busted loose, Shack? Here's somethin' for yuh!"

Orange flames lashed out as Hondo shot through moonlight. Shack threw himself to the ground as the men behind Hondo scattered, too. Horses at Shack's left reared, plunged at the hitch rack. One, struck by a bullet, tore loose and galloped away.

On both sides of the street wild gunfire drowned out all other sounds. Then, as men found cover, the firing settled down to more deliberate sniping.

Hondo Matson had shifted from the lighted front of the Seven-Up Bar as Shack's bullets sought him out. Lead struck the ground near Shack and spun off into space again. Shack threw two shots at the orange flash across the street and came to his feet. He ran at an angle across the street, crouching, dodging.

Guns opened up on him. Shack emptied his guns at the

flashes as he ran. Another bullet went through his hat. A second one nipped at his side. Bar A men were firing to cover his reckless dash.

Shack hurled himself into a dark doorway, panting heavily. His legs were strangely weak. He was getting old, no doubt about it. Breathing hard, he thumbed fresh cartridges into his guns. Shielded in the doorway, he was safe for the moment while his pumping heart steadied.

Lights had been put out all along the street. At the hotel windows, figures were visible, peering out cautiously and jerking back from the threat of stray bullets. The street itself was empty, but the ragged lash of shots, winking streaks of flame, marked where men were standing. It was easy to guess that the whole town was rousing around this block where the battle raged. Innocent people might be struck, if they showed themselves. But it couldn't be otherwise. Hondo Matson and his men had been run to earth here; here they had to be faced, for more reasons than one.

Two doors to the right a gun opened up, firing across the street. Shack thumbed back the hammers of his guns and jumped out, pouring lead as he dashed toward the spot. A dark figure staggered out with gun blazing futilely and went down heavily. He was lying half in the shadows, half in the moonlight as Shack gained that doorway. Catching up the man's gun, Shack thrust it in his own holster.

"Where's Sim Matson?" he asked.

"Damn you!" the man gasped. "I hope they cut you up! You've killed me!"

"Yuh got burnt with yore own fire," Shack told him.

A gun opened up behind the false front of a roof across the street. One of the Bar A men had clambered up there and was coolly sniping at the flashes of the Hanging Noose guns. Between this building and the next a two-foot space led to the back. Shack dashed to it and threw himself back in the black shadows between the buildings. He stumbled over a man, lying flat on the ground there. The man yelled an oath. A wild shot burned Shack's left leg, driving hot powder particles clear through to the skin. Tramping the man hard, Shack turned and clubbed at the rising figure with his guns.

He should have shot but couldn't bring himself to put lead into a man who was down that way. Luckily the head came up first. A hammering gun barrel went home to the skull. The man dropped to stay.

Shack felt his leg. The bullet had only grazed it. He kept on to the back. The next building over was the Seven-Up Bar. Behind it a cigarette glowed in the moonlight as a man stood there, smoking. He whirled, as Shack appeared, and lifted a sawed-off shotgun, plain in the moonlight.

"Watch yourself. I ain't in this!" he warned loudly.

"That you, Tom Craig?"

"Who'n hell do you think it is? Who's that?"

"Shack Anderson."

Tom Craig lowered the gun. "I didn't know you were on this side of the street, Shack. You've sure pried off the lid of hell tonight. Have you gone crazy?"

They were together now, talking in low tones. "Any Hanging Noose men back here?" Shack asked.

"Not as I know of. They're all along the street, throwing lead."

"Hondo's men burnt my place out, took my money, tied the girls up, an' beat Milt's face into a pulp," Shack bit out. "They were masked, but one of 'em showed enough tuh place the blame. The sheriff wouldn't believe it. I had tuh make good or get off this range."

"So Hondo finally came out in the open?" Tom Craig said. "It's been workin' up for forty years, Shack. I guess it had to happen sometime."

"It's come, Tom. Who's in yore saloon?"

"I left Sim Matson an' a couple of men in there. The other customers piled out the back door an' kept going. They didn't want any of it."

Shack had replaced empty cartridges in his gun while he talked. "I might as well tackle Sim next," he decided. "But it's Hondo I want."

"The shootin's sorta falling off out there," Tom Craig commented, cocking his head and listening. "I wonder who's killed who off?"

"Most of my men cut their teeth on this sorta thing long ago," Shack said calmly. "They ain't the kind tuh stand out an' get potted day or night. So long, Tom . . . if I don't see yuh again."

Shack entered the saloon without waiting for Tom Craig's reply. A gun crashed in the front as he eased through the back room. An answering bullet from the other side of the street traversed the long barroom, smashed through the wooden partition, and embedded itself in the adobe back wall.

The partition was closed. Shack opened it softly. The long barroom was dark. The silhouette of a figure moved to the front swinging doors, and shot over them. The man spoke. "I never seen such shootin' fools! You can't keep track of 'em!" It was the surprisingly deep voice of the bowlegged Red Davis, the other new partner of the Hanging Noose.

Sim Matson answered angrily from the other side of the doorway. "They're all crazier'n hell. I'll run every one outta this country before we're through with 'em tonight."

"What makes you so sure we'll get through with 'em tonight?"

"Hell! A bunch of old, busted-down wrecks? We've whipped plenty of real men."

"Gawd knows how many of us are down," Red Davis grumbled. "Slim here is gone, I guess."

"You're talkin' too much," Sim Matson snapped. "Do some shootin'!" He fired an instant later, jumped back just in time. The answering bullet ripped at an angle through the swinging doors and shattered a bottle on the back bar.

Only the two of them stood at the doorway. Shack gripped his guns and played reckless again. "Hands up, yuh two!" he called.

They whirled away from the doorway, guns blazing in a cross-fire toward the voice. A bullet struck Shack in the leg, spinning him off balance against the bar. It probably saved his life, for another bullet clipped his ear as he went. But his two guns were pouring shots as he staggered.

Abruptly it was all over. One dark figure went plunging out through the doors; the other one was down on the floor, groaning.

Blood was running down Shack's leg. The rank smell of powder was strong in his nose as he limped forward cautiously. The fallen man was a dark blob on the floor. Near him was a second form, motionless, silent. The groaning continued as Shack bent over the wounded man.

Red Davis gave a convulsive movement. Moonlight coming under the swinging doors showed his gun twitching up off the floor. Shack kicked it away, stamped his foot on the wrist, and grabbed the gun.

"Like a diamond rattler, you'll kill while yuh can wiggle, won't yuh?"

"Go on an' shoot, damn you. It'll be your turn next," Red Davis wrenched out.

"Yuh suit me like yuh are," Shack told him.

For a moment Shack peered out over the swinging doors. Sim Matson had fled to the right. Hondo had gone that way earlier. It might be possible to find them—and it might not.

Shack was beginning to feel old again. His wounded leg was hurting badly. Luck like he'd had so far couldn't hold up much longer. The next burst of fire might drop him, probably would. Meanwhile, the shooting across the street was getting ragged, slowing down. It didn't seem possible so many Bar A men had been picked off. An inner pain struck through Shack at the thought. Old friends, grand old men who had come to his side when he needed them. He'd asked a lot from them. They hadn't complained. Was it worth the price?

Shack turned quickly as Tom Craig spoke his name from the rear doorway. "Here I am, Tom."

"Thank the Lord!" Tom Craig exclaimed with relief. "I was sure they'd got you this time, Shack. You didn't down Sim, did you?"

"How'd you know that?"

"I just seen Sim an' Hondo makin' a break down the alley. I followed them a little. They went in the bank, Shack."

"Thanks, Tom." Shack limped toward the rear.

"Where you going?" Tom Craig demanded.

"To the bank."

"I'll go with you."

"This ain't yore quarrel, Tom. Stay outta it. You ain't a gunfighter. You've had whiskey an' peace too long."

"I've had you for a friend just as long," Tom Craig said stubbornly. "I'll take my scatter-gun along an' watch your back, anyway. You're wounded, Shack!"

"It ain't nothin'," Shack said as he stepped out the back into the moonlight, reloading his guns again.

The alley was deserted as Shack limped along it. Over the building tops the battle was still raging. They reached the cross street where the brick side wall of the bank rose up opposite them. To the left, in the shadows, spectators were crowding, ready to duck under cover.

No one spoke or offered opposition as Shack limped stiffly across the street to the bank. The curtains were down at the side windows. A dim light burned inside. A buggy had just driven up beside the bank, as Shack emerged from the alley. The man who got out ducked uncertainly away as Shack came up. In the moonlight he was recognizable as a nester named Somers, who lived just outside the town.

"Whatcha doin' here?" Shack demanded curtly.

"Hondo Matson told me to bring my buggy up here beside the bank," Somers said nervously.

"What for?"

"Said he wanted to carry somethin' away from the bank."

"Get yore damned buggy away from here, Somers. You're mixin' in somethin' that'll get you hurt."

Somers leaped into the buggy, sawed on the reins, turned the horse sharply in the street, and drove rapidly away.

Shack tried the door. It was unlocked. Tom Craig, gripping the sawed-off shotgun, stood behind him. "You'll just be in the way with that, Tom," Shack said. "Stand out here an' watch the door. If they drop me, yuh can call some of my men here tuh take over the bank."

Tom Craig nodded. One hand went out and gripped Shack's arm. There was a world of emotion in it. Good luck— and possibly farewell.

Shack looked back down the street. Lone Pine. He'd seen it grow. Might be he'd not see it again, solid and substantial in the silver wash of the bright moon. But the Bar A would go on. Forty years of a man's life couldn't be wiped out in one night by a man like Hondo Matson. Shack turned to the door, twisted the knob, hurled himself inside the bank.

A lamp burned dimly over the cashier's cage. Beyond it, the iron door of the small, square vault stood open. A lamp was lighted inside the vault. Hondo Matson was in there. In the front of the vault, Sim Matson stood tall and powerful. Black-browed, furious, he spat an oath, flipped up a gun, and shot out the light overhead as Shack emerged through the doorway. The vault light went out, too.

Shack lunged to one side in the sudden blackness, and the crashing crescendo of gunfire that burst out seemed to have no ending. Four guns blasting. Three men shifting positions constantly. Ears were deafened by the noise, eyes blinded by the flashes.

Shack's hot guns clicked empty. He dropped them and drew the extra gun from his left holster as he dodged. Only one man was firing from behind the metal grillwork now. Shack ran for the gate, shooting as he went. Three shots— and his third gun was empty. He struck the gate, knocking it open.

To his right a single shot roared out. The shock of a rib giving knocked Shack dizzy, weak. Only that one shot came. Hondo's gun must be empty, too.

Hondo's harsh, furious voice followed. "Damn yuh, Shack! You've killed Sim! I'll get yuh, if it's the last thing I do!"

Shack met Hondo's rush. They both reeled against the vault door, tripping over bags of metal money on the floor. Hondo clubbed his six-gun to Shack's shoulder. The sweep of Shack's gun was broken by Hondo's upflung arm. They grappled and went to the floor—two big, gaunt men, neighbors for half a lifetime, enemies to death. What followed was a blur of clubbing guns, of guarding arms, of straining, writhing bodies. Steel struck Shack's right wrist. His gun fell from the numb fingers, leaving him defenseless.

Hondo struck through his guard, and the blow glanced harmlessly off Shack's head. Strength left him. Hondo piled over on top of him. He seemed to know that the end was near. Wildly savage, his voice rose. "I'll club yuh to death, Shack! I'll settle it for good now!"

Hondo would do it, too, and exult, and go on to Milt, to Flo, Dot—and the Bar A. Crooked, cunning, resourceful, he'd wreck forty years of pride. Only lead and steel and brute strength would stop Hondo. And of that there was none left. Shack's outflung left hand struck a sack of gold coin. It was heavy and solid, almost too heavy to lift.

Hondo was exulting: "I've got yuh now, Shack! An' when I'm through with yuh, I'll go after the rest of yore breed!"

Then Shack dashed the heavy sack to Hondo's head with terrific force. It was gold, heavy, solid. Hondo's gold. Bandit gold. The dull thud was followed by the ringing clatter of gold pieces cascading from the broken sack to the floor. Hondo went limp and slowly slid over to one side.

Shack pushed him off, staggered to his knees, gulping air. His head was spinning; strength had left him. "Tom!" he called. "I got 'em! Hondo's here!"

Shack knew he was swaying over, going down across Hondo's limp body. He couldn't stop it. He pitched down into the blackness and oblivion of insensibility.

The lamplight was bright in Shack's eyes, when they opened. He was in bed. He recognized one of the hotel rooms. Dot and Flo were there, and Doc Burnside, bending over as he worked on a wound in Shack's head.

"Ouch! Are yuh tryin' tuh scalp me?" Shack jerked out.

"Keep still!" Doc Burnside said sternly, screwing his fat, middle-aged face into a frown of annoyance. "I've got too much patching an' mending an' doctoring to do tonight to waste time on a tough, old leather-duster like you."

"Don't tell me I'm goin' tuh live, Doc."

"You're too ornery to die," Doc Burnside snapped. "Short of a game leg, a broken rib, a split scalp, and the Lord knows what, there's nothing the matter with you. You old hellions are all alike. There's no getting rid of you."

Flo was holding a basin of water for the doctor. Dot sat on the bed and held Shack's hand.

"You're the biggest man in town tonight, Dad. Everybody's *proud* of you," Dot said, smiling damply.

"Yuh don't say," said Shack. "What for?"

"The Matsons were all outlaws," Dot said. "You were lying all over the gold pieces that had been taken from all those railroad hold-ups. Hondo Matson had been keeping everything in the bank vault. He and Sim were trying to take it away, when you stopped them. Sim's wounded badly, and Hondo's in jail, with his head all swelled, and some of his men are dead, and part ran away. Lawson has sent a posse out after the rest."

"Huh! Lawson doin' something finally?"

"Kit Erwin made him," Dot said, with a light in her face that wasn't hard to read. "Kit's a Pinkerton detective, Dad. He had a list of all the stolen money. Kit an' Jeff Ryan took charge of things after they found you in the bank."

"So Jeff ain't dead?" Shack said with a breath of relief. "How many of my men are gone?"

"Two or three," Doc Burnside said gruffly. "Rick Jones and Jack Barr are dead. Some of the others are wounded. But the Matsons lost three for your one. Your men slipped around behind the buildings where the Matson men were hiding and rooted them out. One or two of the Matson men have talked already. There'll be some hangings out of all this. The town has decided you saved their money and the bank for them. Hard to tell what would have happened with a bunch of outlaws in control of the bank."

Doc Burnside turned away from the bed for a moment. Flo put down the basin and kissed Shack on the cheek.

"We're all proud of you, Father," Flo said. "And now I've got to run in the next room and look after Milt."

Shack snorted as his eldest daughter departed. "There's too durned much approvin' around here. Dot, yuh needn't hang onto my hand. Go out an' see if yuh can't find a better hand. Erwin'll have some spare time before long. An' tell Jeff Ryan tuh come in."

"You'd better put off gossiping with your friends until tomorrow," Doc Burnside said unsympathetically.

"Gossipin', hell," Shack said testily. "I want Jeff tuh get me a pint of whiskey an' take some orders about the ranch. I aim tuh have the Bar A snortin' along as usual in a hurry. I'm proud of that place, Doc."

"You old-timers are all alike," said Doc Burnside gruffly. "Can't get your mind off your cows and land."

But then Doc Burnside was merely a bone-setter who'd only been around about fifteen years.

The Devil's Lode

"The Quickest Draw" by T. T. Flynn was published in Street & Smith's *Western Story Magazine* in the issue dated December 10, 1938. The editor of the magazine, Jack Burr, remarked in "The Roundup" in the issue dated April 4, 1939 that "since the publication of the December 10th issue . . . we've had so many inquiries concerning the author of this yarn which made such an outstanding hit, that we decided to find out a bit more about him." That short novel has now been reprinted in THE MORROW ANTHOLOGY OF GREAT WESTERN SHORT STORIES (Morrow, 1997) edited by Jon Tuska and Vicki Piekarski. It was followed by the short novel, "Death Marks Time in Trampas," in *Western Story Magazine* (4/15/39) which has been collected in DEATH MARKS TIME IN TRAMPAS (Five Star Westerns, 1998). Flynn completed his third short novel for *Western Story Magazine* on February, 19, 1939 and titled it "The Devil's Lode." It was scheduled almost at once upon receipt and appeared in the issue dated June 24, 1939. The author was paid $600.00 for it upon publication.

I

"PURSUIT"

Paso Brand rode out of Mexico, from down Madera way, near the Laguna Babicora, with four hard-riding *rurales* and a mob of Escobar riders smoking on his trail. It might not have been so bad if the Escobar clan hadn't been lords of that wild empire west of Chihuahua City and the frowning peaks of the Continental Divide. A place where generations of ragged *peones* had taken to the dust before any Escobar and the he-wolf of them all, haughty old Sixto Escobar, gave life and death as he saw fit had been no place for a lone *gringo* to start a flirtation, harmless although it was, with a guarded Escobar *señorita*. But who would have thought the fierce pride of the Escobars would have considered it a matter of death? Or who would have suspected that the girl's two younger brothers, the twins, José and Juan, would take it on themselves to guard the honor of the Escobars by waiting in the moon-drenched shadows under their sister's window? Paso Brand hadn't.

It was perhaps justice—if you were an Escobar. But young José made the mistake of missing with his first shot, and Paso's roaring gun cut down the shadowy figure before Paso knew who it was. Guadalupe Escobar screamed behind the bars of her dark window—and abruptly hell sizzled around that part of the town.

Dodging away through the night, Paso suddenly realized that the border was a long way off, and the Escobars were masters of an empire in any direction. He cursed himself as he ran. *You've done it now, you thick-skulled* borracho! he reflected. *The old wolf himself thought them high-stepping young dandies were where the sun came up! He'll have my hide peeled off in strips and horses pull me in two! Hell, Paso, don't you never get any sense?*

Paso's horse was at a *cantina* hitch rack on a corner of the plaza. Loitering Mexicans stared in astonishment as the *gringo* came plunging out of the night, jerked the reins free, pitched into the saddle, and spurred away.

A rifle and cartridges were in the adobe room beyond the plaza where Paso was staying. He stopped there. Bedroll, war bag, and pack horse would have to be left. He halted as he was leaving the room and jumped back for a canteen.

Tumult had reached the plaza, when he got outside again. Men were shouting; horses were tramping. High, thin, shrill, above all other sounds, came the scream of a frenzied man's shout. An old man's shout that was cracked with age and fury as it screamed death to the *gringo*.

That would be old Sixto Escobar himself. That would be the fierce old wolf whose ranges cowed everyone. Death to the *gringo!*—and death it would be for Paso Brand unless a miracle happened.

The border was a long way off. Scrub land and mountains, deep-frowning *barrancas,* stony desert country with a few widely separated and hidden water holes would have to be crossed. Paso was grim, unsmiling, as he spurred past the adobe houses, past the last of the brush and cactus corrals, past the wildly barking dogs, and the rippling shadows of the little creek into the open country.

They followed him, of course, as fast as they could get horses saddled. With them would be the four, tough, little *rurales* who had ridden in the day before. If there had been a

Join the Western Book Club
and GET 4 FREE* BOOKS NOW!
A $19.96 VALUE!

Yes! I want to subscribe to the Western Book Club.

Please send me my **4 FREE* BOOKS**. I have enclosed $2.00 for shipping/handling. Each month I'll receive the four newest Leisure Western selections to preview for 10 days. If I decide to keep them, I will pay the Special Members Only discounted price of just $3.36 each, a total of $13.44, plus $2.00 shipping/handling ($22.30 US in Canada). This is a **SAVINGS OF AT LEAST $6.00** off the bookstore price. There is no minimum number of books I must buy, and I may cancel the program at any time. In any case, the **4 FREE* BOOKS** are mine to keep.

*In Canada, add $5.00 shipping/handling per order for the first shipment. For all future shipments to Canada, the cost of membership is $22.30 US, which includes shipping and handling. (All payments must be made in US dollars.)

NAME: _____

ADDRESS: _____

CITY: _____ **STATE:** _____

COUNTRY: _____ **ZIP:** _____

TELEPHONE: _____

E-MAIL: _____

SIGNATURE: _____

hundred *rurales,* they all would have followed. The Escobars were heeded as far away as the City of Mexico.

Paso damned himself, damned the lush, bright moon, damned the lazy, sweet madness of Mexico that caught a man and held him until he got into something like this. All the time he was riding furiously into the endless leagues of country, stretching ahead into the northeast. No use to head anywhere else. They'd know well enough he was making for the border, and every lost hour gave them time to close the country ahead.

The only safety was the border. Ride them out, ride them down, ride longer, harder, with less food, less water, less sleep. Keep ahead of them through fresh country where the word was not yet out that the Escobars wanted the death of the lone *gringo* who rode into the north.

A man would try a journey like that only when death was sweeping at his heels, and death was following now. Paso reined up and heard it in the yelping cries, the pounding hoofs far back in the night. They couldn't see him, despite the brightness of the moon. But if they drew close, if his horse stumbled, if something happened to put him afoot, they'd have him there in their sights as plain as day. That moon! That damned Mexican moon that shone so brightly for lovers and equally as brightly for death. No, they couldn't see him— but they all knew well enough he was heading for the Ojo Azul trail and the pass through the mountains to San Miguel, and the hills, the grasslands, the deserts beyond.

Paso cut hard with the rein ends and was thankful his horse was rested, fed, watered. While the moon hung high and the night rolled past, he had to draw ahead of the pursuit, so that sunrise would find him out of sight. After dawn they'd fasten like leeches on his trail; they'd follow like wolves on a blood sign. And if they got him, they'd show no more mercy than wolves would show a wounded beast.

Paso spurred his horse. This was all Escobar land, stretching ahead to the east and far on into the north. Old Sixto Escobar had never laid eyes on some of his sheep and cattle herds that ranged far in the north.

Hour after hour Paso rode, past midnight and into the chill hours before dawn. At last the mountains reared high and black beside the trail, and the howling of wolves was the only sound. The moon was down, when he rode through the pass and took the downward slope through blackness. The faint, gray dawn was in the east, when he stopped for a moment to water his horse and fill the canteen at a little stream tumbling out of the mountain.

Just before midday Paso looked back from a hill crest and saw a yellow column of dust far behind on the horizon. He smiled grimly and went on, searching the rolling country with red-rimmed eyes.

A couple of hours later he saw grazing horses with saddle marks. He untied his rope and rode easily toward them. A bit of maneuvering, a quick, hard run, and his rope settled on a wiry chestnut. The horses were part of some hacienda's *caballado*. The chestnut let itself be saddled without too much fight. Paso scattered the horses and rode on at a fresh gallop.

It had to be this way. A man could ride and keep riding, but he had to have fresh horses. You could be sure the *rurales* and those riding with them would change as often as possible.

Paso rode hard that afternoon and roped another horse an hour before dark and changed again. Rabbits were plentiful, and he was hungry. He shot the head off one, and at the first water tied the horse and had a tiny fire going in a minute. He cleaned, washed, halved the rabbit, spitted the pieces on green sticks over the fire. He watered the horse, filled the canteen, stripped to the waist, and washed.

In twenty minutes Paso was wolfing the half-cooked rabbit meat as he rode on. Water, rest, food helped mightily the night ahead.

Shortly before dawn, Paso circled wide of the trail, rode back a quarter of a mile, looped his arm through the reins, and lay down where the sun would strike his face. When the first blazing rays awoke him, he was back in the saddle.

Never had Paso Brand made a ride like this. That yellow dust haze back on the horizon was the last sight of the pursuit, yet he knew they were back there doggedly holding the trail, hoping he'd crack under the strain, rest too long, or find himself afoot. While he was in Mexico, the Escobars would be trying to come up with him. They were that way, and the shrill, screaming wrath of old Sixto Escobar would ride with them.

A long time—it seemed a thousand years later—Paso came out of the heat and thirst of the Chihuahua desert to San Andres, on the Río Grande. He was sleeping in the saddle, when he rode into El Paso.

He stabled the horse, rented a hotel room, fell across the bed, and slept the clock around three times.

So Paso Brand came across the border after three years, younger than he looked, slender and fined down to a leather gauntness, with gold in his money belt and a fire of wry humor in his eyes as he looked back on the ride out of Mexico. "Never again, pardner," he promised his gaunt reflection in the hotel room mirror. "Women make trouble and this last filled your boots for a long time. Wah! It looks good here after *frijoles, tortillas,* an' dried goat meat." A few days later Paso's gold was cut in half, and El Paso knew a stranger was in town.

Near midnight of the third night, Paso left a saloon,

sucked in the crisp night air to clear up the last two drinks, and walked around the next corner on his way to the hotel. He had not gone more than fifty yards when a voice across the street roared: "Look out behind you over there, stranger!"

Paso jumped to one side, and whirled. A down-striking knife missed his back and slashed through the flesh of his right arm. A man was on him in a furious attack, spitting furiously in Spanish: "For José Escobar, you *gringo!*"

That cleared Paso's head faster than the danger. The Escobars again. He might have known they wouldn't forget. He struck the arm away as the knife flashed in again, only through the coat sleeve this time. When the knife wrist whipped up for another try, Paso caught it. From the corner of his eye he saw a second man plunging in with a drawn gun. Two of them, and there was a third in the background.

II

"A PAYING PROPOSITION"

Paso wrenched at the wrist, whirled around until his back was to the adobe building wall, kicked the attacker away from him into the third man, and streaked for his gun. But the slashed arm had a cold, numb feeling that half crippled it. The gun muzzle was just clearing the holster when the second man fired.

Paso felt the slam of the bullet knock a leg back from under him. Then his own gun roared twice, and the shadowy figure lurched back with arms flying up.

At the first blast of gunfire the other two men plunged away into the shadows clustering darkly here along the side street. Paso threw two shots after the uncertain targets. The buckling leg made his aim uncertain, and they kept on.

Out in the street another gun blasted out. Paso, supporting himself against the wall, swung his gun that way. The same bull-like voice he had heard before roared: "Hey, don'tcha open up on me! I'm trying to help you!"

"It looked like the moon had started raining Mexicans," Paso said wryly as the man came toward him.

"Mexicans, huh? Might've knowed it! I was standin' over there, trying to make up my mind what to do when I saw the three of them ease around the corner after you. They looked ornery, like they might be stalking a drunk."

"Only a half drunk," said Paso.

"I didn't know, stranger. But when one of them went out

ahead of the others, like he was ready for business, I yelled to you. Say, you sure exploded all over them. This fellow don't look like he wants any more of it."

A match blazed out. The stranger bent over the figure that had collapsed on the street. He whistled admiringly as he flipped the match away.

"I guess *he* don't want any more. You got him through the neck and the heart. One hole might be lucky, but two makes you out handy and quick with your lead, stranger. He's a Mex, all right."

"Uhn-huh," Paso agreed. "He's a Mex. How about giving me a hand? He put some lead in my leg."

Other men were running around the corner to find what the shooting was about, and, when the stranger's hand touched Paso's arm, it jerked away. "Lead in your leg? What'n hell'd he put in your arm? You're bleeding like a butchered beef."

"Knife cut," said Paso. "I guess I'd better get to a doctor before most of me leaks away. You can tell the law how it happened, I guess."

"I'll tell 'em plenty and lead a bunch out to find the other two. There's been too many drunks robbed and handled roughly around town lately, they tell me. A few border jumpers strung up may stop some of it. Did you get a good look at either of the others?"

"No," said Paso. "It'll probably be a waste of time, looking for them. How about getting me to a doctor?"

There was no lack of help, and no uncertainty as to what to do. Wounded men near the El Paso plaza were no novelty. Two of the gathering crowd locked hands and carried Paso around the corner and down a block to a doctor's office. The medico took one look and got to work. The slashed arm was easy to sew up, but a big hole had been torn in the back of the leg.

"Stranger in town?" the doctor said. "Well, a hotel room isn't the place for you. We'd better take you over to the Catholic sisters and let them nurse you after I get this leg bandaged."

"If he's short on money, Doc," the bull-voiced stranger offered, "I'll settle with the sisters for his nursing."

"I've got money," said Paso, gritting his teeth against the pain. "And thank you kindly for the offer."

In the lighted doctor's office he was getting his first good look at the stranger who had helped him. Iron-gray hair, a deep chest, a wide, strong mouth under a crisp black mustache, and dark eyes that apparently were never still—eyes with a fiery restlessness that snapped and challenged good-naturedly from sheer force of habit, if a man could judge off-hand.

Paso was weak, listless, when they got the bleeding stopped and the wounds bandaged. He told them where his hotel room was, drank something in a glass that the doctor gave him, and let them put him on a stretcher and carry him through the streets to the adobe building occupied by the Catholic sisters. The doctor's drink must have contained a sleeping powder. Paso was only vaguely aware that he was put between the cool, clean sheets of a comfortable bed. The next thing he knew it was another day, and a smiling nun was waiting on him.

Fever made the first day uncomfortable. The second day Paso felt better, and a smile spread over his face when a nun ushered the bull-voiced stranger into the room.

"I was hoping I'd have a chance to say thanks again," Paso said.

"Don't mind," the stranger chuckled. "I came in to say good bye and tell you I've got a job waiting, if you ever get around to needing one. Gardner's my name, and I can be found over by Concho Pass, in western New Mexico. If you don't know that part of the country, anybody around Three Forks can direct you to Concho. I own the Concho Mine."

"Thanks again, but the first an' last time I tried mining, I swore off for good. Pick and shovel work don't suit me," Paso said good-naturedly.

"I've got work for any kind of a man," Gardner declared. "And the better they like trouble, the faster I'll hire them. I liked the way you tied into those three Mexicans, Brand. Fast and quick, without stopping to see what it was all about. I'd like to have you come up and work for me, and the pay will open your eyes wide."

"When I get broke, I may drop by," Paso said. "Trouble, huh?"

"Nothing," said Gardner with a challenging squint, "that keeps me away." He caressed his chin. "I need a man like you, Brand."

"I guess that settles it," Paso decided. "I'd have had a knife in my back the other night and adobe dirt over my face by now, if you hadn't helped me out. Soon as this leg lets me get around, I'll head for Concho."

"I was wondering if there wasn't some way of getting you to come," Gardner said heartily.

After his visitor was gone, Paso lay, smiling thinly. Gardner hadn't been wondering; the mine owner had been pretty sure that he'd get his man by mentioning that he needed him. Gardner had a look about him that suggested he'd get what he wanted, one way or another. Yet the trouble at Concho couldn't be much worse than getting shot up and cut up here in El Paso.

Two days later one of the nuns brought Paso a small package with his name on it. "You said you didn't have any friends here, Mister Brand," she said in smiling reproof.

"Surprise to me," Paso told her, squinting at his name crudely printed on the brown wrapping paper. He broke the string and unfolded the paper. A keen stiletto tumbled out on the bed covers.

"That," said the nun, "isn't a very useful present for a sick man."

Paso grinned thinly. "You can't tell, ma'am. Got a letter with it, too."

He read the small sheet of paper on which a message was printed in pencil:

For this I no use have. José's knife I carry for José's last wish. I will follow until I am a *viejo*.
Juan Diego de Escobar

"Is your friend coming to see you?" the nun asked cheerfully.

Paso tore the message up and crumpled it in the wrapping paper. "That's hard to say, ma'am. If he gets a chance, I reckon he'll be around."

"That's something to look forward to, isn't it?" she said comfortably.

"It sure is," Paso agreed. "And I take it kindly he let me know he's thinking about me. That reminds me, ma'am, I'd kind of would like my gun belt here on the chair by the bed. I get lonesome without it."

A shadow crossed the nun's face. "Sometimes I pray that all men will forget their guns, Mister Brand," she sighed. "So often they come to us wounded and dying from other guns, and then ask for their own weapons at once."

Paso laughed softly. "It's easy to understand, Sister. When you're a stranger without any friends, you get to looking on your gun as a friend. It'll never go back on you, if you handle it right. And when a man gets on his back, blue and helpless, he wants his friend where he can see it an' handle it."

The nun nodded as she put the gun belt on the chair beside the bed. "I can see how that might be," she admitted. "But you have just heard from a friend. You shouldn't be feeling so blue that you need your gun to cheer you up."

"Two friends are better than one," Paso said jokingly. "Anyway, I'm not sure just when my other friend can get around to see me."

When the nun left the room, Paso lifted the gun belt and holster across his lap, replaced the two used cartridges, and made sure the gun was ready for quick use. He hung the belt on the chair where he could reach the gun instantly, and then picked up the keen steel dagger with a faint smile.

This show of bravado was something you could expect from a haughty young fellow like Juan Escobar. At least, it was a help to know exactly what he had in mind. Paso had recognized Juan Escobar as the man who had slashed his arm. His hunch had been right that he hadn't seen the last of the Escobars. The fact that Juan had come into El Paso with help, had located his man, and had waited for the best time to make an attack was ample proof that the Escobars were on a blood trail.

Now came this warning that another attack might be made at any time in any place. Until he was a *viejo*, Juan Escobar had written. Until he was an old man. Young, fierce in grief and pride, the surviving twin brother was dedicating his life to killing the *gringo* who had shot José Escobar. Paso sighed and put the knife on the chair.

And all over a pair of black eyes where no harm was meant, he thought to himself. *Paso, old son, you sure flirted yourself into a mess. Now I got to kill another one before I can sleep easy. And I ain't got a thing in the world against the boy. Por Dios. I'll have prayers said by a priest for you, Juan, my bloodthirsty young rooster, after I have to kill you. Maybe that'll make José and you and the old wolf himself feel better about it.*

III

"LEAD WARNING"

A little more than two weeks later Paso walked to the stage station with only a slight limp and bought a ticket to Three Forks. He had a debt to pay. The sooner settled, the better.

He saw nothing of the slender, dandified figure of Juan Escobar, but that meant little. Any passing Mexican, any one of the score or so of men loitering about when the stage pulled out, might be watching for Juan Escobar. One thing he could be sure of—Juan Escobar was checking the *gringo*'s movements.

Three Forks was far west of the Río Grande, where the harsh rise of the mountains broke down into the soft, brown swells of a vast plain. Dry grasslands and semi-desert to the south, mountains to the north, high peaks hazy in the blue sky to the east and west, and a little river singing over a rocky bed through the town—that was Three Forks, and there was an overnight wait for the stage through Concho Pass.

In the morning the fat hotel proprietor was talkative in the lobby. "Headin' up to the Concho?" he asked, squinting at Paso.

"Yes."

"Um. Aiming to work for Bull Gardner, I take it."

Paso grinned at the way they'd tagged Gardner's bull-like voice. He nodded. "Gardner sort of hired me in El Paso a few weeks ago."

"Um-hmm," said the proprietor, nodding wisely. "You ain't the only one. Better'n a dozen has gone up to the Concho since Bull went back. Half a dozen came in with him." He rubbed a broad chin that was smooth and pinkly soft after a morning shave. His eyes ran over Paso estimatingly. "Aiming to work in the mine?"

Paso shrugged.

Another wise nod, a half-squinting look, and the proprietor jerked his head toward a girl sitting on the other side of the low-ceilinged lobby. "Bull's daughter is riding the stage. He'll take it kindly, if you put yourself out to help her."

She was looking out a front window. As if sensing Paso's gaze, she turned. Not too pretty, Paso decided, but she looked as if she had spirit and humor. She glanced out the window again and saw something that made her smile.

"Kitty Gardner's some gal," the proprietor remarked.

"Kitty, huh?"

"Named Katherine, I guess. They've always called her Kitty. She used to live around here until her mother died eight, nine years ago, when she went East to relatives and school. She ain't been back more'n twice since then. I better make you acquainted."

Paso assented without enthusiasm. The proprietor led him over and introduced him to the girl with a flourish.

"Miss Kitty, I better make you acquainted with this man who's going to work at the Concho. Brand's his name. He'll be glad to help you in any way on the trip up."

She was not much more than nineteen, and her eyes were gray, cool, estimating. Paso thought there was a lot of her father in the look she gave him.

"Thank you, Mister Brand," she said. "What are you going to do at the Concho?"

"I don't know," answered Paso. "Your father said in El

Paso that he needed men."

A shadow crossed Kitty Gardner's face. "I've heard that men don't stay long at the mine any more," she remarked.

"Your dad did sort of hint at that," Paso admitted.

Kitty Gardner looked at him again. Paso could almost hear her asking him how long he was going to stay. If she had put it in words, it would have been a challenge, but she did not have to put it in words. Her look was a challenge.

Paso smiled. "Maybe we'll come out together," he suggested.

"We might . . . if you stay that long," Kitty Gardner smiled back.

When the heavy stage lumbered out of Three Forks, Paso rode beside the lanky, grizzled driver. Five other passengers and Kitty Gardner were inside the coach. The driver was loquacious.

"Going to Concho, huh?" he said, glancing across his shoulder. "I reckon you're all set to get poisoned quick."

"Poisoned?"

"Lead poisoned," the driver chuckled. "There ain't many besides Bull Gardner that stays long at Concho these days."

"I've been hearing that," Paso said dryly. "Gardner must be plenty man."

"Friend," said the driver, "Bull Gardner ain't a man this last couple of years. He's hell harnessed and whippin' the devil along."

"That," suggested Paso, "calls for more on the subject."

The driver spat and hunched over the reins as he talked from the corner of his mouth. "Concho's way out ahead there to hell and gone, with the border at the back steps," he said, pointing. "The country's cut up with hills an' mountains, and salted an' peppered with hell-for-leather gun artists that don't like decent folks."

"Nice neighbors. I reckon they've got to settle some place."

"They did," said the driver. "The border's near enough for a quick jump, if things get hot. Most of that Concho country is private pasture that's been took over by Shorty Baxter and his bunch."

"Never heard of them," said Paso. "But I take it Baxter and the boys are loaded for trouble."

"That'll say it a little, mister. Those Concho hills make a sweet buzzard's roost where they can sight meat in any direction. An' Bull Gardner squats right there in their faces, workin' a high-grade gold mine."

"You do make it sound kind of interesting." Paso grinned.

The driver snorted. "It's downright murder an' suicide. Any other man but Bull Gardner would have packed up an' moved to other parts after a little of it."

"Gardner looked kind of stubborn to me."

"That ain't the name for it. He's bull-headed. He swears he'll work that mine until hell's out of firewood or his high-grade runs out. When trouble busts, Bull holes up with his men and fights it out."

"Can't blame a man for that."

"There ain't any blame," the driver said, shrugging. "But the way it uses up men is a sight. Bull's payin' double an' triple wages to keep men workin', not to speak of gunfighters he hires. If he wasn't mining on a high-grade vein, there wouldn't be no profit."

"How about the law helping him out?"

"The law has wore itself to a frazzle. The county seat an' the sheriff is a long ways off. The sheriff can't stay up there in the hills the year around. Not to speak of posses getting skittish about pickin' lead out of their teeth to help Bull Gardner. It's reached the point where Gardner's been told, if he wants to work his mine, he better do most of the worryin' an' all of the fighting." Under the grizzled mustache, the driver's mouth split in a meaning smile as he looked at his passenger. "There'll be work for you up at Concho all right, mister. Week before last I brought back a load of Gardner's help that had their bellies full of it. Not to speak of a bellyful of fresh lead a couple was carrying. Anything in pants that'll stay up at Concho an' fight can get on the payroll now."

"Fresh lead sounds like fresh trouble," remarked Paso.

"Nothin' unusual," the driver told him. "Bull rushed a gold shipment out with some of his gunfighters riding guard. They had a running fight with some of the Baxter bunch. Word was got out some way that the gold was moving. I brought down a couple of the men that got wounded in the fight. Bull couldn't stop to take them on to Three Forks with the gold."

"It don't exactly sound like a place for a girl," Paso commented.

"It ain't. I didn't want to bring her," the driver confessed glumly. "Bull Gardner don't know she's coming. He'd have rode down to Three Forks, roaring like forty bulls to head her off. An' don't you think she won't be hustled back, quick." The driver shook his head helplessly. "I knowed Kitty, when she was playin' with dolls. Even then she had a mind of her own. I'm only hoping Bull don't jump me for bringing her up to him."

"He might wonder why you didn't say no to her an' let it go at that," Paso suggested dryly.

The driver gave him an indignant look. "I said no so fast it like to choked me . . . an' Kitty smiled sweet an' said she'd hire a hoss and saddle and ride up alone. She'd have done just that, too. I know her. Sweet an' purty, an' Bull Gardner from bit to cinches when she sets her mind on something. You got any other suggestions to make about handlin' Kitty Gardner?"

"Nope," Paso said briefly. "I'll leave that to her daddy and you. But I don't see where anything much can happen to her. She's a woman."

"And Shorty Baxter," said the stage driver, "is a rattler with his fangs sharpened by nine years in the Yuma pen. He come out sweated down to a sack of bones, a cough that sounds like a dead man, and poison and hate leakin' from every pore. The men he's collected around him ain't any better." He gave Paso a shrewd glance. "For all I know, you may be one of them, headin' to the mine to get on the payroll."

"I might be," Paso chuckled.

"Well, if you are," said the driver, "you know that Shorty Baxter is hungry for gold. And you know that Baxter's took a hate to Bull Gardner that ain't hardly human. I reckon it's because Gardner's shot up so many of Baxter's men an' kept the mine running."

"I don't know all that," Paso told him. "But I reckon I'll soon find out."

"You bet you will, mister."

The miles rolled by, and Paso pondered what the driver had told him. No wonder Gardner needed men. No wonder there had been a challenge in the man's manner in El Paso, and another challenge in Kitty Gardner's look in Three Forks. She must know what her father was up against. Paso marveled that the girl should be coming in this manner, without her father's knowledge, as cool and determined as Bull Gardner might have been himself.

The rough, dusty road struck higher every mile. To the north and south, and in the west ahead, the dry, barren hills rolled higher. Now and then a faint wagon track cut off from the road, but a man could look hard and not find much evidence of travel turning off the road to ranches and mines. A bleak, barren loneliness seemed to blanket the landscape. Perhaps the feeling sprang from what the stage driver had told him. For this was outlaw country all right. This was one of those harsh, deserted, lawless stretches of country where honest men were not welcome and strangers riding through did well to keep out of sight until they knew whom they were meeting.

An hour before noon horses were changed at a small stage station.

"Anyone on the road ahead of us?" the driver asked one of the two men in charge of the station.

"Nope," was the answer. "We're lookin' for some ore wagons through today, but they ain't showed up yet."

The driver's long whip rushed the fresh horses on at a trot. Two hours passed before he said: "Ought to have sighted them ore wagons by now. I most generally pass 'em before this when they're comin' down from the Cocho same day as I go up."

"Could anything have happened to them?" Paso asked.

"Probably not," the driver answered. "But it ain't never any surprise to hear there's been more trouble."

Now the hills were higher. The ascending and descending grades became crooked as the road entered rougher country. In one place a rocky ridge studded with cactus and low growth thrust to the road on the left-hand side. The road swung sharply around the other side of the ridge out of sight. Paso was rolling a cigarette as the stage rolled abreast of the rocks.

A shot and a warning yell called attention to a man who had jumped up into sight among the rocks. His yell reached them. *"Pull up!"*

Two other gunmen with triggered rifles rose up into view as the stage driver cursed and hauled back on the reins.

"Don't stop here!" Paso shouted. "Whip them horses up!"

"They got us covered!"

Paso grabbed the whip, and the long leather lash whistled out over the horses. "Fight it out and run it out!" Paso ordered as he put down the whip and reached beneath the seat for his rifle.

"Damn you! We ain't got a chance!" the driver yelled.

"Only three of them!"

"And thirty more maybe hid around!"

IV

"CONCHO MINE"

Paso was frantically chambering a cartridge as the gunmen up in the rocks opened fire. The lurching stage made a difficult target. They had a chance, if lead didn't drop one of the horses.

Paso had sized up the odds before he grabbed the reins. The gunmen up among the rocks were afoot. If the stage made the turn in the road just ahead, it would put the outlaw guns behind, and there would be a chance in a running fight. Just a chance, but it was worth taking.

A bullet screamed past Paso's head as he swung the rifle back of the driver's shoulders and took a snap shot at the nearest outlaw. The driver was cursing and clawing at the reins, but he was rattled, frightened, and the horses were running hard.

"I'll throw you off, if you pull on them reins!" Paso yelled as he jerked up the rifle for another shot.

"Yuh damn' fool! Yo're crazy!" the driver shouted. "We'll all get killed!"

Paso fired again. His target staggered back and fell. One down. Two up there were still shooting. They must have been so sure the stage would stop that they were rattled some themselves, or they would have shot at the horses instead of trying to knock the men off the driver's seat. Then suddenly the driver dropped the reins and fell over against Paso.

"I'm hit! They got me, yuh damn' fool!"

Paso's hand caught the man as he started to topple off the seat. "Ease back and hang on! We ain't stopping now!"

With a mighty effort, Paso heaved the driver around, half over the back of the seat. Crouching, with one knee on the wildly swaying seat, Paso lifted the rifle again, just as a hammer blow of fire grazed the top of his head and knocked him blind, dizzy, weak. He felt himself falling forward toward the horses and tried to claw back on the seat. Then a terrific lurch staggered him off the side of the footboard into space.

The world was a blur of hoofs and wheels, gunshots and noise as Paso fell. He caught a blurred glimpse of white, staring faces inside the stagecoach, and then he struck hard, and the road battered, pounded, and tore at him as he sprawled helplessly beside the rumbling thunder of the heavy stage wheels.

The wheels just missed him—and then he was alone, half stunned, gasping in the yellow dust cloud behind the receding stage. Paso's first clear thought, as he struggled to his knees, was that he still held the rifle in a death grip. Blood was running into his eyes. The dry, gritty taste of dirt was in his mouth as he staggered up. But he could move, he could see as he shook his head fiercely to clear his senses. The galloping four-horse team was still dragging the careening stage around the sharp turn.

The scream of a bullet sang in Paso's ears. He ducked and stumbled off the road. On this side there were rocks that had tumbled down from the slope and had been rolled aside when the road was leveled through. An instant later the vicious buzz of lead ricocheted off the rock.

The stage vanished around the turn. The shooting had stopped. Only those three men had appeared. Paso swiped blood out of his left eye. His face had dug into the road. It felt as if it had passed through a meat chopper. Danger was whipping his mind clear, driving strength back through his body. Still the guns stayed silent. Paso risked a look from behind the rock. Two running figures were ducking around the shoulder of the ridge. Paso shot at them, missed, and they were gone.

Paso spit dirt from his mouth and considered. The two men must be heading after the stage. That would be the only reason they didn't try to gun him out from behind his rock. Warily he stood up. The third man's gun did not open up at him as he made for the turn in the road. Before he reached the turn, he heard horses drum into a gallop. A moment later the stretch of road around the turn was in sight.

Far ahead the racing stage was throwing up a dust cloud. Two riders were spurring out of a little gully in the side of the ridge and heading after the stage. Paso sat down in the road for steadiness, braced the rifle, sighted carefully, squeezed the trigger. He missed and tried again. This time the rider on the right wove in the saddle, sagged forward, and held on with both hands as he kept going. The other man looked back and rode on hard, also.

Paso stood up, breathing heavily. Now that the furious strain was over, he was shaking. The top of his head burned painfully. He felt the spot and found a raw furrow through the hair roots. Only by a fraction of an inch had death missed him; by a still smaller fraction he had escaped being creased and knocked cold. He smiled wryly. His voice came thick and husky through the dirt taste in his mouth. "Maybe my luck's took a turn for the better. Wonder if it's still gonna hold?"

In the crooked little gully that had washed back in the ridge, Paso found a third horse tied to a mesquite bush. Bruised lips pursed in a silent whistle as Paso surveyed the magnificent, cream-colored animal. The horse had a snow-white stocking on the right foreleg. It was a stallion, clean-limbed, powerful, with unmistakable signs of Arabian blood.

"Some hoss thief sure made a pretty steal," Paso muttered admiringly. "You're enough to make a hoss thief out of 'most anyone. Wisht I knowed your name."

The stallion stood with warily lifted head as Paso approached, speaking soothingly. Its heavy saddle was tooled leather. Bit chains were silver. Silver conchos were on the bridle. Mexican style *tapaderos* boxed the stirrups in front and hung down the sides. An empty rifle boot was made of the same fine, hand-tooled leather.

"If I was curious, I'd say you might belong to this Shorty Baxter himself," Paso murmured softly. "But I ain't curious. We'll just ride on to Concho. Steady, boy, steady."

The stallion looked as if he might fight a strange rider in the saddle. But after standing a moment in indecision, he answered the pressure of the reins and turned to the road. Paso thrust his rifle into the boot and put the horse into a long, easy gallop. Now the country was rougher every mile. The road had few straight stretches. The stage had vanished and did not come in sight again.

Miles from the scene of the fight, Paso marked where the two outlaw riders had turned south off the road. Trees began to appear on the hill slopes, and finally the Concho Mine was not far ahead. The faint, far-off, trip-hammer thunder of a small stamp mill drifted through the hills.

Paso rode around the shoulder of a mountain, and the grade pitched down. The mine was half a mile ahead, in the mouth of a V-shaped valley that knifed back into the mountain. A boiler stack spewed black smoke. A haze of rock dust hung around a small battery of mill stamps. Some of the mine buildings were rock and adobe; others were timber covered with sheet iron.

Surrounding the area of several acres around the shaft mouth was a triple fence of barbed wire. As Paso came nearer, he saw armed guards patrolling the fence. The nearest guard stared in his direction, half lifted a rifle, then lowered it, and waited. The barbed wire came to within a hundred yards of the road, and under one corner of the wire ran a little mountain stream that crossed the road under a short bridge and foamed on down the steep slope in a narrow, rocky channel. Two guards were at the massive wood-and-wire gate as Paso rode up. Heavy ore wagons stood inside the stockade, but there was no sign of the stagecoach.

"Stage get here?" Paso called.

"Yep," said the nearest guard. "Who'n hell are you?"

"I was on the stage."

The guard was a cold-eyed, wolfish man. He wore a saturnine look of disbelief as he eyed Paso. "Only one feller left the stage. He was shot off. What's the idea of ridin' in like this, claimin' you're him?"

Paso eased over in the saddle and shrugged. "I ain't seen my face, but it feels like hell. I was shot off the stage an' fell on my face. Don't it look it?"

"Kinda," was the grudging admission. "Where'd you get that horse?"

"Found him. Did the coach have any more trouble?"

"Nope. One of the passengers drove it in. Bull Gardner furnished a driver to take it on after the horses was changed. The passengers wanted to travel fast beyond any trouble that might come up over the fight."

Men were hurrying toward them, and the other guard was opening the big gate as Paso asked: "What happened to the stage driver?"

"They took him on to get a doctor. He was tore up pretty bad where the bullet came out. Chances are he ain't gonna live. I reckon you'd better ride in an' explain."

"Explain what?"

"Bull Gardner'll tell you."

There was an ominous note in the guard's voice. Paso narrowed his eyes slightly and rode inside the wire. More men had appeared. Most of them looked like miners ready to go to work, but some wore guns and riding boots and had hands that had never been hardened by pick and shovel work. When you looked close, you could see the faint swagger that seemed to grow on many gunmen who lived always on the edge of trouble.

Paso reined up beside one such man, a small, sharp-featured, shrewd-looking one with red hair and a big gun tied down in an oiled holster. The red-haired gunman took a corn-husk cigarette from the corner of his mouth and stared. "Some horse you got."

"I thought so, when I got him," Paso said coolly. "Where's Gardner?"

"He's around. No telling where. Hitch over there at the office an' look."

A small sign across the front of a low, stone building straight ahead read: **Concho Mine**. The windows of the building were small. A massive door suggested a fort rather than a mine office. Paso dismounted at a hitch rack at the side of the building. As he glanced across the saddle, he saw the small, red-headed gunman hurrying into the office.

The hammering steel stamps crushing rock ore to powder in the stamp mill filled the air with an increasing roar of sound. Paso stretched stiffly and looked around. The mine shaft ran straight into the side of the mountain. Here were racing machinery and sweating, working men burrowing into the rock. Here was high-grade ore that meant easy wealth. Here, at least, should be safety, but Bull Gardner's gold mine suddenly seemed like fat, rich meat out here in the wild loneliness. Rich meat for outlaw buzzards to tear and pluck at their leisure. The triple fencing of barbed wire took on a frail and uncertain look against the danger that must lurk by day and night on all sides.

Staring men were beginning to stroll up, as Paso shaped a cigarette and stepped to the office door. He was blocked there at the door by a lean, cat-hipped man who appeared in the doorway.

"Gardner inside?" Paso asked.

"Who wants him?" The man had a knife-edged smile under a black mustache.

"I do," said Paso with a touch of impatience.

"Who'n hell are you?"

Paso drew a breath and shut his teeth over a hot retort. The Concho wasn't giving much of a welcome.

"It don't happen to be your damn' business," he said evenly. "But the name is Brand. I'm the fellow who was shot off the stage. Who in hell are you?"

"Me?" said the other with a thin smile. "I'm Jules Horgan. I run things, when Gardner ain't around. And if you're the hot-headed fool who like to got Gardner's daughter killed on the stage, you ain't wanted around here. Get going."

"Was the girl hurt?" Paso asked quickly, with a sudden wave of apprehension.

"No fault of yours she wasn't," Horgan said unpleasantly. "Get off the mine property before I throw you off. My mouth tastes bad when I look at you an' think of that fool play you made."

A dozen men were near enough to hear what Horgan said, and more were coming.

"Get a gun and throw me off!" Paso suggested.

Jules Horgan put his hands on his lean hips and smiled coldly. "If it's gun play you want," he said, "I'll call some of the boys to cut you down and have it over with. We don't settle arguments with guns around here. Not among ourselves. We've got plenty of that to do with outsiders. Gun talk gets stopped quick inside the wire. Take your choice, fellow, and make it fast. I'm too busy to waste time on you."

Paso lost his head. The instant he unbuckled his gun belt and threw it aside, he knew he had lost his head. Horgan had been goading him to do just this, and the gun belt was still in the air when Horgan jumped at him.

V

"PASO MAKES A NEW ENEMY"

Paso dodged, but Horgan came down off the office steps so fast that no man could have gotten out of the way. Horgan came plunging with his fist cocked for a smashing blow—and, if the blow missed, the weight of his rush would still knock the victim sprawling. Paso did the one thing that gave him a chance. He dropped, ducking forward as he went down—and his shoulder and side knocked Horgan's legs out from under and sent the slightly taller man plunging on in a helpless, sprawling fall.

"*Wow!*" one of the onlookers whooped. "That brought him down fast!"

Paso whipped up and was on Horgan, as the man rose with a skinned hand and the smile wiped from his face. A smashing blow knocked Horgan down again before he could get his balance, but he rolled like a cat and came lunging up, spitting oaths.

The gun crease across Paso's head, the stupefying fall from the speeding stage had taken toll. The edge of his own speed was gone; aches, bruises, weary muscles kept him from responding as he should have. His next blow at Horgan fell short as the man came to his feet, and Horgan's fist crashed into Paso's cheek and staggered him.

Horgan was wild-eyed, furious, as he ducked and rushed behind his flailing fists. Paso staggered back from the blows, jumped aside to the edge of the crowd. As Horgan whirled and came at him again, Paso crouched. He came up inside Horgan's arms with a driving uppercut that snapped the man's head far back. Only Horgan's quick grab saved him from going down again.

Paso tried to fight free from Horgan's relentless grip. Horgan was kicking wildly and trying to trip him. They wrestled back against the nearest men, and a leg that was not Horgan's reached out and tripped Paso. As he went down, he caught one glimpse of the short, red-headed gunman directly at the spot where he had been tripped, then he was on the ground, and Horgan was kicking, stamping him.

A boot grazed Paso's head and half stunned him. He was done for and knew it, as he tried clumsily to roll and protect his head with his arms. He would be lucky if Horgan stopped short of murder with the boots. He'd be lucky if he lived and came out of it with a face scarred for life.

A bull-voiced bellow cut through the noisy cries of the crowd. "What's going on here? Stand back, Horgan! I told you no more of this! Who is he?"

Blood again smeared Paso's face, as he got dizzily to a knee. Bull Gardner's big hand caught his arm and jerked him to his feet.

"So it's *you*, is it?" Bull Gardner exclaimed roughly. He wore a khaki coat, his head was bare, and his face was as hard and dark as the ore out of his mine.

Paso wove unsteadily, trying to catch his breath. He could feel fresh blood on his face, and his head was spinning. Horgan, his own face cut and bruised, was scowling, panting heavily beyond Gardner's shoulder. Paso grinned coldly at Gardner from mashed lips. "It's me," he said thickly. "An' this is about what I had coming for trying to help a lady. I figured I'd ride in and pass the time of day, so you'd know I was all right. But it didn't matter, did it? Not even a man went down the road to make sure what had happened to me. Next time I'll sit back an' let the gun artists have the lady. Maybe you'll sing a different tune, if the Baxter bunch ever gets their hands on her."

Bull Gardner's look narrowed in sharp speculation. "Brand, are you trying to tell me what was on your mind when you whipped the stage on and started a fight?"

"What else?" Paso demanded. "The driver had been giving me the low-down on this Baxter bunch. The hotel man in Three Forks asked me to keep an eye on the young lady until she got to you. What do you figure would have happened if those gunslicks had stepped up to the stage and found your daughter inside? Maybe they knew it already. She was around Three Forks long enough for word to be carried ahead. I saw a chance to get her out of it and grabbed it."

The black look passed from Gardner's face. "I hadn't thought about it that way," he muttered. "The stage driver said you lost your head an' brought on bad trouble when it could have been avoided by giving up pocket money and letting the stage go on. The stage passengers felt the same way about it." Gardner spat and his face darkened again. "The Baxter bunch," he said harshly, "wouldn't dare lay a hand on my daughter."

"Maybe you're sure of it," Paso told him curtly. "I wasn't." He folded his bandanna, wiped blood from his face, and looked around. "Where's my gun belt? I'll be riding on."

Bull Gardner spread big hands. His eyes pleaded for understanding of things he didn't put into words. "What's done is done," he said. "Maybe I was too hasty. It . . . it was a shock seeing my daughter, when I wasn't looking for her, and hearing how close to death she was in that gun brush. It upset me a heap, Brand. You can write your own ticket as to how you'd like all this evened up to suit you."

Paso studied him. Gardner's eyes still seemed to be trying

to say more than he had spoken. "I reckon that covers it," Paso said. "What's done is done. Maybe I'll have better luck the next time I'm jumped."

Jules Horgan had recovered his aplomb and wiped a smear of blood from the corner of his mouth. "This man," he said harshly, "rode in on a horse he got from those gunmen. If you ask me, they might have a damn' good reason why they furnished him with a horse."

"What makes you so sure where I got the horse?" Paso demanded.

Gardner gestured impatiently. "Horgan, you're on the wrong track here. Why should Brand have started trouble if he had any connection with them? His play would have been to set back and let them handle it to suit themselves. Anyhow, I know Brand's all right on that score. What upset me was the thought of Kitty, sitting there with bullets flying. But that's past. Brand, I hope you'll stay here at the mine."

Paso looked at Horgan, and then turned and found the short, red-haired gunman in the crowd about them. He was thoughtful as he nodded to Gardner. "I'll stay."

"Good," said Gardner. "Pick a bunk in the bunkhouse and draw some blankets. Supper won't be long now. After you get settled, I'd like to talk to you in the office."

"Where can I put my horse?"

"Tony Ramos, the hostler over at the stable, will take care of him for you. Ride over behind the bunkhouse. You'll see the corral. Horgan, I want to talk to you."

A big, bearded miner handed Paso his gun belt and gun. "It shore did me good to see you almost whip Horgan, young feller," he said, smiling broadly. "I seen what he was up to when he started proddin' with that damn' sneering mouth of his. When he don't like a man, he hones to get him down an' put the boots to him. An' you was smart not to reach for a gun, with him standing there easy an' unarmed. He'd have plugged you with a Derringer he keeps up his sleeve. We're onto his tricks around here, but he's pizen to a stranger who don't outthink him."

"I'm obliged," said Paso. "I guess I'll be seeing you again, mister."

"Can't miss me, if we both stay around this hell hole. Ask for Ben Davis if you got any questions you want answered. I'll be loafing around, when I ain't working in the tunnel on the evening shift."

The stable was a long, open-front adobe shed fronted by a pole corral. Tony Ramos, Paso reckoned, would be the slender, young Mexican perched on one of the top poles of the corral, smoking a cigarette. He jumped down, took the cigarette from his mouth, and stood staring as Paso rode up and dismounted.

"Tony Ramos?" Paso asked.

"You bet," said the other, still looking at the cream-colored stallion.

"Here's a horse that rates the best you can give him."

There was evidently a fair amount of Indian blood in the Mexican hostler. Broad cheekbones and the magnificent, rugged ugliness of his young face were all Indian, despite the lightish shade of his skin and good English.

"By golly," Tony Ramos said with admiration, "I only seen such a horse once. I bet you had to kill Sonora Joe Riley to get him."

"Hey, what's that you said?" Paso countered quickly.

The young Mexican pointed to the snow-white star on the stallion's forehead and the white foreleg. "Plenty people, I bet, know this horse, if they see him miles away. Me, my frien', I never seen him before, but I've heard plenty about him. Hees Sonora Joe Riley's horse."

Paso whistled softly. "I've crossed that wolf's trail down in old Mexico. He's a bad one. Three years ago some of us rode up to a *hacienda* north of Culiacán a few hours after some bandits led by Sonora Joe had raided the place. I'll never forget what that bunch of wolves left behind. They'd pushed the old don feet first into a bonfire, and there wasn't a young woman left on the place."

Tony Ramos dropped the cigarette and crossed himself. "Ees plenty good he's dead," he said, reaching for the reins. "An' one less to ride with this damn' Shorty Baxter an' make trouble around here. How you keel Sonora Joe, *amigo?*"

"He was one of the bucks who jumped the stage," explained Paso. "Are you sure Riley has been riding with the Baxter bunch?"

"Sure, plenty people know that."

"That's one to think over," Paso decided. "Riley was a big enough wolf himself not to have to ride around under another man."

The hostler nodded.

"Maybe," Paso decided, "things got too hot for Riley down in Mexico, an' he had to jump north of the border and do the best he could. He was so ornery, I guess, most decent outlaws didn't want him around."

"Maybe," suggested Tony Ramos with a flash of white teeth, "maybe Sonora Joe found a bigger wolf than himself when he met thees Shorty Baxter. Hee's a devil, thees Baxter. I tell you!"

Paso laughed. He liked this shrewd, cheerful, young Mexican.

"I hear Baxter's all of that. But the devil's evidently met his match this time in Bull Gardner. There's gold still coming out of the mountain here, no matter what Baxter does about it, eh?"

Tony Ramos replied with an enigmatic look. "Gold's damned funny, I tell you," he said. "Ees gold what keeps Gardner here working the Concho. Ees gold what keeps thees damn' fool men coming up here to work, an' new men coming when the old ones don't stand it no more. Ees gold keeps me, Tony Ramos, here w'en I have nightmares in my sleep, I tell you. *Amigo,* if you t'ink no one else is afraid around here, you watch close for a couple days an' nights an' see what you t'ink then."

Paso smiled. "I'll do that," he promised. "And don't hold Sonora Joe against my horse. The *caballo* couldn't help who rode him."

"Me," said Tony Ramos, shrugging, "I'm not so sure about anyt'ing, my frien'."

VI

"A TRAITOR IN THE CAMP"

Paso laughed and walked off stiffly to find blankets for a bunk and get washed up before supper time. The long, low bunk-house had thick adobe walls. The bunk-lined interior, with eating tables down the middle, was heavy with the reek of hard-working, close-packed humanity. The cook house was built on one end.

Men grouped inside the doorway broke off talk, as Paso entered with his blankets. He looked for a vacant bunk with their staring eyes on him.

"Miner or gun-toter?" a bearded miner demanded from across the room.

"Gun-toter," Paso replied pleasantly, since the man was civil enough.

"Gun-toters' bunks is nearest the door there, where they can get out fustest and fastest. That top bunk, fourth from the end, ain't bein' used."

Paso looked in the bunk. "There's blankets and a slicker in it."

The miner showed white teeth in his beard. "Pitch 'em out, stranger. He's got three feet of dirt over his chin to keep out the rain an' the cold. She's yore's as long as you last."

Half an hour later a great clanging on an iron bar outside brought a rush for supper. After the meal, the men straggled outside, rolling smokes and talking. From one of the men he questioned, Paso learned that in a few minutes a shift would come out of the mine and another shift go in. Two shifts a day. Bull Gardner was ripping rich high-grade gold ore out as fast as he could find men to work. Now and then, when the working force was thinned out, the Concho had to go on a one-shift schedule. All that sounded natural enough, but in the thickening twilight Paso began to sense something inside the barbed-wire enclosure that was not quite natural.

Over the Concho Mine, over the hammering little stamp mill, over the clatter of machinery in the mill shed, and the sight of many men living and working in one spot hung a secretive, furtive tension. Now and then men glanced uneasily past the triple barbed wire to the raw, ragged hills, looming darkly all about. Twilight was bringing a savage, lonely aspect to the landscape.

Paso got a queer feeling that the hammering steel stamps were pounding a noisy defiance to dangers that lurked back in the hills out of sight, and a feeling that most of the men did not share that defiance. Gold had brought them here. Gold kept them here. But they did not like it. A lurking, hidden, secret fear that men tried to hide was something new. Paso wondered what days, weeks of it would do to taut, raw nerves. Hardcased as most of the men seemed to be, the greater part of them evidently was not used to living by the law of steel and lead all the time. They were hard-rock men, used to sledges and drills, picks and shovels, and the dull, heavy explosions of powder down in the mines, not the whiplash snap and snarl of killer guns.

A gaunt, stoop-shouldered man wearing spectacles and a bookkeeper's black-cloth sleeveguards came up and touched Paso's arm. "Are you Brand?"

"Right."

"Mister Gardner would like to see you in the office."

The stone office had an outer and an inner room, and quarters behind where Gardner evidently lived. Gardner was sitting at a desk inside a counter that split the office in half. He got up as Paso entered.

"Come in the back room, Brand."

Paso followed, and leaned his rifle against a desk in the back room. Gardner sat down at the desk. His mouth had a new hardness under the crisp, black mustache. The snapping, challenging eyes were as restless as ever, as Gardner looked his visitor over and caressed his chin. "How do you like it, Brand?"

"Hard to tell."

"Don't like it, eh?"

"I didn't say so."

"You had a sample today on the stage of what we're up against all the time." Bull Gardner dropped a hand to the desk edge and drummed his fingers softly. "Just a sample."

"Next time," said Paso, grinning, "I'll try to keep my face from getting so messed up. It ain't much of a face, but I've got to look at it in mirrors, an' I'm kind o' fond of it."

Gardner nodded. "You're not worried much, I see. I had an idea you wouldn't be. Brand, I'd like to make plain at the start that, when I find a man I can trust, I pay him well. Plenty more than he'd get anywhere else."

"Gold seems to buy everything around here," drawled Paso. "What does all this extra pay get you?"

"Men that will work here at the Concho."

"Regular pay ought to get that."

Gardner scowled. "It ought to, but it doesn't. I'm pretty much alone up here, if you want the truth. These men are all here for what they can get out of me and the mine. Nine out of ten would sell me out, if they thought it would pay better."

Paso lifted his eyebrows. "That many?"

"This isn't a cattle ranch, it's a gold mine," Gardner snapped. "And when men work in gold, they don't give a damn for anything but gold. I'm going to have to put you on night watch tonight, Brand. We're short-handed, and gold is piling up in the safe over there. The outlaws seem to have ways of knowing when gold is on hand."

"I got a whisper of it from the stage driver," Paso nodded. "He had an idea someone on the payroll here was in cahoots with the Baxter bunch."

Bull Gardner slammed both his clenched fists on the desk. "He was right. But I've never been able to find out who it is. We watch for days and don't see anyone around. We send out bagged concentrates to the smelter, and they go through safely. But if there's bar gold from the amalgam tables hidden in the concentrates, chances are we can expect trouble. Bar gold is what they want, and I've got to send it out. The smelter is too far to freight the ore out. We've got to reduce it to concentrates here, take off all the values we can, and try to get them out some way. And it gets harder every month. Somebody is tipping my hand right along."

"Ought to be easy to find who it is," Paso said thoughtfully.

"I'll pay five thousand in gold in El Paso to the man who stops it!"

Paso smiled wryly. "Gold again. I'll be saying it in my sleep. Every move that's made around here butts up against gold. You didn't offer me a job here to spy on your help, did you?"

"No," Gardner denied quickly—too quickly almost, Paso thought. "I spotted you for a good man, and I need good men. I'll be frank with you, Brand. If this mine was twice as rich as it is, it wouldn't be profitable the way things are going. I'm spending a fortune to keep men at work . . . and the damned outlaws are getting more than I make. Men who aren't as stubborn as I am would have closed the mine down and quit before they were entirely cleaned out. I'm running at a loss."

Gardner was blazing with anger. His fist clenched and un-clenched as it rested on the desk, and his eyes were snapping with fury.

Paso looked at him and smiled faintly. "Why not put it up to the wild bunch outside your wire fences? If I was leading a bunch of gunnies, with such easy pickings around, I'd take good care not to make the place close down. It'd be kinda like killin' the goose that lays the golden eggs. And, dammit, there *I* go tossing my loop over gold talk, too."

Gardner's reply was harsh. "Shorty Baxter would rather have the mine closed down, flooded out, ruined, abandoned, and me run out of these parts busted, than get his loop on all the gold we take out."

"Something personal in it?" Paso suggested.

"No!" Gardner denied violently, but his eyes narrowed.

"And that offer of five thousand gold still holds?" Paso asked.

"I'll make it ten thousand," Gardner offered quickly. "Ten thousand in bar gold, paid over to your say-so in El Paso."

"Gold again," said Paso. "I'm gettin' so I don't like the sound of it. Mister, I didn't come here lookin' for bar gold. I had a tally against me to check off. You saved my hair in El Paso, and, if helpin' you keep your gold mine open will make us even, I'll take that way. I always aim to pay off, when I can."

Bull Gardner leaned back in the chair as if he were re-lieved. "Fair enough, Brand, if that's the way you feel about it. And I'll insist on you taking the gold, also. Your work will give you the run of the mine and any outside riding you want to do. I suggest you don't seem too friendly with me. We're on our own, pretty much, as far as the law is concerned. Murder is easy. Watch your step."

"I usually do," Paso said dryly. "I'll count on you, keeping this under your hat. Who else do I take orders from?"

"Jules Horgan. No one else."

"Horgan, huh?" said Paso, touching his face reminiscently. "Friend of yours?"

"He does what he's told to do. He misjudged the way I felt about you today. He'll not make you any more trouble. I've given him his orders."

"That's good," said Paso mildly. He picked up his rifle and turned to the door. His hand was on the knob, when he heard Kitty Gardner say in the front room: "Good evening, Mister Horgan. Is Father in here?"

"I was just comin' in myself to see, Miss Kitty."

Paso opened the door. Kitty Gardner was coming around the end of the counter. Jules Horgan was halfway to the inner door, waiting for her. Horgan turned as the door opened. The smile wiped off his face at sight of Paso. "We're looking for Mister Gardner," he said brusquely.

"If you'd kept on coming, you'd have found him," Paso pointed out. He came out of the doorway and stepped aside with a wary nod of recognition at Kitty Gardner, waiting for her to pass. But she stopped with her gray eyes on his bruised face, and her sympathy was instant.

"It *did* hurt you badly, didn't it? We thought you were dead and . . . and no one seemed to be able to do anything about it back there on the road. Father told me what you did . . . and why you did it. Will you believe I'm awfully grateful? No one else would have thought of doing anything, I know."

Paso smiled at her earnestness. "I'm glad you made it here

all right, ma'am. I'm fit an' fine an' going to work tonight. I reckon we'll both enjoy the Concho a heap now that we're here."

Jules Horgan was impassive, as Paso walked on out, but Paso had the feeling that the man's eyes followed him out. When the dark evening closed around him outside, Paso spat. *Just comin' in, was he? And so far ahead of her she didn't see him until she got inside. The skunk eased in there an' was listening. An' I'd give a bar of that damn' yellow gold to know how much he heard. Gardner can give orders from now till hell freezes over, an' it won't make that* hombre *like me. Or me like him.*

The mine shifts had changed. Food was being served in the bunkhouse again. Lighted lanterns on poles drove back the night inside the barbed wire. The thunder of the stamp mill beat endlessly over all other sounds. Lights in the mill shed and other buildings made the Concho a gaudy, light-spangled scar against the vastness of the night. Out there in the night, death. And inside the barbed wire, a devil's brew of greed, fear, and distrust. Paso grinned coldly, as he strolled toward the mill building.

About as bad as the Laguna Babicora country and old Sixto Escobar's hate, he said to himself. *All this needs is Juan Escobar around to stick a knife in my back, an' hell would be calm and peaceful.* Paso spat. *And Juan won't be far behind. Paso, old son, you shore started gray hairs a-sproutin' when you got off the main trail down there in old Mexico.*

VII

"SHOTS IN THE NIGHT"

Two hours later Paso was outside the wire, doing night guard. Four others were out there patrolling the wire. Not many, but they could give the alarm and throw lead if anyone tried to rush the camp. They were afoot, so they could get back through the wire fast if they had to.

One of the other guards, a bowlegged, hook-nosed desperado who said his name was Tex and let it go at that, was resentful at being forced out of the saddle. "I ain't been so much on my feet since I was a kid. Gold money an' plenty of it is all that'd keep me pushing my toes in the dirt all night long. It's a hell of a job. Don't get lined up long afore any of them lights," he warned Paso. "We get shot up every now an' then in the middle of the night just to keep us on our toes. They tie their hosses out of hearing, sneak in close, fan a few shots, an' give us the horse laugh as they leave."

"What does that get them?" Paso demanded. "There ain't any gold in that."

"How'n hell do I know?" Tex said viciously. "But it keeps us shot up an' the whole camp worried. Maybe they figure it keeps us softened up, so we're easier meat when they make a jump after gold. If you ask me, they want the mine closed down an' strangers out o' this border country. Long as the mine is running, they never know what the law'll decide to do. An' they can't keep their hands offen the gold as long as

202

it's here for the takin'. If I was sure I'd make more ridin' with them, I'd cash in here and look the wild bunch up."

"I reckon a heap of the boys feel the same way," Paso judged.

"I reckon so. Why not? We're all lookin' for all we can get, ain't we?"

"Seems so," Paso agreed.

For a time laughter and some singing from men off duty came through the roar of machinery in the camp. But outside the wire the night brooded under the cold, bright stars. Coyotes yapped and howled in the hills. Now and then the far howl of a big loafer wolf drifted on the night breeze. The water rushed and poured in the rocky, little channel.

Paso thought of Bull Gardner and his explanation of all this. The reasons he had given for the mine raids didn't make too much sense. Since when would outlaws rather close down a mine and stop future chances at the gold the mine might produce? Why should the Baxter bunch go to all the trouble of picking off the guards at night and keeping the camp terrorized? Gardner had said there was nothing personal about it. Well, maybe. But now out in the night, beyond the wire, Gardner's words became even less convincing.

The more Paso thought about it, the less he liked the set-up and the chore he'd let himself in for. But he'd passed his word, and it was backed by the debt he owed Gardner. If it hadn't been for Gardner, they would probably have buried Paso Brand quickly back there in El Paso, and young Juan Escobar would have headed back over the Río Grande to boast far and wide that the Escobar dead was avenged.

You owed a man something for saving your life, and, when he put it up to you that he needed help, you couldn't shrug it aside. At least, Paso Brand couldn't, even when he knew the other man was skillfully hazing him around to repay the favor in this manner. Maybe, though, you couldn't blame Gardner for snatching at all the help he could get. He has a war bag full of trouble, and his daughter, showing up the way she had, didn't make it any easier.

Paso wondered about the gray-eyed girl who seemed as stubborn as her father. Had she known how bad things really were at the Concho when she left Three Forks? Probably she had. Paso guessed it wouldn't have made any difference. Probably it would have made her more determined to come. She was that much like her father. Paso considered her without any sentiment. She shared in the debt he owed her father. Helping her was helping Gardner. By tomorrow she'd be out of the picture. Gardner would pack her back to Three Forks in a hurry. And there you had a problem. If word could get out of the Concho camp about secret gold shipments, why couldn't it get out that Bull Gardner's daughter was in camp and fixing to travel back over the road tomorrow? If word did get out to the Baxter bunch, what would they be apt to do about it?

Paso didn't know. He wished he did. He wasn't even sure that the stage hold-up had any connection with the girl. Nobody could be sure except the men who had been there, and of those three, Sonora Joe Riley, and perhaps one of the other two, was dead by now. If they hadn't known Kitty Gardner was on the stage, they hadn't had a chance to find out during the fight.

Once more Paso drifted out of the night and met the bow-legged Tex. "Anybody ever go out through the wire at night?" Paso inquired.

"Hell, no! You figuring on ketching someone at it?"

"I was just making talk, I guess," Paso chuckled.

"Your job," said Tex, "is to make sure the camp ain't jumped by surprise. With them damn' stamps makin' so much noise most of the night, it ain't any trick for riders to come up in our face almost before you hear 'em. Keep watch on your share of the fence an' you'll be doin' enough to stay on the payroll."

Tex was right according to the way he felt. The other guards probably felt the same way, and it would make spying on the mine easy. Information must be going out at night before the racketing mill machinery closed down. The guards on the fence might know about it and might not.

Paso had been assigned to that part of the fence nearest the road. The chances, he decided now, were not great that anyone would slip out through the wire on this side of the camp. Behind the camp was the steep mountain, the nearly inaccessible little river gorge. Paso stood in the starlight and surveyed the lay of the land as best he could. A man would not get anywhere at night by leaving the camp at the back. He'd go out one side or the other.

On the right was a steep shoulder of the mountain around which the road had dropped to the mine. Hard climbing that way. But if a man slipped out the other side of the camp, he'd find an easy downgrade running alongside the road for almost a mile. He could cross the road at any point—and it would take him down in a deeply thicketed hollow with another hard climb to get out the other side. But anywhere on down the road one could wait at night and be out of sight of the camp. The guard on that side of the camp was Tex.

The next time Paso met the bowlegged little Texan at the fence corner, he growled: "I've had a plenty hard day. Can't hardly stay awake. Any chance of a little sleep out somewheres without gettin' into trouble?"

"It's been done, feller. Gardner an' Horgan gits around now an' then to see how things is goin', but it's mostly after midnight. Git off some'eres now for forty winks an' you won't be caught." Tex spat. "If you kind o' drop out o' the way a little, an' anybody shows up, I'll tell 'em I just seen you. What the hell does it matter?"

"Thanks," Paso said. As he walked away in the night, his smile was cold. Gardner's gold could buy powder, drills, shovels, guns, and men to work them. But the one thing he needed in a set-up like this, he didn't have. Gardner had to have loyalty, and he didn't have loyalty and never would with the kind of men his gold kept up here at the mine.

Paso stopped when he was out of sight of Tex. He waited until the Texan would be toward the back of the camp. Then he returned to the fence corner and kept on going into the night on the other side of the camp that Tex was watching. Beyond the strip of cleared ground, Paso vanished in the undergrowth, moved warily and carefully to the road, and kept going.

The camp lights dropped back. The sound of the mill machinery grew fainter. The cool, clean, quiet night enveloped Paso as he walked halfway to the shoulder of the mountain, and then a little farther, and turned off into the undergrowth. He sat down against a small tree and relaxed. The stamp mill roar was a murmur now. No one could approach the mine from this direction without being heard. Paso waited patiently, fighting off drowsiness that came with the quiet.

Hours passed, and nothing happened. Maybe nothing would happen tonight. Maybe he was on the wrong track. But if he'd sized things up right, word would be passing out about Gardner's daughter and the safe arrival of the man who'd stopped the stage hold-up and killed Sonora Joe Riley. The border and the outlaw country were on this side. Anyone approaching the mine from this direction or anyone heading out from the mine would have to pass near this point.

Half an hour later Paso jerked his head up as a faint sound

drifted from the south. It came again. He eased stiffly to his feet, chambered a shell in the rifle, and made sure his holstered six-gun was loose and ready.

A horse was coming toward the mine at a slow, cautious walk. Crouching behind a bush, Paso watched. There was enough starlight to reveal the dark bulk of the rider, who seemed to be peering into the undergrowth as he passed.

Paso drew a slow breath of satisfaction. He'd hit a bull's-eye. When the rider was past, Paso eased out of the undergrowth and followed. He shifted the rifle to his left hand and drew the six-gun. If he was spotted, gun talk would come first and questions later.

He had almost decided to hail the man and try to pass himself off as the one from the mine, but that was running the odds too fine that he would have any luck finding out who was expected from the mine. The slow-walking horse moved on ahead toward the mine lights. The machinery roared louder. Then the horse stopped, and the rider dismounted.

Paso stopped and began to stalk the spot a step at a time. Presently he caught the sound of cautious voices. He thought he could make out the horse, but the starlight was too faint to be sure. The two men, standing at the edge of the road, were invisible.

Paso hooked a thumb over the six-gun hammer and made each step with care. The horse moved restlessly, and chains jingled softly. Then the horse's bulk loomed just ahead, and an impatient voice lifted slightly.

"Who gives a damn about that part of it? You heered what was wanted."

"Sounds like a fool trick to me," a second voice grumbled. "I don't know whether I want any of it or not."

"You better."

"Listen. . . ."

"Damn list'nin'! Shorty knows what he wants, an' what he says goes unless you're willin' to stand up with gun talk an' have it out with him. You got that on your mind?"

"I never said so. But we got plenty to think of around the mine here. If *he* was to get an idea of this, he'd go proddy without callin' his first shots."

"Tell it to Shorty. I'm only bringing you what he said. What'll I tell him back?"

"Anything you damn' please!"

"That ain't what Shorty'll want to hear."

"All right," the other man growled after a moment. "Tell him OK if he wants it thataway."

Paso didn't recognize the voice, but then he'd heard few voices at the mine, and these two men were talking in slurred, low tones. He wasn't close enough yet to have much luck with a gun. A couple of dozen steps more and he'd have a chance.

Then the horse tossed its head, snorted, changed position restlessly. Paso could almost see the pricked ears of the horse and its eyes staring warily at the intruder, slipping close in the dark. Paso had been afraid just this might happen. He ran at the men, and a harsh voice blurted: "There's one of them in the road!"

The horse bolted toward Paso. A gun spit livid flame at him. His own six-gun blasted back, as he jumped aside. The horse flashed past like a destructive shadow, its rider lacing the night with a drum roll of shots and Paso firing back. Paso was sure he hit the man for the other gun stopped firing. The mad run of the horse went on down the road, and, if the rider had been knocked out of the saddle, he left no sign of it.

Paso had jumped to the edge of the undergrowth. Now with his gun almost empty, he crouched for half a dozen breaths, waiting for the second man to show his hand. But the second man had vanished. The shattering reports of the guns had covered his movements. Ears ringing with gunfire echoes and the pound of the retreating horse, Paso could catch no sign of the man. He might be a dozen feet away or a dozen yards.

Silently Paso cursed himself for a weakness he had never been able to help. He could have put lead in the running horse, but he'd never yet shot down a horse to get at the rider. Something always stopped him. At the moment of firing he would always think that the horse couldn't help its rider and didn't deserve killing, and he'd try to get the rider, instead.

Quietly Paso reloaded. He moved toward the spot where the two men had been standing, and nothing happened. Now the horse was almost out of hearing. The noise of the mine machinery drifted clearly once more. The camp would have heard the shooting. The guards, Gardner, some of the men would be out to see what had happened. If that second man wasn't hiding nearby, he was making his way through the undergrowth back to camp. Paso turned toward camp and ran hard on the road. This way, running fast, he still had a chance to get back to the wire before the fellow slipped through.

Paso was panting, when he reached the belt of cleared ground outside the wire. The twinkling mine lights looked close and bright, and the unending hammer of the stamps was loud and friendly as Paso cut over from the road toward the wire.

Tex would be there in the darkness somewhere, and the other men, too. Paso was halfway across the cleared space, when a gun opened up behind him. A shout that followed a burst of two shots rang loudly and clearly. "There he is! Get him!"

The gun opened up again. The man who was firing it had run out of the undergrowth as Paso cut over the open ground from the road. It was probably one of the guards.

"Tex!" Paso yelled. "That you, Tex?"

A bullet whistled past his ear. He fired back and retreated toward the wire. The other man came on after him. Paso damned the night that hid faces and got everything mixed up like this. The man they wanted would dodge away and get back safely into camp. Just then a second gun farther back in the cleared swath opened up in Paso's direction.

Swearing, Paso ran toward the wire. He was challenged loudly: "I see yuh comin'! Speak out! Who is it?" It was Tex, standing near the wire.

"Don't shoot!" Paso called back. "This is Brand!"

"Come up and show yourself, Brand!"

"I'm after a fellow who met someone down the road. There's a chance to grab him, if he ain't got back already."

"Who did that shootin' down the road?" Tex demanded, as Paso came up.

"I did," Paso panted. "Two of them was talking. One got away on a horse. The other came back here. I'm trying to head him off."

Tex moved close, and his gun shoved against Paso's side. "I heard you comin' at a fast run," Tex said coldly. "But damned if it looked like you was followin' anybody. Who was it came after you with a gun?"

"Take that gun out of my ribs," Paso said violently. "I thought it might be you, not knowing who you was shooting at. Who went out there?"

Tex jabbed harder. "Drop them guns quick, Brand. I ain't takin' chances."

"You fool!" Paso raged. "I haven't got time to mess up in a mistake like this."

"Who said it was a mistake? Are you gonna drop them guns an' reach up? Last chance!"

The six-gun and rifle hit the ground by Paso's feet. He

lifted his hands. Tex was a man to do just what he threatened. "I got him!" Tex yelled. "Over here! Hold off on that shootin'!"

Now men came running toward the spot inside the wire. The one who had shot at Paso came running across the cleared ground, panting: "Hold him! I got him cold!"

"What's it all about?" Tex demanded.

The man plunged up to them. He was short like Tex. He gasped for breath, before biting out: "I follered him down the road to where he made a talk with one of the Baxter bunch. They heard me move an' started to shoot. The Baxter one high-tailed off on a hoss. I chased this feller back here. Who'n hell is he, anyway?"

"Brand," Tex answered. "The one who come in this afternoon an' had a fight with Horgan."

"I might've knowed it. He looked wrong, when he rode that hoss in. The talk that started about him hit the nail on the head, didn't it? Hell, we might as well kill him right now an' get it over with. The men'll hang him for pullin' a trick like this."

Plain enough now, that voice. Paso made him out as the small, shrewd-faced, red-haired man who had tripped him during that fight with Jules Horgan. The red-haired man was set for a killing before others, ducking through the triple wire fencing, got to them.

VIII

"LYNCH TALK"

With Tex's gun hard against his side, Paso leaned to make a fight of it. At that moment Bull Gardner's shout lifted a few yards away. "What's this all about? What've you men got there?"

The redhead swore under his breath and hesitated. That instant of waiting was enough for Bull Gardner to reach them.

Tex explained to Gardner. "Got a *hombre* who slipped down the road for a talk with one of the Baxter bunch. Sandy Cole here caught him at it an' chased him back. I collared him, when he ran up. It's Brand, the one that was put watchin' the wire out there along the road."

Bull Gardner's bawl of anger blasted over them. "Brand? Dammit, it'll go hard if it's so. Brand, what about it?"

"A damn' lie an' a slick trick, I'll give him that," Paso hit back. "I was the one who caught him talking to the Baxter man. When the shooting down the road was over, the Baxter man got away, an' I headed back fast to the wire to stop the feller who went out from the mine on foot. He beat me back an' turned the dirt on me."

A dozen men were swarming through the wire to the spot, and more were coming. Armed men, muttering with anger as they heard what had happened.

"String the dirty pup up!" one called out.

"Yeah, somebody get a rope!"

"Never mind talking about a rope," Gardner ordered. "There won't be anybody strung up before I know who's guilty. An' then I'm man enough to hand out all that's needed." Gardner spat. His voice grew ugly. "We know damn' well someone here's guilty. But one of you ain't. Which one?"

"How much proof you got to have?" the red-haired Cole asked complainingly. "Me, I've been scoutin' outside the wire night after night. Tex told me tonight he seen someone sneakin' off down the road. So I follered to see what was up. And then I butted into them, an' chased the feller back here to camp, an' fanned him right up to the wire with my gun, what else do yuh want? Tex'll tell you how I follered Brand. Wasn't that you shootin' at him off to the left there, Mister Gardner?"

"Yes, it was," Gardner assented grimly. "Tex, how about this story?"

"You heard it," Tex said readily. "Cole an' I were hunkered down over there near the road, havin' a smoke, an' I heard someone sneakin' past down the road. Cole said he'd look into it, an' followed. I didn't have no idea it was Brand. Just before that, Brand told me he was plenty tired an' might be ketching himself a little sleep. It looked to me like maybe someone had sneaked out his side of the fence."

"Asleep?" Gardner said angrily. "While he was supposed to be doing guard on the fence? Brand, is that true?"

"I did talk of some sleep," Paso admitted. "But I was laying to move on down the road and see what might happen tonight. And plenty happened . . . the way I told it. You've just heard two of the slickest liars that ever thought fast. They're pulling together like a matched team on it, so both must have had a hand in it."

"I've kilt men for callin' me less than a liar," warned Tex, past clenched teeth. "An' right here's where. . . ."

"Don't throw that gun on him," Gardner blared.

"Put a gun in my hand and give him a chance," Paso invited. "They've got one yarn. I've got another. We'll see who's right."

A man in the back of the gathering crowd of miners called: "That's just a slick trick to get him a gun an' a chance to run for it. Hell, didn't he ride an outlaw hoss in here today? Ain't it plain them gunmen this afternoon give him a horse to ride in here an' get set for a dirty trick? An' the first night he goes to work an' does it."

"Pete Jensen's went for a rope," another one called.

They were a dark, uneasy mass of angered men crowding close. Nerves were keyed up, tempers flaring. A few more of the right words would set them off like sparks in an open can of blasting powder. Paso had seen crowds go out of control before. He'd come out of Mexico ahead of a mob that had been inflamed by the Escobars. Now two men that this crowd knew were calmly swearing his life away. He'd gotten the information that Bull Gardner wanted—and the pay was being tendered in death instead of gold. The grim humor of it made Paso smile bitterly while his mind raced.

He could see there was not a chance of making a break. He didn't want to, anyway. Running away would only mark him with the guilt he was denying. He had to talk them out of it—a stranger's word against that of two men who had been among them day after day. The ugly mood of the listeners made that almost impossible.

Paso lifted his voice. "Anybody here who don't want to see justice done?"

"We'll give you justice," Sandy Cole snapped from where he stood at Gardner's elbow.

But other men called: "Sure, we want the right man."

"What do yuh call justice, stranger?"

"If you were innocent, you'd get all the chance you needed."

"All right," said Paso. "I only reached your damn' mine late this afternoon. I came from El Paso, where I've been laid up in bed for weeks. Gardner himself asked me in El Paso to come here and take a job. I never heard of this mine until he spoke to me about it. Gardner, how about it?"

"They're fair facts and right," Gardner admitted. "I was the one who met you an' got you to come here."

"If I rode into camp and made a deal in a few hours with somebody outside of camp," Paso asked ironically, "then who in the hell has been selling out to the Baxter bunch before I showed up? You can't pin dirt on me that was done while I was laid up helpless in El Paso."

The silence that followed might have meant anything. The ugly mood of the crowd was still heavy, electric. Tex broke the silence with a brittle challenge. "We're talkin' about tonight. An' there ain't any. . . ."

"Shut up!" Bull Gardner told his hired gunman with grim finality. "*I'm* thinking about more than tonight. Brand is right. Plenty happened around here before I ever bumped into him in El Paso. He couldn't have had a hand in any of that. It's been going on all the time. Common sense says what was done tonight wasn't done by a new hand at it. I should have thought of that."

"That's straight thinking, boss," a calm voice behind Gardner said. "Brand would have been a fool to have rode that horse into camp here if he was guilty of anything. He could have turned the horse loose a couple of miles away an' walked in after dark. I've noticed it's most generally the innocent man who looks worse when there's some slick lying going on."

That voice belonged to Ben Davis, the big, good-natured, bearded miner who had been friendly to Paso after the fight with Jules Horgan. Davis had struck the mood of the crowd, or at least found men who respected his way of thinking.

"Davis is right!"

"Sure thing," another agreed. "We ain't gettin' justice done, hangin' this new man. Maybe he ain't any good, but he sounds good the way he explains this."

"Is anybody callin' me a liar?" Sandy Cole demanded angrily.

"Didn't you hear?" said Paso. "I called you an' your sidekick both liars. I'll say it again an' back it up with a gun."

"None of that, I said!" Bull Gardner exploded. "You all know the rule against gun play here among ourselves. Cole, Tex . . . you two put those guns up and get away from Brand. There's been a mix-up here that won't be settled with two different sets of stories. So I'm going to call it off. Nobody got hurt. We'll go back to my orders that nobody goes outside the wire at night. That goes for the three of you . . . Brand, Tex, Cole! If anyone, or all of you, don't like it, I'll pay off tonight or tomorrow, and you can get going."

"Suits me," said Paso curtly.

"It don't suit me," said Sandy Cole shortly. "But I'm staying just to see this straightened out."

"Me, too," said Tex sourly.

"All of you back inside the wire, then," Gardner ordered. "You three men, too. I'll put new guards out tonight in your places. Back in, men. It's all over."

"The hell it's over," someone said caustically. "Them three'll take care of that. It oughta be good when they pay each other off."

IX

"A DEATH NOTICE"

Gardner must have had his reasons for not asking further questions at once. Paso expected them, but the mine owner said nothing more to him. The crowd broke up, seeming to agree with the man who expected more trouble between Paso and the other two. Tex and Sandy Cole stalked off toward the bunkhouse, while Paso retrieved his weapons.

Big Ben Davis fell into step beside him. "Plenty of trouble, huh, Brand?"

"Seems so," Paso agreed. "Thanks for speakin' up. I needed a good word."

"I figured so," Ben Davis said laconically. "For a minute I wondered if anybody would be able to stop it in time." He spat. "I knowed where the truth was as soon as I found out who was callin' the other fellow a liar. Ain't this camp in a dirty mess? One of these nights hell is gonna bust right through that fancy fence wire an' clean everything out."

"Got any reason for being so sure about it?"

"Just the way things is going, my friend. Word has been sent in time and again that any man working for Bull Gardner is cold meat if he's caught outside the camp. I've got a hunch that Shorty Baxter is trying to make sure the place is so unhealthy that Gardner'll find himself short of men some week. Then it'll happen."

"It ought to be something to write home about, if it does

happen," Paso said thoughtfully.

"Don't be afeerd it won't," Ben Davis said confidently. "I look for Shorty Baxter to try and bust open the powder house and blow up the mine. I'm only hoping I ain't back in the tunnel, when it happens. I'm a hard-rock man, but I don't hanker to lay in seep water an' pitch-black cold inside a mountain while I take a week or so to die. An' it'll be just my luck to do so. This is my day off, but I go back on the night shift tomorrow. You didn't hear what was said down the road there to the Baxter man, did you?"

"I didn't get close enough to hear much of anything," Paso said briefly.

Ben Davis hesitated. "What I'm going to say now ain't any of my business, Brand. You probably know it already. But if I was you, I'd climb that big, purty-lookin' stallion you rode in today an' leave. I'd do it tonight. I'd do it as fast as I could hang a saddle on that hoss. You've got two hard an' ornery *hombres* layin' for you now. A man can't watch his back twenty-four hours a day."

"I'll be a fool not to leave," Paso agreed soberly, "but I'm staying over a little to see what happens. Chances are they won't make a move tonight, while I'm catchin' a little sleep in the bunkhouse. Everybody'll be watchin' for them to try it. And tomorrow's another day."

"Uhn-huh," Ben Davis agreed. "And around here a new day is apt to be more trouble. Well, if you stay, your eyes is wide open about it."

Paso was weary and stiff, when he entered the bunkhouse where thick-muscled miners were snoring heavily. He put his rifle and gun belt on the inside of his bunk, and, when he was in that top bunk under the blankets, he slid the keen stiletto sent him by Juan Diego de Escobar down beside his leg where his hand could touch it instantly. He smiled, thinking that the blade of the Escobars might protect Paso Brand. Then he noticed that Ben Davis had strolled in and seated himself on a box under the dim oil lamp hanging in the center of the long room.

The big, bearded miner was calmly smoking a short-stemmed pipe. He looked as if he might sit there a long time tonight. It appeared as though Davis was sitting there, silent and watchful, to see that Paso Brand slept safely. Now and then you ran across men like Davis, honest, square, quick to help a man who was in a tight. Bull Gardner in El Paso had seemed like that. Now Paso wasn't sure of anything about Gardner. He had expected that mine owner to approach him with further questions tonight. Paso tried to figure out why he hadn't in the few moments before heavy sleep claimed him.

Sometime during the night the noisy hammer of the stamp mill stopped, and the night shift came off work. Paso roused briefly as the night miners began to straggle to their bunks. Then, before he knew it, the sun was bright, machinery was hammering again, and the Concho sounded like any other busy mining camp.

At noon Kitty Gardner still had not started back to Three Forks, and Bull Gardner had made no move to probe further into what had happened last night. Sandy Cole and Tex were keeping away from Paso. Which might mean anything. By afternoon it was evident that Gardner's daughter must be staying over another day. Paso stopped at the stable for the third time during the day to feast his eyes on the big, cream-colored stallion.

Tony Ramos joined him outside the corral and smiled as he followed Paso's gaze inside. "Plenty come to look at him," said the hostler. "By golly, they never see soch a horse, I tell you. Me, I give one damn' year's pay for heem if ever I have so much pay."

Paso fingered tobacco into a paper and rolled a cigarette. "He ain't for sale. I wonder where Sonora Joe Riley got him."

"Las' night I remember somet'ing I hear once," said Tony Ramos. "Thees horse belonged to a *rico grande* . . . what you say? . . . a great man in Méjico. Sonora Joe keel him just for to get thees horse. Now Sonora Joe ees dead, too. Maybe for thees horse so big, so beautiful, death ees the price, eh? Death ees the one price greater than money, my frien'."

Paso chuckled. "Maybe so. But I wasn't after this horse when I shot Riley. Ain't he a beauty, though? He rides like a cloud an' runs like the wind, an', if he ever gets tired, he didn't show it on the way here."

Tony Ramos rolled a cigarette, too. The rugged ugliness of his smile was shaded with doubt. "*Sí*, a beauty, *señor*. Soch a beauty that the devil must see heem long ago. I don't know . . . maybe I don' like to own thees horse, after all."

"You ain't going to get the chance," Paso said, and turned as his name was called.

It was Gardner. With him was Jules Horgan, and walking between them was a ragged Mexican, leading a bony, old mule that had a sheepskin tied on for a saddle, a bridle mended with old rope, and reins of rope.

"This here man," said Gardner brusquely as he came up, "rode here to leave a note. The men brought him to me. He claims he was stopped by strange men who ordered him to ride here for them. This is for you, Brand."

Paso opened the folded, crumpled sheet of wrapping paper. A pencil had crudely printed:

Send my Big Star hoss back with this Mex or I'll kill the *hombre* who's got him. Maybe I will anyway for shootin' at me.

Sonora Joe Riley

Paso whistled softly. "So Sonora Joe ain't dead, after all?"

"Evidently not," Gardner said grimly.

"He won't get the horse by sending for him," Paso declared. "I got the horse just like Riley did, and I'll keep him the same way. Was that what you wanted to hear?"

"You're the one to decide," said Gardner. "It's your horse as long as you can back it up."

"I'll try," said Paso, and turned to the Mexican. "Savvy?"

Unshaven, stoop-shouldered, vacant-eyed, the Mexican carried a ragged, old, straw sombrero in his hand and looked stupid as he shrugged and shook his head.

Paso spoke in Spanish. "Ride back and say that another owns the horse now."

The Mexican ducked his head humbly. *"Sí, señor,"* he muttered.

Horgan's smile was hard under his black mustache. "This'll mean more trouble for us to worry about," he said to Gardner. "Sonora Riley won't let it go at this. I've heard he killed three men in getting that damn' horse, the owner and two men who were riding with him. Riley will have the animal back one way or another, if he has to start killing again to do it."

"Mister," said Paso mildly, "I don't know as much about Sonora Riley as you seem to, but I'm keeping the horse until he comes after it. Riley and I will talk about that stage hold-up first. If that don't suit the Concho Mine, I'll ride on."

"That's all I wanted to know," said Gardner. "Horgan, take this man to the gate and send him on his way."

With ill grace, Horgan walked off with the ragged Mexican.

Tony Ramos caught Paso's eye and flashed white teeth in a wry smile. "No, I don't think I want that horse, *amigo*. Hees price ees still death, eh?"

X

"DANGEROUS PLANS"

"Step over here, Brand," Gardner said. When they were off to themselves, the mine owner stared for a moment, hands on his hips, and then demanded: "Do you know who Sonora Riley is?"

Paso nodded.

"And you're ready to tangle with him?"

"Why not?"

"Brand, you're a hardcase."

"I never figured so."

"You are," Gardner said. "You proved it last night. And I'm satisfied now that I can trust you."

"How am I supposed to feel about that?" Paso asked with a trace of sarcasm.

Gardner's gesture was impatient. "Considering what I'm up against, Brand, my trusting a man says a lot."

"I suppose so," Paso conceded. "What about Horgan? You trust him plenty, I reckon?"

Gardner's cold, gray eyes stared for a moment before he nodded. "Brand, when the day comes that I can't trust Horgan, I'll know there's not much use trying to keep the mine open. If I can't trust Horgan, I'll never be able to trust any man."

"And that," remarked Paso, "is saying a lot."

"That's the way it is," Gardner said. "I'm sorry you and Horgan got off on the wrong foot. Horgan's a good hater and bound to run things when he can. Yesterday he thought you were in the wrong and backed it up his way." Gardner paused, considering. "Maybe Horgan hasn't changed his mind about you, but he'll take my orders about it. So forget him."

Paso changed the subject without committing himself. "Was that what you wanted to say?"

"At the moment," said Gardner, "it is. I just wanted you to know that I'm trusting you in anything that comes up. I want you to know that you're among a very few whom I'm depending on."

"Thanks," said Paso. "You ain't wrong about it. But you didn't show it by not asking more about what happened down the road last night."

"I've been hiding what I believe about last night," Gardner said coolly. "I'm giving out plenty of rope and hoping those two will get reckless or hurried, and hang themselves. I want to find out who they talk to and what they do. Did anything more happen last night that I should know about?"

"Maybe not," said Paso. "Shorty Baxter sent word for Cole to do something that Cole didn't have the stomach to try. He tried to back out. The Baxter man told him it'd mean gun play with Baxter, if he didn't go through with it."

"What was it?" Gardner asked quickly.

"I'd like to know. Cole said it'd start you shooting fast, if you found out. He'd just agreed to do it, when the Baxter man's horse spotted me, and hell was all over the road. I'd run them two snakes out of camp, if I was you. They're up to something dirty."

"I've had plenty of it all along," Gardner growled. "I guess I can handle this. Are you up to a hard, fast ride?"

"On Riley's horse I am."

"Any horse you like," said the mine owner. "Better go over your guns and draw more ammunition if you need it. I want you ready, if I call on you."

Gardner turned on his heel and walked away. His shoulders were back, head was up, and he was scowling thoughtfully. Paso watched him go and reached for the tobacco sack again. So Gardner trusted Horgan above all others? Yesterday Sandy Cole had hurried in to see Horgan while Paso was dismounting beside the mine office. Cole had carried word of the stranger's arrival—and Horgan had come to the office door primed for trouble. Cole had edged forward in the crowd and tripped Paso during the fight. Cole and Horgan were evidently thick. How did that stack up beside Gardner's feeling about Horgan and the fact that Sandy Cole was linked with the Baxter bunch? Then Kitty Gardner had all but stumbled over Horgan, listening in the outer office, while Gardner was talking to Paso.

The amused voice of Tony Ramos spoke behind Paso. "I t'ink I study hard, too, if Sonora Riley send for my horse."

Paso turned with a faint smile. "Who wouldn't be scared green? What do you know about Horgan?"

Tony Ramos spread his hands out open and empty as he shrugged.

"Any reason why Horgan an' this Sandy Cole should be good friends?" Paso questioned.

"No savvy."

"You ain't any good to me," Paso said good-naturedly.

"Sure, I know . . . I'm jus' a horse hand," said Tony Ramos with a flash of white teeth. "Now I ask you som't'ing about that *pelado* what come here. Hees mule ready to fall down. Hees old clothes almost fall off. Hees whiskers two, t'ree days old. You bet me he don' have ten *centavos* to spend, huh?"

"I reckon not," agreed Paso.

"Who he ees? W'at he do to eat an' live?" Tony Ramos asked with a peculiar smile.

"How do I know who he is? Maybe he's got a shack and some sheep or goats somewhere or works around. . . ."

"He work to live, huh?"

"I reckon so. It don't rain grub in these parts more'n once a year. What are you driving at?"

"Nothing," said Tony Ramos. "But hees hands, *amigo,* so soft and fine like one of the *gente fina.* Hees hands don' do a *peon*'s work. Hees feet don' walk right in those *huaraches* he wear. Hees feet too small, like one of the *gente fina.* An' hees eyes don't miss nothing, I tell you, that damn' *pelado.*"

"Why'n hell didn't you say some of that while he was here?"

Tony Ramos shrugged. "I am pay to watch horses," he remarked. "W'at I do to put my face in the beeg boss' business? If he ask me, I say so. Eef he don' ask, Tony Ramos watch the horses."

Paso made a break for the front of the camp, but, when he got there, the ragged Mexican and his mule were not in sight.

"He kicked that bag of bones into a run down the road," a guard at the gate said. "I've had a smoke, since he's been outta sight."

Paso swore under his breath. The cream stallion could catch the old mule, if one could be sure where the mule had gone. But Baxter's men might be waiting just out of sight. They might be hoping such a fool move would be made. Reluctantly Paso abandoned the idea. But it made a man feel sheepish to know that one of the Baxter bunch had ridden in under their noses and ridden safely out again. And it left Paso wondering whether Riley's horse had been all the Mexican had come for.

The afternoon dragged to the steady roar of the stamp mill. Little ore cars trundled out of the mine, and dumped rock was clattering into the ore bins. Gray-black smoke drifted in an uneasy plume from the black boiler stack. Far back in the mountain, one knew, lights were flickering dimly in the damp darkness where sweating men ripped out the high-grade rock. Out here in the sunlight men were busy at the mill. The night shift men were waiting to take their turn at labor.

Nothing about all this should make a man nervous. This was a rich gold camp. It should be solid, safe with the might, the power of yellow gold. But it wasn't safe, and everyone in the camp knew it. Under the bright blaze of the brassy sun fear hung like the everlasting dust around the mill stamps. Fear of what might strike from outside the wire, suspicion of others inside the wire. As Paso walked about, he caught men eyeing him furtively. He noticed stares that lacked friendliness. Ben Davis gave him the answer.

"Word has traveled around," explained Davis, "that we'll have more trouble over the hoss you rode on here. Some of the men are still mixed up about last night. They ain't sure about you. Hell, they ain't sure about anyone around here. A couple of weeks makes them mighty jumpy. They get so they expect anything and believe anything. I take it there's been no move from them two skunks who double-crossed you last night."

"Not yet," said Paso.

"It'll come," Davis warned. "It'll come, and there won't be no warning."

"I'd give a heap for two pairs of eyes," Paso admitted, smiling thinly. "But I'll try to make out. How come Horgan stands so high with Gardner?"

"You ain't the only one who's wondered," said Davis.

"I'm one of the oldest men here now. Horgan was here, when I come. I've seen things that would indicate Horgan an' Gardner ain't exactly crazy about each other. But mostly they run along together like a bull and a bear caught in a forest fire an' no time for personal fights."

"Funny," mused Paso.

"Damn' funny," Davis agreed. "But you get used to expectin' anything around here."

Paso could believe it. He found his own nerves tightening, his attention sharp, a feeling going with him that anything might happen at any time.

Half an hour before the night shift was due to troop back in the tunnel, Gardner's hail brought Paso around near the mill. Gardner came striding hurriedly.

"Saddle up, Brand. As soon as I get out the dynamite for the night shift, I'm starting a fast buggy and guards for Three Forks."

The sun had slid down behind the mountain. The first steel-gray somberness of twilight was moving into the sky.

"Night trip, huh?" said Paso, looking at the sky. "I reckon we're taking the young lady back?"

Gardner frowned and nodded almost reluctantly, as if he hated to talk about the matter. "She's got to go back fast, Brand. A night ride will be safest. No one has any idea but what she's staying on. I'm taking the gold on hand, also, and men whom I think I can trust. No one else knows we're leaving. There won't be a chance for word to get out until we're well on our way. Four horses to a light buggy will travel faster than we can be caught." Gardner's face darkened. "Then," he finished grimly, "with the gold on hand out of the way and my daughter safe, we'll have a showdown. I'm bringing back every gunman money will hire. I'll have them deputized. I'll rawhide Baxter and his wolves until they're killed or run out of these parts."

"You're on the right track," Paso approved. "I've been wondering why you didn't use some of your gold that way long ago."

"A good reason," said Gardner. "Baxter can call on twenty or thirty outlaws. Maybe more. A showdown fight to clean out the country between here and the border will bring more gunmen to help Baxter. They can't afford to be run out of this border strip. They'd never be as safe anywhere else."

"It's a hell of a job, at that," Paso agreed. "Maybe I'd have strung wire and set tight like you did."

"It didn't work," confessed Gardner. "They're bleeding me to death. Now I'll jump them, while I've got the gold to give me a chance." Gardner slammed a clenched fist into a palm. "We'll get the gold out safely and bring men back. So get ready to ride."

Gardner started to turn away. Then they both stood rooted to the spot as two fast gunshots knifed thinly through the stamp mill racket. Gardner's hand went instinctively to the gun at his side, as he broke into a run toward the spot. Paso followed at his heels.

XI

"AN EXPLOSION"

The shots had been fired at the back of the camp, where the wire enclosure reached into the rocky, little cañon which spawned the mountain stream. The hammering steel stamps had all but blotted out the gunshots. As he started to run, Paso noticed a man or two staring curiously. But that was all. No one else seemed to know that anything was wrong, and it would take time to spread an alarm. Paso knew why Gardner was bolting like a wild man toward the sound of the shots. Back there in the little cañon, around a jutting shoulder of rock from the camp and the mine workings, was where the powder stores were kept.

In the rock side of the narrow little cañon an old prospector's tunnel had been enlarged into a storeroom. A solid steel inner door was fronted by the wooden outer door, each triple locked, with a man on guard night and day. Two steel rails ran from the powder room to the mine tunnel. Explosives were loaded on one of the little ore cars as needed and rolled to the mine.

Now Gardner was running toward trouble near the stored explosives. A shoulder of rock at the cañon entrance cut off view of the spot. If the stored explosives went off, it would shake the mountain, demolish the camp, kill, maim, stun all men nearby. Paso drew his gun as he ran.

He was at Gardner's heels as they bolted around the shoulder of rock and saw the steel rails, stretching up the cañon. On the left the cañon side was steep, brush-covered. On the right rocks and brush covered a rough, low bank beside the cold, swift water of the little stream. The track had a slight upgrade. One of the ore cars was coasting slowly down the grade toward them. Up at the end of the track, where the explosives were stored in the living rock, four men were standing.

Paso recognized the stooped, gray-haired bookkeeper and two overalled miners with their hands in the air. Tex had them cowed with a six-gun. He fired a shot down the track as Paso and Gardner dashed into view. Then a jump put Tex behind his three prisoners where he was safe from flying lead. At that moment Sandy Cole backed out of the powder room, paying out line from a coil that hung over his arm. He saw Paso and Gardner and went hurriedly about what he was doing without drawing his gun.

Tex fired again. Gardner did not stop. An oath burst from Paso as he realized what Sandy Cole was doing. That coil over the red-headed gunman's arm wasn't rope. That coil was fuse that Cole was laying from the explosive room.

Tex yelled something. Sandy Cole dropped the fuse, slammed the massive wooden door, went to his knees, grabbed up the end of the fuse, and struck a match. That told its own story. Shorty Baxter had ordered all this. Paso could see the dead guard lying where Tex and Cole had shot him down.

Now Tex was shooting past the prisoners. Here in the cañon it was quieter. Paso heard the loud *whang* of a bullet, smashing through the thin steel side of the slow-rolling little ore car. The two miners sprawled down on the ground. The bookkeeper started to follow. Tex yanked him up, held him for a shield, and aimed carefully again. Another bullet smashed into the ore car.

"Why don't the dirty skunk stand out alone and fight?" Gardner cried with furious helplessness.

Tex snatched a rifle off the ground as Gardner shot twice. The little bookkeeper staggered and fell. Tex whipped the rifle up to his shoulder.

"Get down, Gardner!" Paso yelled. "He ain't shootin' at us! That ore car must have dynamite in it! He's trying to blow it up, an' he can't miss with that rifle!"

Paso leaped off the track and went flat, sprawling on the ground amid the rocks and bushes. Gardner halted. Standing there, he emptied his six-gun so fast the shots made one burst of sound. Only then did Gardner get off the track and go to the ground some yards ahead.

Paso lifted his head. Tex was weaving, obviously hit hard, but he got the rifle against his shoulder and fired. The world blew up in a crashing, gigantic, thundering roar of sound that deafened, crushed, unmercifully beat at the senses. It was as if the hand of a mighty giant had slammed down a destructive force. The little, steel ore car dissolved in a sheet of flame and smoke. The force of the explosion beat Paso hard against the ground, crushed at his ears. For a terrible moment breath was torn away. Then the clattering rain of débris started.

Rocks, metal, bits of bushes and trees showered down. Ears deafened by the blast could barely make out the rumble of bigger rocks as they rolled down the steep cañon side. Instinctively Paso shielded his head with his arms. It was no protection, if a big rock struck him, but it was all he could do. Small fragments pelted him. One great boulder crashed over the mine track, missed his head by less than a yard, and bounded into the creek. His face was rawhided by the rock fragments it struck off in passing.

A small avalanche poured down near the spot where the ore car had exploded. Paso remembered Gardner and struggled up. The mine owner lay there, half buried by the rocks. Bright blood was flowing over the side of Gardner's face. He was motionless, when Paso reached him. On up the track where the powder-room door was closed and the lighted fuse was burning only Sandy Cole was on his feet. Cole looked unsteady, as if he, too, had been hurt by the explosion. Paso had instinctively held onto his gun. Now he broke into a lurching run toward Cole.

Cole fired at him. The small gunman's face was snarling. His bullet must have passed close, but Paso didn't think about it. His mind was on the awful thought of what would follow when the fuse burned into the powder room. Cole fired again and again—and Paso held that dogged, weaving run toward him, holding shots until he got close.

Cole's gun emptied. He started to reload, and then suddenly turned and ran up the cañon. The shots Paso fired missed, and the gunman vanished in the underbrush.

Only Cole knew how long the fuse would take to burn—and he was running. Paso wanted to turn and run the other way. He was still trembling from the ore car blast. Thought of a far mightier explosion made nerves crawl helplessly. But here was still a chance to do something. Paso kept on. He was still many yards away, when one of the miners staggered up to the powder-room door, stooped, caught the fuse in both hands, and jerked back with all his strength. The fuse broke. Blood was streaming down into the miner's right eye, and he was dashing it away with the back of his hand and feverishly examining the end of the fuse when Paso ran up.

In that instant the fuse spit fire from the end. The miner hurled it down. His clear eye seemed to be bulging in the socket.

"Got it just in time," he blurted hoarsely. "A few seconds

more an' it'd been too late. He locked the damned door."

Sandy Cole had slammed the massive wooden door and snapped one of the triple locks. The fuse led under the locked door. No power on earth could have stopped an explosion by the time Paso would have reached the spot.

"Mister," Paso said weakly, "you sure carry a rabbit's foot."

"Ain't it the truth. Something hit me on the head an' knocked me clean out. First thing I thought of, when my eyes opened, was that fuse. What's the matter with Bill there?"

Bill was the other miner, a big, broad-chested, powerful man, who lay doubled up on the ground, groaning, holding his middle. Bill spoke thickly as Paso bent over him. "I tried to get up, an' he shot me. Why'd I ever come to this hell spot anyway?"

A shrill, panic-stricken falsetto broke out on Paso's left. "Oh, Lord, let me get away from here, and I'll never be back. It's hell and the devil stays here! The gold's cursed, and we're all damned for trying to get it out. Oh, Lord, let me live to get away from here!" The thin, elderly, stoop-shouldered bookkeeper was ashen-faced, shaking as he stood there, crying dazedly.

"The Lord's done his share of helping you just now, buddy," Paso reminded him. "Don't ask for more favors before you earn 'em. Get back to camp and crawl under your desk an' keep quiet."

He had to shake the bookkeeper's shoulder before the man drew a shuddering breath, looked helplessly at him, and then broke into a stumbling run down the track.

"You look after this man, while I see to Gardner," Paso told the miner. "He's hurt bad."

"How about the dirty killer?"

"He won't be back," guessed Paso. "The men'll tear him

to pieces, if they catch him. Here they come now."

Men had burst into view from the camp. Ben Davis was one of them. He reached Bull Gardner a few seconds before Paso got to the spot. "What'n hell happened?" Davis demanded.

Paso told them as he helped move Gardner's inert body.

"We should've hanged them last night and had it over with!" Davis said angrily. "Looks like this blood on Gardner's face is where a rock struck him. Is he breathing?"

Paso felt inside Gardner's shirt and nodded. "His heart's still going. I don't know whether he's shot or not. Better get him to the office. Can't do anything here. Another one up the track there is shot. I think Gardner killed that bowlegged Tex. I hope so. The dirty snake lived long enough to set off a car loaded with dynamite."

There was no lack of help. Brawny miners locked hands under Gardner's body, lifted him as gently as they could, and started down the track.

Jules Horgan came running to meet them. Paso stopped and outlined what had happened. Now Horgan was not smiling under his black mustache. For the first time his dislike of Paso Brand was not evident. Paso's cold, probing stare could find no sign that Horgan might have known something about this. No sign that any guilt was attached to the man. But Horgan was clever. He would be able to hide his feelings.

"There's no use sending anyone after Cole," Horgan decided curtly. "We haven't much chance of catching him now. I'll put men guarding the powder in case anyone else has a try at it. Are you hurt, Brand?"

"Shook up is all."

"Tell 'em to put Gardner in bed. I want the medicine chest and hot water, plenty of it. Sims, the bookkeeper, will take care of that. I'll need a few minutes to get things straightened out here and more guards posted." Horgan's stare was searching. "Gardner seems to think you can be trusted, Brand. I'm counting on you to be where I can use you."

This was a new Horgan. Maybe, Paso thought as he hurried toward the office, Gardner had more reason to speak well of Horgan than a man would believe. Yet, Sandy Cole had been thick with Horgan, had tripped Paso in that fight with Horgan. How could you be sure of Horgan after that? How could you have much idea what was on Horgan's mind now that Bull Gardner was down and helpless? Horgan might have been waiting for this to happen. Here at the Concho Mine you could believe anything of any man. The bookkeeper was right. The place seemed to be cursed, the devil to have a hand in the rich, high-grade, yellow gold which was being won by blood and death.

Kitty Gardner, Paso saw, was out in the open before the stone office. She looked slimmer, younger than ever, as she ran to meet the men carrying her father. She did not try to hide an agony of fear and apprehension when she saw who they were carrying. Her voice shook. "Is he dead?"

"Not yet," said Paso, and could have bitten his tongue at the scant hope he gave her.

Tears were in her gray eyes. Her hands clenched, her face was pale as she said: "Bring him to the side door. It's closer to his room."

She ran ahead to the door. Paso kept with her, speaking of hot water and the medicine chest.

"I'll see to it," she said. "Sims ran to the bunkhouse. I don't think he'll be much help."

Now she was cooler than Paso would have thought possible. No tears, no wringing of hands, no walking and crying.

She led the way to Gardner's bedroom, and then hurried off for hot water and the medicine kit. Her heart must have been breaking, for Bull Gardner was a gruesome sight. Blood smeared the mine owner's face and clotted in his hair. A gash in his arm had soaked blood into a bandanna which had been hurriedly tied about the spot. In the small, quiet, low-ceilinged bedroom where the miner's heavy boots shuffled uneasily, Gardner looked like a dead man, or a man close to death.

"Get the medicine chest, wherever it is," Paso directed as he opened Gardner's shirt to look for a bullet hole.

The man had not been shot, but the ribs on one side of his chest looked sunken and queer. Paso probed the spot gently with his fingertips, and felt broken bone where a rock had crashed into Gardner's ribs.

Jules Horgan came into the room with his quick, cat-like tread. "Get back from the bed . . . get outside the room, men," Horgan ordered. "You, Brand, stay in here. Davis, too, I guess. I may need you. Where's the medicine chest and hot water? How is his heart?"

Horgan went into action as he talked. He must have learned some medicine. His hands had a sure, deft touch that Paso had to admire.

"Heart seems all right," Horgan decided. He shook his head as he felt the broken ribs. "Get his boots off," he said to Paso. "Watch that right leg. Something is wrong there."

Paso had not noticed. He saw it now as Horgan examined the leg below the knee.

"Broken," Horgan said, and turned back to the great gash at the scalp line which was smearing Gardner's face with blood.

Two men brought in a small, stout, wooden chest. Another passed in a kettle of hot water and a basin. Kitty

Gardner hurried in with towels and a sheet. "How is he?" she asked anxiously.

"Good," said Horgan, rummaging in the chest. "Maybe you'd better wait outside the door, Miss Kitty."

"I'll stay," the girl said. Now her eyes were dry, her pale face calm.

Horgan worked on the head wound first, and Gardner stirred, groaned, opened his eyes. For a moment Gardner looked around vacantly. His hand fluttered uncertainly to his face.

"Father!" Kitty Gardner said, and there was a sob in her voice.

A faint, grim smile lighted Gardner's blood-smeared countenance. "I'm all right, baby," he mumbled. He looked at Horgan, Ben Davis, Paso. "Did it all go up?"

"No," said Horgan. "You got Tex. Cole escaped."

Gardner closed his eyes. "Baxter's work. There'll be more coming. Get the gold out and Kitty along with it. Can't have her here, if trouble busts loose. Brand can take her. Need you here, Horgan."

"Brand?" said Horgan. Some of the old distrust was in the question.

"Brand," Gardner muttered. "Want all the gunmen hired he can get. Pat Thompson at Three Forks'll give him help. Get Kitty away."

"I'll not leave you like this, father," Kitty Gardner said unsteadily.

"Got to get you away," Gardner mumbled. He was grayfaced, weaker with each word. He tried a deep breath, and a spasm of pain crossed his face.

"She'll start as soon as you're fixed up," Horgan promised. He looked over his shoulder at Paso. "The men are saddling at the corral, Brand. The gold's ready to load in the buggy. You're in charge. Miss Gardner will be ready."

"No!" Kitty Gardner refused.

Paso was leaving the room as Horgan answered coolly. "I'm running the Concho now, Miss Gardner. You'll do as your father says."

XII

"BUSHWHACK LEAD"

Twilight was deepening fast, when Paso reached the corral. Men were roping and saddling horses. Seven, nine men Paso counted. Men he didn't know. Strangers.

Tony Ramos stepped up. "Your horse, too, *señor?*"

"*Sí,*" said Paso. "I'm bossing this, Gardner and Horgan said. Can you ride and shoot?"

Tony Ramos shrugged. "I'm jus' wan horse hand."

"I know what you are," said Paso. "I'm asking you what you can do. Horse herding ain't all you know."

"I theenk maybe so," Tony Ramos said quietly.

"Saddle up an' come along," Paso told him. "I like your looks. We're riding to Three Forks with bar gold an' Gardner's girl. I want plenty of guns, an' someone I know along."

A smile flickered behind the rugged ugliness of Ramos's young face. "So? Maybe you like my Mexican guts, *señor?*"

"I'll tell you later," said Paso. "Get a good horse an' guns. Somebody else can watch the corral tonight."

The big, cream stallion stood in the dusty corral, proudly reserved while other horses milled around. His head was alertly up. He seemed to know work was ahead. Yes, a man like Sonora Joe Riley would kill for a horse like this and would kill to get him back, Paso thought, as he led the stallion out of the corral for saddling.

In ten minutes they were ready, including Tony Ramos, whose saddle, gun boot, rifle, and twin six-guns he had not worn until now showed hard use and care. Four small, speedy-looking horses were hitched to a two-seated buggy. A man on the back seat had a shotgun and a rifle. The driver had a rifle. He was a wizened oldster with a drooping, brown mustache, an old hat canted over one eye, and no expression on his face, when Paso reined in beside the buggy and asked: "Think you can take it fast all the way in the dark?"

The driver chewed in silence for a moment. He spat over the wheel and drawled: "I reckon so, if Jake hangs on tight back there. Jes' keep out o' my way an' give me room."

"You've got it from now to Three Forks," Paso chuckled. "Drive over to the office an' load up."

It was as simple as that. The men accepted his authority silently, but whether they liked the gaunt young newcomer over them or not was hard to tell.

Ben Davis was giving directions at the office. Men staggered out with two small, iron-bound chests. Only gold could have made those chests so heavy. They were put by the feet of the man in the back of the buggy and roped there.

Paso had dismounted. Ben Davis joined him. "Wisht I was going along," he said.

"Come along. I'll need you."

"Horgan wants me here. Gardner's gal will be out in a few minutes."

"So she decided to go?"

"Hardest thing she's ever faced, I reckon," said Davis. "She's got a feeling that Gardner won't leave the Concho alive. But he wants her to go, an' she's not going to worry him by being contrary."

"Good girl," Paso said, and looked at the darkening sky.

"I'd rather do a heap of things than start to Three Forks with that girl."

"An' that gold," added Ben Davis slowly. "Brand, there's men here in camp who'd kill their own mother for a chance at that much gold . . . not to speak of outlaws outside."

"How about these men I'm taking?" Paso asked under his breath.

"I wisht I knew," Davis admitted. "Better watch sharp. If you ask me, hell has finally busted loose around here. What's due to follow ain't gonna be nice."

Kitty Gardner walked to the buggy through the deep, purple twilight. She was solemn and quiet. Paso could not help contrasting her with the girl who had left Three Forks only the day before.

Sims, the bookkeeper, pushed through the crowd of miners which had gathered for the departure. "I'm going!" Sims cried shrilly. "Not another night in this cursed place."

One of the guards rode forward and blocked him from the buggy.

"You've got to take me!" Sims begged frantically.

"Can't we take him, Mister Brand?" Kitty Gardner asked.

"Ride in the back seat, Sims," Paso decided. "First trouble you make, I'll have you pitched out on the road."

The buggy rolled off a moment later. The heavy gate opened for them. The armed riders poured through, then the buggy followed to the road, and the long whiplash sent the four-horse team running hard eastward into the somber cloak of night.

Paso glanced back at the mine as he topped the crest of the first grade. Lights were beginning to wink back there. The faint beat of the stamp mill reached through the drumming hoofs like the restless strokes of a heart that would not stop—like Bull Gardner's heart that stubbornly defied all odds.

Four men rode behind the buggy, four in front, including Paso. The effortless run of Sonora Riley's horse would make any man glow with pride.

"Caramba w'at a horse, *amigo!"* Tony Ramos called over through the last purple light. "But that buggy, she's coming plenty fas', no?"

The droop-mustached old driver was driving the fast four-horse team with reckless skill. The racing buggy bounced, lurched, swayed along the rough and winding road and careened around the sharp turns.

Night blotted out the road, and the bouncing, swaying buggy came on faster than ever. Kitty Gardner would never forget this ride. Mile after mile the road wound down through the bleak and lonely hills, the stars were cold and bright, and the black shadows wrapped the way with protection. Each mile put them nearer Three Forks and safety for Gardner's gold and Gardner's daughter. Riding ahead with Ramos and two more men, Paso felt his spirits begin to lift with relief.

The devil himself could not have struck with less warning. It might have been the devil himself, waiting on that stretch of road where low-stunted trees grew close and the road shadows between them were blacker. Tony Ramos and another rider were just ahead of Paso and barely visible in the starlight. The first warning was a wild yell from Ramos. Both of the men and the horses they were riding plunged helplessly down on the road.

Paso's horse snorted, tried to leap the tangle of fallen horses and men, and went down in a plunging fall himself. Paso kicked his feet out of the box stirrups, as he was hurled from the silver-mounted saddle. A kicking hoof knocked him rolling to the side of the road. A horse screamed in fright, and the bawling curses of the old buggy driver were audible as the hard-running harness horses bolted into the tangle that blocked the road. More horses went down. The buggy overturned as guns blazed from the side of the road.

"Shoot them men riding behind!" a voice bawled.

Paso came up by the side of the road with his left arm numb and useless where the floundering horse had kicked him. His rifle had gone down in the saddle boot, and the horse wasn't visible. Snatching out his hand gun, Paso turned past the floundering horses toward the overturned buggy. Something in the darkness tripped him. He came up from the second fall, knowing that a rope had been stretched taut between the roadside trees at the right height to bring down running horses.

Ambushed gunmen beside the road were pouring shots. The muzzle flashes were like vicious fireflies. Back on the road other guns were retreating. Paso swore helplessly. All Gardner's gold could not make his hired gunmen stand in the murderous crossfire of a surprise ambush.

A shotgun bellowed just ahead. In the trees a man yelled with pain. "Come on, yuh dirty killers an' get more of it," the buggy driver challenged in shrill fury.

Paso blundered into the front wheels of the overturned buggy. "Miss Gardner!" he called.

The driver answered from the other side of the buggy. "She got out safe? Where are yuh, lady?"

A riderless horse almost knocked Paso down as it bolted back along the road. The thin, crying fright of Sims, the bookkeeper, pierced through the gunshots. Snorting, floundering harness horses were pulling in all directions and dragging the buggy along the road.

"Miss Gardner?" Paso shouted again.

"Here!" her voice answered. She was up at the head of the plunging team. "One of these horses is down! I think his leg is broken!"

"Keep away from them!" Paso yelled, sick at heart as he ran forward. Bull Gardner himself could not have avoided this trap. But Gardner wouldn't believe that. The numbed shoulder became usable again as Paso dodged around the maddened horses and bumped into a slender figure. His quick catch saved her from falling. "This way," Paso said huskily.

Flashing guns along the roadside showed that they were vastly outnumbered. But bullets weren't striking around the overturned buggy. Paso guessed Kitty Gardner was the reason. The bandits were trying not to hit her.

"Put down them guns an' you won't be hurt!" a strident voice yelled from the trees.

Paso looked desperately about, as he reached Kitty Gardner, and ran her forward in the road. He saw a lighter shadow and made for it, thanking God when he saw he was right. The big, cream-colored horse stood uneasily with the reins dragging, so well trained he had not bolted after regaining his feet.

Speaking soothingly, Paso caught the reins, led the horse a step to make sure it was not crippled. "Hold onto the stirrup," Paso told the girl.

He forked the saddle, reached down and swung Kitty Gardner up before him, and yanked the big stallion to the left off the road as other riders poured out of the trees ahead of them and blocked the road. A wild yell announced their discovery.

"There's one of them on a white hoss! My Star Blaze hoss, by damn!"

Paso ducked, trying to shield the girl, as the big horse burst in among the trees. Behind them the pursuit came thundering, and the bellow of Sonora Joe Riley warned: "Don't shoot my hoss! I want him sound!"

Three branches slashed Paso's face. A low-hanging limb scraped the top of his head and almost knocked him from the saddle. Behind them, guns were crashing, but they were aiming high in the dark, trying not to hit the horse. Paso's rifle was still in the hand-tooled saddle boot, but the rolling of the horse had broken the gun stock. No use firing a six-gun back at them. Muzzle flashes would only give the outlaws better aim. Suddenly Paso stifled an oath as the stallion swerved sharply to dodge a tree, and the saddle slipped.

Helplessly Paso realized that the rolling fall on the road had loosened the saddle. Any second now it might turn and throw them under the driving hoofs, and the pursuit was following so close there wasn't a chance to dismount and tighten the cinches.

The horse swerved hard again. The saddle slipped badly this time. Paso reined hard to a stop. "Saddle's coming off!" he ripped out. "Let's try to give 'em the slip in the dark!"

Kitty Gardner dropped lightly to the ground. Paso hurled himself after her, and so quickly did they dismount and run that for an instant Paso had hopes they might be swallowed in the night's blackness. But the pursuit roared up with heartbreaking speed. Men yelled when the empty saddle was discovered.

"There he goes!" one called.

A gun crashed, riders ripped among the trees after them, and Paso knew this was the end. "There's a lady here!" he shouted. "Hold your guns!" Panting and bitterly helpless, Paso spoke bleakly to Kitty Gardner. "It's the best I could do. I'm sorry."

"We tried, anyway," the girl said unsteadily.

Then riders were all about them. Men swung down with drawn guns, and they were prisoners.

"Hell, it's the gal! He must've got away with her."

"Who is he?"

"He was ridin' Sonora's hoss," a rasping voice said. "Maybe he's the feller Sonora wants. Hey, Sonora! Take a look at this man!"

A match was struck. Other matches flared out. Faces leaped into view—unshaven, hard faces, some leering, some scowling.

"Ain't she a purty little trick?"

"Shorty'll do a buck and wing over this! He swore he'd ruther have her than all the gold that come out o' the damn' mine."

"Shorty ain't so dumb. I kind o' feel that way myself after gittin' a good look at her. Ain't seen nothin' so sweet an' purty in a year."

Kitty Gardner groped for Paso's hand. She was trembling as she clutched his fingers for comfort.

"Keep steady!" Paso comforted her, but in his heart he could find no comfort for this girl, small hope that she would escape. There was a venom and hatred between the outlaw, Shorty Baxter, and Bull Gardner which was hard to understand or explain.

A man shouldered to them, struck several matches together, and held the flame close to their faces. Tall, lean, and saturnine, with two six-guns tied low, a knife sheathed on his hip, wearing a gaudy Mexican jacket with silver *concha* buttons, there was nothing reassuring about the man who peered at them. A high-peaked Mexican sombrero hung back on his shoulders, held by braided leather thongs, a bandage was tied around his forehead, and a thin, cold smile twisted his mouth as he surveyed Paso.

"It's the one," he said. "By hell, he's the one who shot a rock splinter in my face yesterday an' stole my hoss. This is shore a lucky night."

"How about the gal, Sonora?"

Sonora Riley dropped the match ends as his grin broadened. "She's Shorty's. Tie this hoss thief an' walk him back. The gal rode right purty on my saddle gettin' here. I'll cuddle her back on the same saddle myself."

Talk would be futile. Paso kept his teeth locked tightly while his arms were roped to his sides and a rider took the end of the rope and drove him on foot back toward the road. Kitty Gardner, too, was silent as Sonora Joe Riley swung her up on the big horse and rode ahead.

XIII

"SHORTY BAXTER'S REVENGE"

Hope had left Paso Brand. The four guards, riding behind the buggy, had bolted back toward the Concho Mine. Paso had heard or seen nothing of Tony Ramos after the first warning yell as Ramos fell. Now all shooting back in the road had stopped. They were vastly outnumbered. The Concho and any help that might be sent were long miles back into the west.

A fire of dry branches crackled and blazed in the road by the overturned buggy, when Paso walked out of the trees. Two dead horses lay in the road. Near one horse lay the dead guard who had ridden beside Tony Ramos. The other guard was there, a sullen prisoner. The gray-haired driver of the buggy was holding a wounded arm. Sims was cowering in terrified silence. The man who had been guarding the gold in the back seat was not in sight. The outlaws had dragged the two iron-bounded gold chests to the fire.

As Paso approached, a short, fleshless man with a clean-shaven face held a six-gun close to the lock of one of the chests and shattered it with shots. He worked a moment, then threw the lid back. Whistles and exclamations greeted the gleam of small, yellow gold bars in the firelight.

"We c'n buy out South America an' live off the white fat down there from now to then!" one man whooped.

The outlaw who had opened the chest faced them with the smoking gun slack in his hand. For a moment a racking, terrible cough shook his emaciated body. Then his voice cracked at them like a lash. "Forget this gold until there's time enough to spend it. We got plenty more to do."

"Nothin' that'll get us anything like this, Shorty."

Paso stared in fascination at Shorty Baxter, whom he was finally facing. The bandit leader seemed to shrink and crouch and coil as he faced the speaker. "You don't like the way I'm running things, Johnson?"

The man he called Johnson would have made two of Baxter. He wore twin guns, also. But his denial was hasty and fervent. "Everything suits me, Shorty. I was just puttin' in my word."

"I don't need your talk to run this bunch."

Shorty Baxter turned to Paso. Blazing branches fell in on the fire, and the flames leaped up. The light flickered and danced over a face that was like dry leather stretched taut over a bony shell in which sunken eyes blazed malevolently. The stage driver had said that nine years in the Yuma pen had sweated Shorty Baxter down to a sack of bones. It had. Baxter was like a death's head on a body that had wasted away to bone, a few sinews, and skin. Looking like a living skeleton, Shorty Baxter stood there with a flame burning inside of him, a fire glowing back of his eyes that was like nothing human. He was vicious, venomous, malevolent. He looked as if the fire of life inside him fed on hate and cold, inhuman fury that included all men.

At Paso's left Sonora Riley held the arm of Kitty Gardner. In the firelight Riley's face was bold, reckless, and cruel, but it lacked the bitter hate that seemed to ooze from Shorty Baxter. Paso wondered again why a hard-bitten border jumper in his own right like Sonora Joe Riley should be taking orders from any outlaw leader. Even Shorty Baxter.

Baxter's eyes were burning at Paso. "So you're the one

who's under my feet every move I make?"

"What moves," asked Paso, "are you making?"

Shorty Baxter had that coiling look again, as if he were posing to strike without warning. "The stage yesterday," he said. "An' that little play at the mine just before dark. You were in both of them up to your damn' neck."

Sandy Cole must have gotten away clean and made contact with the outlaws. Paso looked around, but among the dozen and a half men crowding close to the fire he failed to see Cole. It was plain, however, that this outlaw bunch had been close to the Concho before dark. They had been waiting, Paso guessed with a flash of insight, for the great store of explosives to wreck and stun the mine camp before they poured down like buzzards to pick the bones that were left. Baxter had planned it all, when he sent orders to Sandy Cole last night.

"Your business is your own," Paso said shortly. "I've been tackling things as they come up."

Baxter's death's head smile was ghastly. "You tackled me too many times, mister. We had a spyglass on the mine while you were fixin' to leave. You didn't have a chance."

"Wish I'd known," said Paso. "Maybe we'd have had a chance."

Baxter looked around at the prisoners. "These men say Gardner's flat on his back an' helpless. Maybe dead by now."

"He'll take a heap of killing," declared Paso, and added against his better judgment: "Maybe you've found that out."

Baxter jumped at him, striking with the gun barrel. The fury flaring on that fleshless face was murderous. Paso dodged, and the blow struck his shoulder instead of his head. "Don't laugh at me," Shorty Baxter was screaming, "or I'll give you some of what I've been savin' for Gardner for ten years!"

You could almost see froth on the screaming lips, then icy reason blotted out the insane fury. Baxter shuddered and stepped back, shaken by a spasm of coughing. His voice came forced and husky.

"Gardner'll never die until I settle with him. He'll live to suffer an' think an' eat his heart out. He'll die a thousand deaths every time I send word to him about what's happening to his daughter down below the border. With his mine gone an' his daughter gone, he'll think of Shorty Baxter day an' night until he's dead."

Silence had fallen over the ring of outlaw gunmen. It was as if something gruesome and terrible beyond their own hard-bitten sins had silenced them. Paso slid a look at Kitty Gardner, so pale, young, and helpless now. The firelight danced against tears she was holding back as she bit hard on her lower lip.

"What have you got against Gardner?" Paso asked Baxter carefully.

Baxter had his harsh, dry voice under control now. "He framed me into the Yuma pen because his sister acted like a fool, when I throwed her over," he said. "Walked out in a blizzard an' froze herself to death. Gardner an' that damned Horgan, who was in love with the gal himself, twisted the evidence and had me put in hell for nine long years to pay for it. Told me privately they was aimin' to make me pay, one way or another." Baxter spat. "I warned them that I'd settle ten for one. God, the years I spent waitin' to get at them. And now I've got Gardner like I want him. He'll wish he'd died like that fool sister of his, when he hears what's going to happen to his daughter." He lapsed into silence, grim satisfaction on his long face. Then he said: "Brand, here's a man you know. An old *compadre,* he says. Where is that fellow?"

"*Compadre,*" said Paso, glancing at the man who stepped

forward, "how'd you get friendly so quick with these wolves?"

The *compadre* was worn and dusty from hard travel, but he was still slender, aristocratic, dandified; he was still Juan Diego de Escobar, whose family members were lords of that wild empire west of Chihuahua City and the frowning peaks of the Continental Divide. *"Gringo,"* Juan Escobar said stiffly, "I followed."

"I figured you would," nodded Paso. "But I did plan on havin' both hands free when we met up." Paso's lip curled. "You can go back an' tell old Sixto an' the other Escobars what a *caballero* they sent out to drag down a lady as good as your own sister."

Juan Escobar was staring at Kitty Gardner. "With her I have nothing to do," he mumbled in Spanish.

Shorty Baxter grinned. "Some of the boys caught him trailin' that Three Forks stage. They knowed him from Mexico an' brought him to me. When I heered what he was after on this side of the border, I made a deal promisin' you to him, after we cleaned out the mine. He talked so damned bloodthirsty that we're all primed to watch his showdown with you." Then Baxter wheeled on the men as if regretting so much talk. "Get that buggy ready now. The gold'll stay like it is until we're ready to divvy up an' scatter. Jump fast, boys, while things is runnin' our way."

XIV

"ESCOBAR HONOR AVENGED"

The prisoners were put on horses and their feet roped under their horses' bellies. Kitty Gardner rode once more in the buggy with the gold. The outlaws backtracked a mile or more, then turned southwest across the harsh, open country. The gold bars, weighing so heavily in the buggy, acted like fiery trade whiskey on the outlaws. They were jubilant, frolicsome, joking and laughing. Paso gathered that they had raided other gold shipments from the mine, but never had such a one as this fallen into their hands. Even Shorty Baxter seemed to share in the jubilation, but it was not gold that affected Baxter. Hate was running like drunken fire through the veins of that emaciated, malevolent gunman. No wonder Gardner had known no peace, had been fearful for his daughter's safety, and savagely stubborn in keeping his mine open.

The blood trail that young Juan Escobar had taken after Paso Brand was the childish exasperation of a harmless young man compared to the venomous purpose of Shorty Baxter. Not that young Escobar was less dangerous now. Moodily Paso reflected that he was about washed up. The Escobars would have blood for their blood, and pass the story of Escobar justice down to their children's children.

But it was Kitty Gardner and Bull Gardner of whom Paso thought with bitter regret. He'd failed Gardner, when the man needed him most. Small return to give for the saving of your life. No imagination was needed about Kitty Gardner. Far down in Mexico she wouldn't have a chance. Paso had seen tawdry, hard-faced girls in the *cantinas* and dance halls south of the border who once might have been Kitty Gardners. They never came back home.

Paso judged it was well past midnight, when they traversed a narrow little valley between frowning mountain slopes. The valley narrowed to a long bottleneck, and then widened again. Under the star-studded sky in the south, Paso could make out vast reaches of descending lower country. They splashed through a tiny mountain brook, and just beyond found corrals filled with horses, and low, badly weathered adobe buildings.

Waiting men greeted them. Questions were called and answered as riders dismounted. This, Paso gathered, was one of the outlaw hide-outs. His horse had stopped beside the one ridden by the grizzled, old buggy driver. "I had a hunch we was headin' tuh here," the old man grumbled. "Hit's the old Diamond O spread that usta be owned by a feller named McCarty. Rustlers from acrost the border cleaned him out, an' he left. Ain't more'n six, seven miles to the border. Dadblame this arm! Hit's still oozin' blood. I blowed the head offen the feller who done it, though. Things looks bad fer us, don't they?"

"Kind of," Paso agreed.

"Gardner's durn gold packs a curse, if I ever seen one," the driver said bitterly.

"It seems to," Paso agreed.

Guns covered them, as they were taken off the horses. Lanterns were being lit, men were heading to the corrals for fresh horses, as Paso and the other prisoners were hustled inside the old ranch house. Half an eye could see that the place had long been abandoned. Only crude repairs had been made.

"Ain't this luck, now?"

Paso looked around into the cold-lipped grin of Sandy Cole, who was using a stick for a cane and limping badly when he moved.

"The company don't improve," Paso remarked. "I'm surprised you didn't crawl down in a snake hole so's to feel at home."

Cole's grin was half a snarl as he struck Paso in the face.

Juan Escobar had brought Kitty Gardner in, and he jumped forward as Paso's head snapped back from the blow.

"Thees man is mine!" the young Mexican protested.

"Who'n hell are *you?*" Cole demanded.

Shorty Baxter intervened. "Git away, Cole. I promised Brand to that young feller."

"I've got a score with Brand," Cole blurted angrily.

"You heerd me," snapped Baxter. "I know what I'm doing. You want to argue about it?"

Sandy Cole shrugged and turned away, glowering.

Juan Escobar spoke coldly to Paso. "That is not the Escobar way."

Paso tasted blood on his lip as he smiled thinly and replied in Spanish. "The Escobars like a knife or gun better, *verdad?*"

"We show no mercy to our enemies, *señor.*"

There was so much stiff-necked, youthful pride in the answer that Paso laughed. Juan Escobar was a handsome young don, following his code as to what was right. Another time, another place, he might be likable.

In the next room coffee and food were being hurriedly prepared. As fresh horses were saddled and made ready to ride, more men crowded into the room. Black coffee, plates of beans, bacon, and cold Mexican tortillas were hurriedly put away. The prisoners were offered nothing, but Paso saw Juan Escobar bring coffee and a plate of food to Kitty Gardner and urge her in broken English to eat. Finally she drank a little coffee and ate a few bites of food. Chalk that good deed up for the Escobar gallantry, at any rate.

Shorty Baxter, Sonora Joe Riley, and half a dozen other men were arguing in low voices at the end of the room. Finally Riley left them and began to eat.

When most of the plates were empty and cigarettes were lighted, Shorty Baxter lifted his voice. "Here's what we're doin'. The gold's going over the border tonight, where it'll be safe. The girl goes, too. An' that feller Brand goes with the young Mex I promised him to. There's a hide-out a coupla days south where they'll wait for us. We'll know the gold is safe there, when we want it."

An uncertain silence was broken by a sullen question. "Is that Mex gonna take our gold acrost the border?"

Shorty Baxter's fleshless face was almost ghastly as he grinned. "You're the right feller to ask, Pres. Your two brothers, Joe and Lon, are gonna take a coupla more men to make sure the gold don't sprout wings when it gets out o' our sight. Pres, you're gonna come along with us, so we'll all be damned sure your brothers don't get tired of waitin' an' move on with our gold. If it ain't there when we come lookin' for it, there'll be a Purdy brother filled full of lead fast an' quick, Pres. An' it'll be you. That suit everybody?"

Paso judged most of the men were against it. One bearded, broad-shouldered man spoke for the others. "What do we get by wipin' the mine out, Shorty? It'll have more gold, if it keeps on running. I'm for spending this gold now."

Baxter had the crouching, coiling look again as his voice lashed with contempt. "The gold's got you fools blinded. This whole end of the country will be up in arms over the girl. Ain't a one of you'll dare stay around. An' she goes with me. I'll kill the first man who don't like it."

"Nobody arguin' about that, Shorty."

"Use your head, then. With Gardner's mine blowed up an' Gardner's pockets empty, nobody's gonna give a damn what Gardner thinks. His hands'll be tied. The quickest way to have all this blow over is to clip Gardner's wings, while we got the chance. They won't be lookin' for us at the mine today. Not in broad daylight. They'll figure we skipped over the border."

"What's Sonora Joe think about it?" a doubtful voice asked.

"I'm stringin' along with Shorty. The sooner we start, the better."

Riley's decision carried the doubtful ones. Hurried preparations started for departure.

In the confusion, Kitty Gardner had a chance to move close. "Can't we do anything?" she whispered through stiff lips.

"Both bound and helpless," Paso shrugged. "None of them even care enough about us to cross Baxter, ma'am."

"The young man who brought me food was kind."

"Young Escobar," Paso said quietly, "followed me out of Mexico to put a knife or a bullet in me."

"But . . . but he was so kind to me. . . ."

Paso's eyes narrowed at a sudden thought. "Be nice back at him, ma'am. He's the only chance you've got. When you get down in his own country, he might weaken an' help you, if he's handled right."

Flushing, Kitty Gardner nodded. A few minutes later Paso noted with satisfaction that she was again talking to Juan Escobar, and it seemed to Paso that young Escobar's eyes were hungry, troubled, as they rested on the girl. Even that slight hope for her cheered Paso.

The gold was stowed in leather sacks lashed on two pack

mules. There were seven who were making the long ride into Mexico. The two Purdy brothers, Joe and Lon, were big men, bearded and gruff. There was an outlaw named Jake, and another called Tonopah, a lank, leathery, saturnine, slow-moving man, but a dangerous *hombre*, Paso guessed. Juan Escobar, Kitty Gardner, Paso, and two more pack mules made up the party. Behind them they left the other prisoners, and the main body of the outlaws who were getting ready to ride to the Concho.

Paso's final salute was from Sonora Joe Riley. "If the Mex don't kill you, Brand, I shore will, when we meet up."

Paso chuckled grimly. "If he don't, Riley, I'd like a chance to get that horse back."

Riley laughed ironically as he turned away. "I like your nerve, Brand. But you said the surest thing to make me kill you on sight."

Once more the night swallowed them. The trail they rode wound down through descending, broken country into the wilderness south of the border. South into old Mexico, toward those vast lands where the Escobars were lords, and young Juan, a don in his own right, would one day fill the shoes of old Sixto Escobar.

Paso didn't exactly see how it happened, but after a time he noticed Juan Escobar riding often beside Kitty Gardner. Their low-toned talk was not audible. Paso grinned coldly to himself. Kitty Gardner was working fast. Even an Escobar don had his weak spots.

Two hours of that and dawn was near. They'd ride through the day, Paso was curtly told by Lon Purdy, the big outlaw who rode beside him.

"The lady ain't strong enough," Paso objected.

"Who gives a damn? We'll tie her on."

Juan Escobar presently reined back beside Paso, and Lon

Purdy growled: " 'Bout time yuh got away from that girl. She's Baxter's."

"Thees *hombre* Brand ees all I want," Escobar said stiffly.

"Gonna cut his throat like yuh swore yuh would?"

"I theenk now ees good time."

Lon Purdy chuckled. "Can't wait, huh? Well, go ahead. He's yores."

"I theenk I do it here and catch up later."

"Hell, you're cold-blooded," said Purdy. "I don't want to see it. Bring his horse when yo're through."

"Purdy," Paso said coldly, "I wouldn't let a dog get butchered like this."

"If yuh was gold," Purdy retorted, "it might matter. Yuh ain't none of my business, anyway. Argue with the Mex there."

Purdy spurred ahead as Juan Escobar yanked Paso's horse to a stop. It was still dark. Paso reached carefully inside his shirt, under his belt. His wrists, tied with rawhide, allowed him awkwardly to handle the knife he brought out. It was the knife of the dead José Escobar, which the outlaws hadn't found.

"I got something to say to you," Paso said, heeling his horse so that it danced aside on the trail. Turning the knife, Paso sawed the blade awkwardly up inside his wrists against the rawhide thongs.

"What you say?"

One thong parted—another—and a third. Paso's hands were free, and only his ankles were tied under the horse. He gripped the knife, gathered the reins in the other hand, and tensed to spur closer and strike hard. Escobar steel slashing for an Escobar life. Fate, Paso thought, took some queer turns.

259

XV

"ESCAPE"

Then he held back in amazement as words tumbled out of Juan Escobar. "They don' hear now! By the Holy Mother, *Señor* Brand, you mus' help me!"

"What's that?" Paso jerked out in amazement.

Escobar shifted into excited Spanish. "The *señorita!* Ah, so quickly am I loving her! She must go to her father! He must be helped!"

A long, silent breath escaped Paso. So Kitty Gardner had put it over. "I help you, an' then get your knife in my back?" he asked skeptically.

"*Por Dios,* no! How could I kill the man who helped the girl I love? *Amigo,* the past is dead! How this happened I do not know. I am mad with love. She is an angel. A little dove, so helpless, so *bonita,* so . . . so. . . ."

"Don't gag on all that sweet talk," Paso said dryly, as he slipped the knife back under his belt. "After she's safe, we can listen to it. Got an extra gun?"

"Only my rifle," Escobar confessed glumly. "And they are four."

"Four ain't so many. Two of them are ridin' up ahead with the pack mules. Gimme your six-gun. Use that knife you were savin' for me, an' then your rifle."

"*Amigo,*" said Juan Escobar in a voice that shook, "the *señorita* and I will never forget your friendship!"

"Every time you call me *amigo*," said Paso, "I get boogery and don't believe it. We'll get drunk together, if we come out of this. Maybe then it'll sound all right." He tensed. "What's that?"

Paso wheeled his horse to the back trail and cocked the six-gun as a low voice cautiously whispered. "*Señor* Brand?"

"Who is it?"

"Tony Ramos."

"Hell, I must be drunk already!" Paso exclaimed. "Where'd you come from?"

Tony Ramos appeared magically under the nose of Paso's horse. Afoot, he had approached with Indian-like stealth. "Two of us have followed," Tony Ramos said cautiously. "Who ees thees man?"

"A friend. We're fixin' to help Miss Gardner escape."

"I theenk I hear so when I listen to you," Ramos said. "How many mus' we keel?"

"Four . . . an' damn' good men."

"You wait."

Tony Ramos vanished again. Even Paso could not hear him leave. Minutes later two horses came along the trail. Tony Ramos rode one; the guard, who had vanished with him at the fight, was on the other.

"Follow us," Paso directed after describing what was ahead. "Watch out for Miss Gardner. She'll be right in front of the first trouble."

Paso still found all this hard to believe, as he rode on behind Juan Escobar.

"Yuh finished him off mighty quiet," Lon Purdy's voice called as they rode up.

"Oh, *sí*," said Juan Escobar.

"Ride back here with Jake. I'm going up front."

"One minute, *señor*," said Escobar, reining over beside Jake.

Paso spurred hard, was up beside Lon Purdy before the man realized the second horse still carried a rider.

"What the hell!" Purdy blurted as Paso chopped hard with the gun barrel, trying to knock Purdy out. Purdy's head jerked, the weapon struck his shoulder, and he was drawing his own gun in the same instant.

A strangled cry ended in a gasp behind Paso—and he dragged his gun barrel down over Purdy's shoulder and triggered. At that it was almost too late. Purdy's shot followed an instant later as the man was blasted backward. But he was already a dying man, shooting wildly. As Purdy plunged into the darkness, Paso spurred forward.

"Ride back!" he called as he passed Kitty Gardner.

Ahead Joe Purdy shouted: "Lon, are yuh all right?" When no answer came, red flame spit at Paso. A second gun joined in, as Paso rushed at them with his own gun blasting.

The pack animals were snorting and rearing away. An unearthly, screeching Indian yell lifted behind from Tony Ramos. A bullet grazed Paso's arm. He fired his last shot and snatched the knife from his belt just as he reached the gunman who had shot at him. The man was a dark, weaving blot on a rearing horse. Paso leaned over and stabbed hard as he rode by—and set himself for the shot he expected. The knife went in to the hilt and was torn from Paso's hand. And there was no shot.

Paso heard the other outlaw, galloping off through the low brush off the trail. With a whoop, Tony Ramos followed. When Paso wheeled back to meet the man he had stabbed, he found an empty saddle.

Guns began to fire from where Tony Ramos had ridden. Then a distant yell of triumph told that Tony had caught his man.

It was over that quickly. The pack mules had run off the

trail. Paso and his guard who had come with Tony Ramos went after them. Tony galloped up to help.

"T'ree dead, one *muy malo!*" Ramos called.

Juan Escobar was comforting Kitty Gardner, when they were all together again on the trail. The lanky Tonopah, who had been shot through the mouth, had just died.

"Miss Gardner, we'll get you to Three Forks first," said Paso.

"Not now. I've got to know how my father is."

"I won't argue," Paso yielded. "An' I guess the mine has got word out for help long ago. The best we can do is kill these horses, getting back there, and hope we're in time. Baxter wasn't figuring on doing anything until long after daylight. Maybe later in the day. We'll have to hide the gold as soon as it gets daylight. If Baxter wipes out the Concho, there ain't any use carrying the gold back to him."

"I teenk so, too," agreed Tony Ramos.

Two hours later, in the first gray light of dawn, north of the border and west of the old Diamond O Ranch, they stopped to cache the gold in a little side cañon. At the foot of a little rock slide they laid the heavy, leather sacks, and covered them with rocks until the spot looked natural. Miles farther on, they unsaddled the pack mules, turned them loose, and continued the hard, grim ride into the north.

Hour by hour Kitty Gardner drooped visibly with increasing weariness, but, when Paso halted to give her rest, she insisted on going on toward the Concho. Juan Escobar rode beside Kitty. His attention was unflagging. Concern, devotion were in his every look and speech. Paso, watching, felt sorry for the handsome young Mexican. Kitty Gardner couldn't be blamed for encouraging him, but the truth was going to be a bitter pill.

Tony Ramos was guiding them. He had been through this country and knew it well. Paso tried not to think of what would happen this time, if they again met the Baxter bunch. The dead outlaws had furnished them with plenty of cartridges and guns, but four men couldn't hold off the Baxter bunch.

The mid-morning sun was high and bright, when Paso recognized the low, harsh hills ahead. "Not far now," he said to Tony Ramos.

"Not far, *señor*."

Half an hour later, from a high ridge they were crossing, Paso saw a little plume of dark smoke some miles ahead. Under that smoke would be the Concho mill and rest and help.

"The mine isn't blown up yet, anyway. I guess we're all right now," Paso cheered them.

That wasn't exactly so. The closer they got to the mine, the nearer they were to the Baxter gunmen. They were riding up a deep, brushy draw when the keen eyes of Tony Ramos first discovered trouble. Ramos whipped up his rifle and fired to the left, at the top of the high slope.

XVI

"FRIENDS"

Paso had his rifle up even before he saw what Ramos was shooting at. His sights swung over a magnificent, cream-colored horse that was being savagely reined around at the slope. Sonora Riley must have ridden out into view there without knowing anyone was down in the draw. Tony Ramos had missed his hurried shot. Paso's finger was squeezing the trigger—and suddenly he couldn't put a bullet in that horse. In another moment Riley was out of sight. They heard him fire three quick shots. His yell drifted back.

"Ride like hell!" Paso cried.

"I t'eenk you moch better shoot that horse then, *amigo!* Ees better he die than you."

Paso nodded. A minute later Tony Ramos looked back and grimly jerked a thumb. Behind them Sonora Riley and three other riders were racing down into the draw. As Paso looked, two more men flashed over the crest and followed. And then another. Then a turn in the draw cut off sight of the pursuit for the moment. But you could be sure Baxter hadn't let his men scatter much. They'd all be coming on fresher horses that had rested some. The broken country gave cover of a sort, but it made the going harder for tiring horses.

Twice guns opened up behind them for brief moments, when they were in sight. Then the long, serpentine draw narrowed sharply, and they drove their horses up the steep side.

Behind them guns burst out again. Over his shoulder Paso saw a dozen riders trying to keep up with Sonora Riley's great horse. And more were coming.

"Ramos!" Paso shouted. "Try to get Miss Gardner to the mine! The rest of you back me up!"

Paso swung from the saddle, as he topped the draw slope, and opened fire. Juan Escobar and the mine guard were throwing shots beside him an instant later. It caught the Baxter men by surprise. Two of them dropped, and a horse went down before the outlaws swerved up the side of the draw.

"Now they'll be more careful," Paso growled as he hit the saddle again and spurred on.

Ramos and Kitty Gardner were already out of sight. Paso was satisfied. Now the outlaws would have to pass the three of them before they could overtake the girl. It had turned into a running fight through the harsh broken foothills. The gunfire came in crackling bursts as the pursuit sighted them, lost them, and sighted them again and again.

The lathered horses were blowing hard and weakening fast, when Paso saw the mine smokestack not more than a mile away. Kitty Gardner would have covered half that mile already.

"Ride for it!" Paso yelled as guns opened up on them again.

Now he saw that they were south of the mine, south of the road, in the broken, little hills through which the creek from the mine camp ran. A short run and they'd reach the creek—and, as Paso thought that, a bullet knocked his horse over at full gallop.

Paso kicked himself from the saddle as the horse fell, and the rifle was knocked from his hand as he struck the ground hard at one side and rolled helplessly. The horse came to a kicking stop in a cloud of dust. Paso scrambled back on hands and knees for his rifle. A knife-like pain told of the bad sprain there in his hand. At that moment Juan Escobar hit the ground beside him.

"On my horse!" he cried in English.

"Ride on, you fool!" Paso shouted. "Your horse won't carry two of us!" He lurched over behind his dying horse, knelt, and opened fire on the crescent line of outlaws galloping at them. Juan Escobar stood calmly in his tracks and started to shoot, also.

"By hell, you're a man!" Paso jerked out in admiration.

"I am a friend, *Señor* Brand, because you have helped me," Juan Escobar retorted.

The guard galloped back and joined them. "I might as well lose my hair, too," he called.

Now the outlaws were close—a dozen and a half of them— a wave of hard, angry killers fired by the knowledge that their gold must be gone. Well out ahead of all of them rode Sonora Riley, lean, grim, dangerous.

Paso got his rifle sights on Riley and squeezed the trigger. He missed. It would be far easier to knock the cream stallion over, but Paso locked his teeth and sighted on Riley again.

Bullets were whistling about them. Behind, Juan Escobar's horse staggered away and fell heavily as Paso shot again. Sonora Riley flung himself up and back in the saddle and clutched for support.

Juan Escobar's rifle cracked sharply. Riley's horse had stopped. Riley pitched out of the saddle, and the stallion stood there with the reins dragging as the other outlaws began to scatter to circle the three men on foot.

"I think," said Juan Escobar in Spanish, "it is not long now. Look! More of them!"

The young Mexican had swung his gun toward a wooded

slope not a hundred and fifty yards away on the right. On that slope, bursting into the open, came a second wave of riders, spurring toward them.

A dozen—two dozen armed men—still more were pouring down the slope.

"Don't shoot, Juan!" Paso yelled. "That's Tony Ramos riding in front! And that's Horgan from the mine! They're *all* from the mine!"

Until then Paso had not seen Shorty Baxter. Now he made out the venomous, little, outlaw leader on a big, black horse that pulled up sharply as Baxter shouted orders to his men. But a rolling storm of gunfire from the mine riders and the thunder of their charge drowned out all other sounds. The outlaw charge had already broken. One man turned back. Another followed him. Half a dozen other men, who were galloping over to Shorty Baxter, lost their nerve and spurred away in retreat when they saw how they were outnumbered. Yesterday the Concho had not had this many armed riders.

Only Shorty Baxter stood his ground. Hunched on the big, black horse he poured shot after shot from his rifle. When you knew the emaciated, little gunman's hate, you could see that he was firing only at Jules Horgan, who led the charge toward him.

Paso was feverishly reloading, but Juan Escobar beat him to it. Standing coolly, Juan Escobar took careful aim with his rifle and fired. Shorty Baxter fell not fifty yards from where Sonora Joe Riley lay in the short grass.

Satisfaction was on Juan Escobar's face, as he lowered the rifle and crouched down beside Paso, to whom his flowery Spanish had a note of pathos in its futility. "Now I theenk my beloved will always be safe," Juan Escobar said, and Paso was sorry he would soon have to learn that the beloved would not be Kitty Gardner.

Tony Ramos threw himself off his lathered horse and joined them. As the mine men thundered past after the outlaws, they yelled encouragement to Paso and the others.

"The sheriff's men, the ranchers from T'ree Forks, the mine men were come to ride out w'en they hear the shooting," Tony Ramos blurted. "Ah, *Dios,* now ees all over."

Paso staggered as he stood up. Tony Ramos caught his arm. "*Señor,* ees eet help you need?"

"I sure do," said Paso. "Run out and get that damned white horse before he wanders away. He's mine now, an' I'm keepin' him."

The hammering stamp mill was shut down, the mine machinery was silent as Paso and the other three men rode to the gate in the wire. Only armed miners on foot were there to greet them.

While excited questions were asked and answered, Juan Escobar cried: "Where ees the *Señorita* Gardner?"

"With her old man, I reckon. That's where she headed," one of the miners told him.

"*Señor,* I must see her!" Juan Escobar appealed to Paso.

"I reckon you might as well get it over with," Paso agreed. "I'll take you."

Outside the mine office Juan Escobar helped Paso down and supported him on the injured ankle as they went inside. The door of Gardner's room was closed.

"Wait back there in the office," Paso directed.

When he was alone, Paso knocked, turned the knob, and limped in. Kitty Gardner jumped from the edge of the bed where she had been holding her father's hand. She stared at Paso as if he were a ghost, then color flooded into her face. "Are you all safe? Were they in time?" she asked anxiously.

Gardner's face was half hidden in bandages, but he looked better. His voice was stronger as he said: "Thank God, you got through all right, Brand. And got here when you did. A little more and all the riders would have been gone, looking for Kitty. What's happening out there?"

"Baxter's dead," Paso said. "And so's Sonora Riley. The others are high-tailin' it with your men after them."

"So Baxter's dead?" Gardner said heavily. "Well, that saves me a job hunting him down later on. Kitty's just told me what you've all been through."

Kitty Gardner's color was fading again. Her eyes were big, frightened. "The rest of you . . . ?" she faltered.

"We're all right," said Paso, grinning. "But you've got a problem in young Escobar. He's head over heels in love. It'll take a lot of talkin' to make him ever think different."

"I don't want him ever to think different. I love him. Where is he?" Kitty cried, turning to the door.

Paso's mouth was open soundlessly as she left the room, running toward the office. Silently he questioned Gardner with a look and got a nod in return.

"I reckon it's so," the mine owner conceded. "Kitty says he's from a good family and swears they both fell in love in a few hours. Know anything about him, Paso?"

"His family's good enough," said Paso. "Plenty good." He coughed and put up his hand to hide a grin. "Hell, yes. We're friends. Mighty good friends."

"I guess it's all right, then," Gardner decided with relief. "Maybe it'd have to be all right, anyway, the way Kitty feels." He chuckled ruefully. "I didn't bank on getting a son-in-law out of all this. But I guess it's all right. I've talked to Ben Davis, and Kitty has told me what Ramos did. I'll take care of those two men. They're the kind I need. You, too, Paso."

"Thanks," Paso said, and chuckled. "Gardner, your daughter got a husband out of this, you got a son-in-law, and I got the best damn' horse a man ever rode. So I guess everybody's happy."